An Unexpected Guest

August 27, 1918.
The War is finally coming to an end.
The Jazz Age is preparing to take center stage and
The Grove Park Inn - *the finest resort hotel in the world* -
is now catering to the rich and famous, politicians and
industrialists - from Thomas Edison, Henry Ford and
Harvey Firestone to Presidents Hoover, Coolidge,
Harding and Roosevelt. But along with famous
celebrities come secrets hidden behind those
towering, granite walls - - secrets swirling
around the mysterious death of a young,
beautiful woman in a pink, silk gown.
Secrets no one wants to talk about.

"A fascinating blend of history and mystery."

"A carefully crafted story.
It left me wanting to know more."

"A journey back to the golden era of grand hotels."

"What a night! I wasn't ready for it to be over."

An Unexpected Guest

Bruce E. Johnson

Knock On Wood

K o W

Publications

Harvey Firestone, Thomas Edison, Harvey Firestone Jr.,
pose for photographers outside the famed Grove Park Inn

Copyright 2011 © by Bruce E. Johnson. All rights reserved.
Published by Knock On Wood Publications,
a division of Wood-Care, Inc.
800-E Fairview Road, Suite 176, Asheville, N.C. 28803.
Printed in the United States of America.
www.AnUnexpectedGuest.com
ISBN 978-1-4507-3571-1

Photographs courtesy of The Grove Park Inn Resort and Spa.
www.GroveParkInn.com

owner Edwin Wiley Grove, Henry Ford and host Fred Loring Seely
on Tuesday, August 27, 1918, during a break from a camping trip.

No. 322 of 500 copies of an Author's Special ~~First~~ Edition.

Bruce E. Johnson

This novel is a work of fiction. While many of the names, characters, events and
descriptions in this novel are historically accurate, they are all used fictitiously.
Any resemblance between actual persons, living or deceased, and any of the
characters portrayed in this work of fiction is entirely coincidental.

Unless otherwise noted, quotations at the beginning of each chapter are from a
1918 promotional brochure written by Frederick Loring Seely, published by the
Grove Park Inn and currently residing in the author's collection.

Books by Bruce E. Johnson

Grove Park Inn Arts & Crafts Furniture
Built for the Ages: A History of the Grove Park Inn (2nd edition)
Hand Wrought: The Artistry of William Waldo Dodge, Silversmith
The Official Price Guide to American Arts & Crafts (3rd edition)
The Pegged Joint
Fifty Simple Ways To Save Your House
The Wood Finisher
The Weekend Refinisher
Gustav Stickley's 1912 Craftsman Furniture Catalog
Dedham Pottery Catalog
Arts & Craft Shopmarks
How To Make $20,000 a Year in Antiques
Knock On Wood Antique Repair and Restoration

Websites

AnUnexpectedGuest.com
ArtsAndCraftsCollector.com
Arts-CraftsConference.com
AskBruceJohnson.com

For Leigh Ann -

Who gave me confidence

to make the leap....

Women golfers on the Asheville Country Club course below the Grove Park Inn.

An Unexpected Guest

Bruce E. Johnson

The Grove Park Inn is located on the side of Sunset Mountain,
a mile from the top. It was built by hand in the old-fashioned way,
full of rest, comfort and wholesomeness. The front lawn
is the hundred and twenty acre, eighteen-hole golf links
of the Asheville Country Club, and with it sixty acres of lawn and a
thousand acres of woods and mountains belonging to the hotel.

Frederick L. Seely, President
Grove Park Inn, Inc.
1918 Brochure

Some of the 400 men who attended the opening banquet on July 12th, 1913.

Preface

*The four hundred guests were greeted by an army
of gray-coated attendants as they entered the great doorways.
There was no confusion in the reception or in the allotment of guests,
and the elaborate menu was served with perfect precision.
A first-class orchestra discoursed sweet music during the banquet,
and when the last dish had been cleared away,
the diners settled back in their seats to prepare
for the rich oratorical feast in store.*

The Asheville Citizen
Sunday, July 13, 1913

9:45pm
Saturday
12 July 1913
The Grove Park Inn
Asheville, North Carolina
The Opening Night Banquet

Edwin Wiley Grove, founder and owner of the famed Paris Medicine
Company in St. Louis, Missouri - and now of the newly completed, 150-room Grove Park Inn - prepares to address an audience of
nearly 400 distinguished guests who have gathered to celebrate the
completion of "the finest resort hotel in the world."

Each man in the room had been carefully selected by Frederick Loring Seely, the president and general manager of the hotel. Seated around him in the spacious Plantation Dining Room are the presidents of every major Asheville bank, numerous prominent business and civic leaders, United States Senator Luke Lea and the featured speaker of the evening, Secretary of State William Jennings Bryan.

As the room grows quiet in anticipation, E. W. Grove glances down at the back of the envelop on which he has jotted a few notes, then begins:

A man never grows too old to build castles and dream dreams. Standing here tonight in the midst of my friends and invited guests, I find a dream realized and a castle materialized.

After a long mountain walk one evening, at the sunset hour, scarcely more than a year ago, I sat down here to rest, and while almost entranced by the panorama of these encircling mountains and a restful outlook upon green fields, the dream of an old-time inn came to me – an inn whose exterior, and interior as well, should present a home-like and wholesome simplicity, whose hospitable doors should ever be open wide, inviting the traveler to rest awhile, shut in from the busy world outside.

It affords me far more gratification than I can express in having in my immediate family Frederick Loring Seely, a friend to all of you, my son-in-law, and an architect and a builder, who, by his artistic conception and by his untiring zeal, has studied out the very minutest details, making my dream a reality, indeed, and accomplishing what in so short a time seems almost beyond human endurance.

Grove looks down at his son-in-law seated a few feet away.

That which a man builds, that which a man creates is a true index of his character. These massive boulders, placed by skill and endurance into this wonderful structure, fittingly represent the sturdy character of Fred Seely.

In his untiring efforts to build a monument to me and my wife, to me and my children, to me and my grandchildren, to me and my friends, he has built an even greater monument --- to himself.

As the evening drew to a close, Secretary of State William Jennings Bryan, the three-time presidential candidate, paused to gaze across the room, then concluded with an observation:

Why should not this hotel stand for all time, for it has none of the elements of decay?

It will be here, as an eloquent monument to its founders in the centuries to come. It was built not for the dead, as were the tombs of the kings, but for living human beings, that they might find delight here.

Is it not better to build such a monument than a tomb?

Tonight, we stand in this wonderful hotel built not for a few, but for the multitudes who will come and go.

I congratulate these two men,

Edwin Wiley Grove and Fred Loring Seely.

They have built for the ages.

The Palm Court housekeeping staff viewed from the 6th floor.

Chapter 1

*The third floor Palm Court above the Great Hall occupies the center
of the Main Inn. Extending to the roof, it is capped with an
enormous skylight which admits an ocean of sunlight.
The effect is a most delightful sun-parlor to be enjoyed on cool days,
as well as a sitting-room for evenings.*

Frederick L. Seely, President
Grove Park Inn, Inc.
1918 Brochure

9:15pm
Tuesday
27 August 1918

She lay on her back, her long blond hair silhouetted by a small pool
of blood slowly creeping out from beneath her head. He avoided
looking at her eyes, bright blue eyes staring blankly at the skylight
sixty feet above the Palm Court. Her long, delicate fingers quivered
once, then slowly relaxed. He stood looking down at her, thinking he
should check her neck for a pulse, but hesitated, somehow sensing
there would be none.

"Black boys don't touch no white girls," he could hear his mama say. *"Never! They done lynched a boy down in Hazelhurst -- same age as you -- jus' cause his feet fit some ol' shoe they found near this dead white girl. Dragged 'im back to the place where she died, Robert, and done tied 'im to a tree. Then her daddy poured gasoline o'er him. Gasoline, Robert. He begged 'em for mercy, oh, lordy, how that boy begged 'em. But her ol' daddy just spit in his face, spit in his face, then set 'im afire. Set 'im afire, Robert. They all jus' stood there and watched 'im burn. Listened to that poor boy scream and watched 'im burn - burn 'til he died, Robert. You hear me? Burn 'til he died. Now don't you touch no white girls up at that fancy hotel.*

Don't you touch 'em. Never!"

Robert looked around for someone, anyone, but the third floor atrium was deserted. Two long rows of wicker chairs, rustic rockers and oak planters stood facing each other, the chairs empty, their tufted, red leather cushions wiped clean of any dust. Dellie had cleared the tables of any glasses and polished the heavy Roycroft oak and copper ashtrays until they looked as new as the day they had arrived five years earlier.

Mr. Seely accepted no less.

The potted palms reaching upward toward the starry skylight rustled as an August breeze hurried through the open transom windows over the guest room doors, rushing up past the fourth, fifth and sixth floor balcony walls ringed with their stenciled friezes, frozen like figures on a Grecian urn.

Up toward the skylight and freedom, cool freedom.

Run.

Escape.

A door carefully clicked shut somewhere down one of the upper wings, but no one appeared, no one stood looking down at Robert and the young woman in the pink dress who lay dying on the floor. Twelve inches of steel-reinforced concrete beneath her body had muffled any sound from the guests below in the Great Hall, guests gathered to watch the movie *Her Final Reckoning,* starring the beautiful Pauline Frederick.

No one, Robert thought, *probably even glanced up at the ceiling when she slammed into the hard tile floor, decorated with rugs Mr. Seely had ordered all the way from France.*

"Don't you touch no white girls," his mama whispered in his ear.

He had to find Mr. Seely.

"Never!"

Mr. Seely would know what to do.

Scanning the deserted balconies above him, Robert slowly stepped back from the young woman in the pink dress, then turned and hurried to the night watchman's station near the elevator.

Hands shaking, he fumbled with the small brass key tucked into the pocket of his starched white pants, then opened the small, square door recessed into the wall. Inside he found a single brass light switch framing two ivory buttons.

He pushed the upper button, closed the door and locked it, hoping Mr. Seely would see the small white bulb now glowing in his office behind the front desk.

Heywood-Wakefield wicker rockers ring the six rock pillars in Great Hall.

Chapter 2

The "Great Hall" or lobby of the Grove Park Inn is one of the most wonderful rooms in the world. It is 120 feet long by 80 feet wide, and can comfortably entertain 1000 people. The two great fireplaces in it burn eight-foot logs, and each required 120 tons of boulders to build. The men worked under instructions that when the Inn was finished every piece of stone should show the time-eaten face given to it by the thousands of years of sun and rain that had beaten upon it as it had lain on the mountain side.

Frederick L. Seely, President
Grove Park Inn, Inc.
1918 Brochure

9:17pm
Tuesday
27 August 1918

Fred Loring Seely stood near the bellstand guarding the front entrance to the Grove Park Inn. From this precise vantage point, which, late one night --- soon after the Inn's opening banquet --- he had carefully tested and marked with a small dot of India ink, Seely could observe everything and everyone in the Great Hall.

To his left, he could watch Edward Higgins and his front
desk staff as they dealt with each guest, directing new arrivals to the
south elevator just a few feet further away. To his right, he could see
the north elevator at the opposite end of the lobby and the twin oak
doors leading to two sets of stairs: one leading up to the third floor
Palm Court and the surrounding guest rooms, the other down to the
basement offices, the indoor swimming pool, the recreation room
and the barber shop.

With just a turn of his head he could also observe and greet
anyone approaching the main entrance by automobile, horse-drawn
carriage or on foot.

Seely had first named the cavernous, two-story granite lobby
the Big Room, but lately his staff and guests had begun calling it the
Great Hall. It irritated Seely that they assumed he had modeled the
room and its two towering fireplaces after a European medieval castle. Yet, he felt less inclined to confront them with the truth: he had
taken the idea for the hotel lobby from Robert Reamer, the talented,
young architect who, in 1904, had designed the Old Faithful Inn at
Yellowstone National Park.

When it had been announced that E. W. Grove was going
to build a new hotel in Asheville, Robert Reamer had written Fred
Seely, hoping to gain consideration for the coveted position as architect for the famous millionaire. Reamer proposed a hotel similar
to that of the Old Faithful Inn, wisely suggesting, however, that in
place of pine logs they substitute granite boulders hauled down from
Grove's 1,200 acres of surrounding mountainside.

Seely, who had been recommending a clapboard structure
similar to their main competitor - the stately Victorian queen of
Asheville, the Battery Park Hotel – had immediately realized the
value of Reamer's suggestion. Anxious to both design and oversee

the construction of the Grove Park Inn himself, Seely had quietly slipped aboard a Union Pacific sleeper car and traveled to Wyoming to see the Old Faithful Inn for himself.

Playing the role of a curious tourist, he meticulously stepped off the lobby's dimensions, took photographs, made sketches and filled a notebook with ideas. Before returning, Seely had decided to include not one, but two enormous fireplaces in the lobby of the Grove Park Inn, making it even larger than the Old Faithful Inn.

When E. W. Grove saw Fred Seely's sketch of a six-story hotel built of granite boulders, he immediately turned the project over to his son-in-law. Later, after the hotel had been completed, Seely destroyed Reamer's drawings, along with all of the other plans and proposals they had received from architects across the country.

At this moment, however, the Great Hall was shrouded in darkness, except for the temporary movie screen suspended over the massive south fireplace. Several hundred people sat on oak chairs and brown wicker rockers or stood around the fringe of the room watching the movie, intent on each subtitle as the plot neared its climax, accompanied by Mr. Longhurst blasting out chords on the Inn's pipe organ.

Fred Seely typically made it a point to personally preview each film in his private basement office before a showing in the Great Hall, but in the rush to prepare the hotel for its four famous visitors --- Henry Ford, Thomas Edison, Harvey Firestone and author John Burroughs --- now all four seated near the front of the room, he had simply run out of time.

Seely, too, had been mesmerized by the stunning Pauline Frederick, but his eyes were suddenly drawn to a small, solitary bulb now burning in his darkened office behind the front desk.

With a glance Seely saw that his head bellman, Theodore, had also spotted the light in Seely's office. With a barely perceivable nod of his head toward his boss, Theodore quietly left his post at the bellstand, walked noiselessly on his polished rubber-soled shoes behind the front desk and slipped into Mr. Seely's office, where he pushed the ivory button turning off the small bulb marked "3-PC."

Third floor, Palm Court.

Robert's watch.

Theodore turned around, but Fred Seely was already gone, the solid oak door to the stairway behind the north fireplace clicking shut in his wake as he took the spotless grey-tiled stairs two at a time.

At age forty-seven, Fred Seely considered himself in excellent health. He generally ate only two meals a day – breakfast and dinner - making it a point to always have a serving of prunes each morning. The dining room staff knew to expect him promptly at six forty-five, serving him at his personal table next to the window in the east corner of the Plantation Dining Room.

He awoke at five each day to personally inspect every public hallway and staff room in the entire 150-room hotel, including the rest rooms, the ladies' lounge, the lower recreation room, the shower rooms, each of the storage rooms, the laundry and the kitchen, making notes which he left for his secretary, Miss Hatch, to type in duplicate and hand to each of his department heads as they reported to work.

On Mondays, Wednesdays and Fridays he followed breakfast with a brisk walk down to the stable where Thomas would have Mica, his fifteen-hand quarterhorse, saddled and ready for a ride up one of the old logging roads cut into Sunset Mountain.

Seely had been introduced to morning horseback rides by his friend Elbert Hubbard, head of the Roycrofters in East Aurora, New

York, who was fond of proclaiming, "There is nothing better for the inside of a man than the outside of a horse."

On occasion Fred Seely would ask one of his more important guests to accompany him, but lately found himself growing irritated at their inevitable tardiness and preferred riding at his own pace. More often, he also discovered, guests were displaying a preference for golf over horseback riding.

Privately, Fred Seely considered golf a waste of time. But he recognized its importance to many of his guests, especially to men like Wall Street mogul Charles Schwab, Manhattan banker George Baker, and Asa Candler, owner of the Coca-Cola empire and now a powerful Atlanta real estate developer, men who regularly came to Asheville and the Grove Park Inn to relax, play golf and, he quickly discovered, to indulge in some late night, private indiscretions.

But as Seely topped the third flight of stairs, he paused to draw in a deep breath, as the tightly buttoned vest of his white homespun suit began to feel more like his wife's laced corset.

Robert stood waiting for him a few feet away, beneath the overhanging balcony of the fourth floor. Fred Seely had given each bellman explicit instructions that they were only to use his light system for emergencies -- and he knew this was the first time in his five years at the hotel that Robert had ever pressed the ivory button.

Robert stepped forward as Seely paused to catch his breath, pointing nervously through the open doorway leading into the Palm Court at the crumpled body thirty feet away.

"I was making my nine o'clock rounds, just like I always do, Mr. Seely, when I found her. Lying there. Right there. I didn't touch her. I didn't, Mr. Seely, I swear."

Seely silenced him with a raised right hand as he brushed past Robert into the brightly lit Palm Court. His eyes swept the long, narrow room as he crossed over, knelt down and touched two fingers to her limp neck, searching in vain for a pulse. As he pressed against her smooth, cool skin, her head rolled unnaturally to her left.

Broken, he surmised, biting his lower lip.

He immediately looked up at the fourth, fifth and sixth floor balconies ringing the room. Half-expecting, half-hoping to see someone.

Could she have fallen...?

He studied her clothing, a medium-length, pink silk dress with a laced bodice, revealing just a tantalizing hint of her young, firm breasts.

Expensive. Not bought in Asheville.

Instinctively, he smoothed her dress back down, covering her partially exposed white thighs from Robert's view.

He studied her face closely, sensing he had seen her, somewhere, but could not recall where or with whom.

But not a guest. At least not one registered....

He glanced down at her outstretched hand.

No wedding ring.

He ticked off the possibilities in his mind.

College girl, perhaps. Home for the summer?

Traveling with her parents?

Maybe a nurse at Vanderbilt Hospital?

Or over at Van Ruck's tuberculosis sanitarium?

Her trim figure triggered a distant memory of the young secretaries he had watched on their lunch hour in Atlanta.

Could it have really been that long ago?

That crisp, wonderful fall of 1905 -- a fall of hope, of promise -- the fall when he had moved Evelyn and their children to Atlanta, leaving behind a promising career working for his famous father-in-law as vice-president of the Paris Medicine Company in the ware-house district of sultry St. Louis.

'*Promising*,' he silently snorted. *That describes Grove, the man of many promises....*

The spreading crimson stain on the imported French rug caught his attention.

Ruined, he muttered.

One hundred and thirty-nine dollars.

He pulled from his suit coat a monogrammed silk hand-kerchief, custom-designed and ordered from Italy through Solomon Lipinski, the Jewish merchant who owned the downtown Bon Marche department store. Carefully sliding his fingers beneath her neck, he lifted her head, then rested it on his handkerchief to stem the flow of blood onto his carpet.

Without raising his voice or even looking in Robert's direction, Seely started firing off questions.

"Did you see anyone?"

"No, no, sir."

"Has anyone seen you - or her?"

The young man was silent.

"Robert! Did anyone see you?"

"I, I don't think so. No, sir. No one," Robert stammered.

Seely stood and scanned the balconies again.

Still no one.

She must have been alone.

He waited another few seconds, but no one appeared.

No one around.

No need to upset everyone.

Not right now....

We can handle this later.

He looked around the Palm Court, then quickly strode over to room 347 and put his ear against the oak door. Drawing a deep breath, he gently knocked on the yellowed varnished boards.

No answer.

He reached into his coat pocket and withdrew his master key, unlocking the door with his left hand as he pressed down on the smooth iron thumb latch with his right.

"Mr. and Mrs. Chiles?" he called softly into the room.

Still, no answer.

Seely stepped in, quickly checked to make sure neither Liliya nor Harold Chiles, a wealthy banker from Miami, were asleep in the twin oak beds, then grabbed a hand towel from the sparkling, white-tiled bathroom. He quickly walked back into the Palm Court, where Robert still stood a few feet away, staring in disbelief down at the young woman in the pink silk dress.

"You take her feet," Seely ordered as he gently lifted her blond head and wrapped the towel around it.

Sliding his arms under her head, neck and shoulders, Seely lifted her torso as Robert slid her feet together and reached under her calves. Seely estimated her to weigh no more than a hundred and eighteen pounds.

Twenty, maybe twenty-one years old.

Young, way too young.

As they shuffled across the atrium, making their way between the wicker rockers and through the door into room 347, Seely studied the young woman's face. She still seemed familiar, but not in a way that led him to believe they had ever met.

Who are you?

And what are you doing here....?

He remained convinced she was not a guest, at least not one officially registered that day, but with Ford, Edison, Firestone and Burroughs staying at the hotel this night, there were scores of people in the hotel whom he did not know -- including more newspaper reporters than had been inside the hotel since the opening banquet five years earlier.

And what he could not have right now was a dead body -- a dead girl -- in the Palm Court.

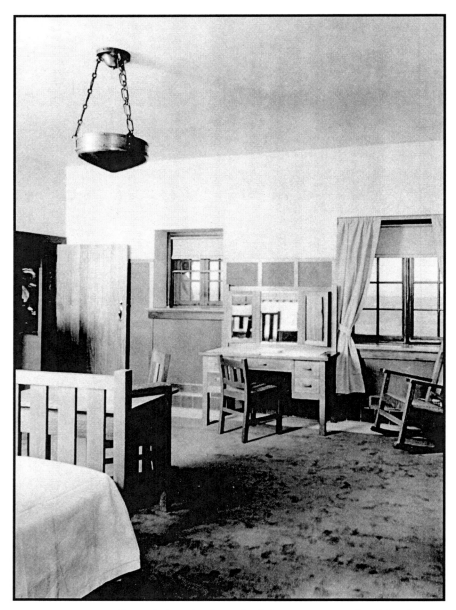

Room 262 at the Grove Park Inn as it appeared in July of 1913.

Chapter 3

In the main section of the building there are sixty-four guest rooms,
every one a double room and every one with private bath.
All bedrooms connect and all walls between rooms
are double fireproof walls with air spaces between.
The walls between the corridors and bedrooms are
double tile partitions, nearly one and one-half feet thick,
through which it is practically impossible to hear noises outside.
They are nearly sound-proof.

Frederick L. Seely, President
Grove Park Inn, Inc.
1918 Brochure

9:22pm
Tuesday
27 August 1918

Fred Seely pushed the door closed with his right foot as the two men carefully lowered the young woman's body to the carpeted floor, taking care to keep the towel beneath the spreading red stain in her hair.

"What happened, Robert?"

"Like I said, Mr. Seely, she was just laying there. There weren't no one else around. I don't know what happened. I swear."

Seely believed him. Robert had been with him since the opening night and the young Negro had never given him any reason to doubt his word.

Seely checked his watch, a gold-plated Hamilton pocket watch his father, Uriah, had given him on his eighteenth birthday. *Nine twenty-three. The movie would be over in just fourteen minutes.* Mrs. Chiles had been complaining to Seely of indigestion, which came as no surprise given the enormous amount of food he had watched the obese woman consume at dinner. She had first devoured the roast prime rib, plowed her way through a large helping of the shrimp newburg, then finished her husband's broiled chicken on toast, all before inhaling both the peach tarts and his slice of custard pie.

Given all that Mrs. Chiles had eaten, he suspected the couple would make their way back to their room directly, despite the fact that Harold Chiles, an avid amateur ornithologist, had hoped to hear more about John Burroughs' sighting of a painted bunting in Tucker County, West Virginia. Fleeing the Miami heat, the Chiles had been in Asheville since the first of August and had extended their stay when Seely announced to the press that the four internationally known campers -- along with their entourage, including Sato, Mr. Ford's personal Japanese chef, who had immediately begun making life difficult for Seely's kitchen staff -- were going to be staying at the Grove Park Inn tonight.

Seely had worked for weeks to persuade his friend Henry Ford to include the Grove Park Inn on the itinerary for their nationally-publicized camping trip. Ford, who had stayed at the Inn with his wife in November of 1916, had eagerly accepted the invitation, but Edison proved to be a challenge. The famed inventor -- who had insisted on being the navigator for the group -- remained adamant that this was to be a true camping trip and not a publicity stunt for Henry Ford's rising political career.

"We can't be coddling ourselves," the 71-year-old inventor had been quoted admonishing the group in the newspapers. Ford promised Seely over the phone that he would try his best, so on August 18th, the campers boarded their three open touring cars -- Edison's Simplex in the lead, followed by the rest, all Fords -- and pulled out of Pittsburgh. Three trucks laden with personal staff, tents, cots, chairs, food and cooking equipment followed, along with a platoon of national newspaper reporters.

Burroughs, at 82 the elder statesmen of the party, questioned whether he was up to the rigors of the trip. Henry Ford figured on using the naturalist's frail health to convince Edison that Burroughs would need a few nights' rest in a soft bed at the Grove Park Inn to recuperate from a week of sleeping on the hard mountain terrain.

Though trained as a pharmaceutical chemist, Fred Seely had learned during his six-year stint as the founder and publisher of the *Atlanta Georgian* that wherever politicians, entertainers and celebrities traveled, the press would follow. He had scored a major coup when his friend William Jennings Bryan, then Secretary of State under President Woodrow Wilson, had agreed to come to Asheville in 1913 to deliver the keynote address at the hotel's opening banquet.

On his coattails had come a covey of Washington and New York reporters, about to discover that in addition to appearing at the Grove Park Inn on Saturday evening, the Secretary of State had also accepted two lucrative speaking engagements on the North Carolina chautauqua circuit.

While the self-righteous Bryan remained unruffled, the uproar in the press over the paid appearances proved embarrassing for President Wilson. The quiet scholar and former head of Princeton

University had never warmed to Bryan's old school style of bombastic oratory. In 1912, however, Wilson's political advisers had convinced him they needed to promise Bryan a cabinet post just to keep the "Great Commoner" from running for president an historic fourth time – and in doing so splitting the Democratic party vote. Bryan's popularity had waned in recent years, especially with younger voters, but they feared he could still pull enough votes away from Wilson to cost the Democrats the White House.

The Republican strategists did not fare as well that year. They had their own version of a pulpit pounder in Teddy Roosevelt, but their's was a former president. Roosevelt had reluctantly declined the opportunity to run for re-election in 1908, letting his handpicked successor, William Howard Taft, take over the reins. Never comfortable as a politician, William Taft had always had but one lifelong goal: to become Chief Justice of the Supreme Court.

But his ambitious wife had other aspirations. With Teddy Roosevelt's endorsement and his wife's astute political maneuvering, William Howard Taft sailed into the White House in 1908 -- where endured four of the most miserable years of his life.

In 1911, yearning to again be president, Teddy Roosevelt launched an all-out attack on his former friend President Taft. When Roosevelt was unable to usurp the incumbent president at the national Republican convention, he bolted the party to lead the upstart Progressives. Teddy Roosevelt, like William Jennings Bryan, no longer could excite the younger electorate as he once did, but the former president pulled enough votes away from the weary incumbent Taft to let Woodrow Wilson slip into the White House.

The new president's staff had planned to make Bryan's role as Secretary of State largely ceremonial, enabling Wilson to push forward a number of domestic plans on which he had successfully campaigned. Instead, Wilson was forced to deal with two explosive international conflicts: one with the Mexican insurgents along the Texas border and the other with Germany's saber rattling in Europe. Rather than accepting the menial tasks Wilson's advisors had planned to occupy the Secretary's time, William Jennings Bryan entertained the press with a constant stream of solutions for ending both international disputes.

Evelyn and Fred Seely, who, as publisher of the *Atlanta Georgian*, had been an early and vocal supporter of Wilson, had received an invitation to the presidential inaugural ball. Since then Seely had maintained friendships with both President Wilson and Secretary of State Bryan – and while he publicly lamented the strained relations between his two friends, privately he reveled in the publicity the chautauqua controversy provided for the Grove Park Inn in the days after the opening banquet.

And tonight represented the most important night since the opening banquet five years earlier -- a night designed to garner national praise and recognition for the Grove Park Inn, not a scandal involving a dead girl in the Palm Court.

In truth, Fred Seely had never intended to design, build or manage the Grove Park Inn. His public endorsement of Wilson and Bryan in the 1912 election had been carefully calculated to land him a post in the new Democratic administration, hopefully in the state department. His boyish enthusiasm back in the spring of 1905 over the prospect of founding, editing and publishing his own newspaper had soon soured, as his plan to overtake the powerful *Atlanta Constitution* and the well-established *Evening News* had effectively been throttled by inside political power and influence. Although the Atlanta public embraced it, major businesses failed to support it -- and Seely's *Atlanta Georgian* struggled to stay afloat.

E. W. Grove, his reluctant financial backer and unofficial partner, complained incessantly about Seely's inability to make the newspaper profitable -- and continued every chance he got to remind Evelyn of Fred's missed opportunities back in St. Louis.

But when the president's telegram inviting him to become a part of his new Washington staff never materialized, Fred Seely pounced on the opportunity to escape Atlanta with his dignity intact by offering to manage the Grove Park Inn. The memory of those first years working for his father-in-law at the Paris Medicine Company, however, years laced with Grove's constant criticism of his business methods, had been seared into his mind -- and he had no intention of repeating that mistake.

Instead, Fred Seely presented E. W. Grove with a proposal: after overseeing construction of the hotel for his father-in-law, Seely would lease the Grove Park Inn from Grove, operating the hotel as if it were his own and paying Grove a fixed percentage of the gross receipts as rent.

Grove, who had shown only passing interest in either the design or construction of the hotel and who had no experience in hotel management, quickly accepted Fred Seely's offer. Grove's motivation for building the Grove Park Inn had been quite simple: he believed a resort hotel would generate interest and spur lagging sales in his new housing developments on the nearly 1,200 acres of land he owned around the site.

Grove also recognized that having someone as talented, as organized and as driven as Fred Seely as his general manager would free him from any worry – and would net him 8% a year in revenues. Seely's efficiency would save him tens of thousands of dollars in construction costs – and Seely had already negotiated the sale of the *Atlanta Georgian* to William Randolph Hearst for far more money than the young newspaper was worth. Hearst's money financed the construction of the Grove Park Inn, which, in Grove's mind, was far more likely to show a profit than a struggling newspaper in Atlanta.

But for Fred Seely the failure of the *Atlanta Georgian* had represented more than just a poor business investment.

It had left him broke.

He had long since sold the shares of Paris Medicine Company stock his father-in-law had given him and Evelyn as a wedding present to support his household in Atlanta: a nurse for the children, a housekeeper for Evelyn, start-up expenses for the *Georgian* that Grove refused to cover, new cars, vacations, private schools. The list seemed to grow by the week.

Their house on Peachtree Avenue had been a gift in 1905 from Grove, who never questioned how much money Seely had profited from the sale of it in 1912 when the Seely family moved to Asheville. That same year, as compensation for designing and overseeing construction of the hotel, Grove had paid him $7,500 and, in addition, had deeded nineteen acres of land on top of Sunset Mountain to Evelyn.

> *It was all carefully planned,* Seely knew, *to persuade him to build a house and settle down in Asheville, enabling Grove to spend more time with his only daughter and grandchildren.*

Still stinging from the failure of the *Atlanta Georgian* and his inability to land a position within the new Wilson administration -- an appointment he had foolishly assured Evelyn would be forthcoming -- Seely decided to build her a home atop Sunset Mountain so unusual that not even her famous father could equal: a 30,000 square-foot castle modeled after the medieval Forde Castle in Northumberland, England.

Seely began construction in 1913, just as he was finishing the Grove Park Inn. To his dismay it quickly swallowed all of the profit from the sale of their Atlanta home, the $7,500 Grove had paid him to serve as contractor for the hotel and nearly $20,000 more he had to borrow -- without telling either Evelyn or her father -- from the Battery Park Bank.

Now, six years later, Overlook Castle still was not finished. Seely had sent all of the stonemasons packing when he realized he wouldn't have enough money to finish the east wing. He also had discovered a loophole in the local tax law: the annual property tax would not be levied until the house was finished. Leaving the last wing covered with tarps did not prevent him, Evelyn and their children from living in the rest of the castle, but it saved him thousands of dollars a year in taxes. Judging from the letters he had been receiving from the tax office attorneys, though, it wouldn't be much longer before the statute was rewritten and his taxes due.

Furnishing a 30,000 square-foot castle, he also discovered, cost him as much as it would to buy a comfortable house in north Asheville. Regular furniture was dwarfed by the eighteen-foot ceilings, meaning almost every piece of furniture had either been custom-made or imported from England.

And then there was Biltmore Industries. Seely did not regret paying Edith Vanderbilt for the motley crew of semi-illiterate woodworkers and weavers, plus their looms, machinery and inventory of wood and wool, but the $10,000 cost had wiped out what was left of his personal savings.

Ever since the hotel had opened, Seely's relationship with Grove had grown more strained by the year, as they continued to disagree over where to advertise, how many employees to hire and whether or not to expand the number of guest rooms. Seely knew the day might come when he would have to lay down his keys to the hotel and walk out the door, so he had to make sure he could continue to provide for his growing family.

Biltmore Industries, he was convinced, would give him that option -- once it was up and running. Right now, however, he couldn't sell the four completed buildings, plus one still being built, for what he owed on them. He had spread his construction loans over three different Asheville banks, disguising to each just how deep he had sunk in debt. Each bank president knew full well that Seely's buildings next to the Grove Park Inn stood on land Seely only leased from E. W. Grove. While they had no reason to yet suspect that Grove and Seely were having personal difficulties, they reasoned that E. W. Grove, if necessary, would repay any loans made to his son-in-law.

Publicity surrounding the opening of what Seely had declared nationwide to be "the finest resort hotel in the world" had generated hundreds of reservations in 1913, but exactly one year later, in July of 1914, war had erupted in Europe. While President Wilson assured the American public he had no intention of asking congress to declare war on Germany, uncertainty over America's role in the war prompted many Americans to forego their annual vacations.

Rather than boarding one of the plush club cars on the Southern Railway to escape the South's searing summers or the North's brutal winters, people were opting to remain home, forcing Seely to again turn to the Asheville banks, this time for help in meeting his weekly payroll. For the past two years his debts continued to mount, as he struggled to both keep his employees paid and to fend off a nervous T. S. Morrison at Wachovia Bank & Trust and Charles Brown, president of the Central Bank of Asheville.

Both of whom, Seely knew, *were sitting in the Great Hall tonight....*

Only days ago, however, his friend William Jennings Bryan had disclosed to Seely that an armistice was expected to be signed in the coming weeks.

But he had to find a way to hang onto the Grove Park Inn until then.

Once word of an impending end to the war began circulating, he reasoned, the American public would release their pent-up desire to travel. Losing the hotel now would mean that the Grove family would get it back just as tourists started returning to Asheville in droves.

Fred Seely had been so confident that the war would soon end and the economy would quickly recover that he had begun pressuring E. W. Grove to do the unthinkable: add a new wing to the hotel. He pointed out to Grove that this was the time to take advantage of the number of unemployed workers and available contractors –- all willing to work for less than they had a few years earlier.

What he also knew, but dared not state, was that Grove's real estate, mining and cattle investments, coupled with a steady flow of revenues from an assortment of successful pharmaceutical products –- including Grove's Tasteless Chill Tonic, Grove's Laxative Bromo Quinine Tablets, Grove's Cold Tablets, Dr. Porter's Antiseptic Healing Oil, Grove's Pazo Ointment for Piles and Grove's Tasteless Syrup of Quinine -- would easily surpass ten million dollars.

Ten million dollars.

One small wing on the Grove Park Inn wouldn't even leave a dent in it.

Yet Grove wouldn't even listen.

Each night Evelyn sat and nodded as Fred recited the figures and repeated his arguments. He was so sure of himself that he was ready to offer to reimburse Grove for any part of the cost of the new wing that had not been paid by increased revenues in the first three years of operation.

Finally, though, it dawned on him.

> *Grove knew he was right -- he just didn't want to admit it.*
> *He did not want Fred Seely to succeed.*
> *He wanted Evelyn to know her famous father would always be more successful than her husband.*
> *And he wanted his hotel back. He wanted the Grove Park Inn.*
> *Not for himself,* Fred knew, *but for Edwin.*
> *Edwin Wiley Grove, Junior.*

The 28-year-old Edwin Grove was the only child of E. W. Grove's second marriage. Grove had met his first wife, a beautiful young woman by the name of Mary Louisa Moore, in his small drug store on the square in Paris, Tennessee. They named their first daughter Evelyn, but two other girls died as infants, victims of malaria.

Then, in September of 1884, tragedy again struck the Grove family. The frail Mary Louisa went into premature labor, but was unable to deliver what would have been their first son. While Grove sat by her side, with Evelyn huddled in the next room with their neighbors, Mary Louisa bled to death in their bed.

He buried his young, beautiful wife and son together, next to their other two children in the Paris town cemetery. For two years E. W. Grove ran his business and raised Evelyn by himself, but, then, in 1886 he remarried, this time to Gertrude Matthewson, who in 1890 gave birth to a son, Edwin Wiley Grove Jr.

Although E. W. Grove eventually found it necessary to move his business and his family from the rural Tennessee countryside to St. Louis, he always maintained close ties with the town and his many friends who lived there. He continued to provide for the up-keep of the Paris cemetery where Mary Louisa and their children were buried and remained a benefactor of the Presbyterian Church where they had been married. Those in Paris who recalled Mary Louisa never failed to comment what a striking resemblance Evelyn bore to her mother.

The Grove family began vacationing in Asheville about the time Evelyn was 21 and her half-brother Edwin was eight. After renting for a few years, E. W. Grove eventually bought a spacious Victorian home on the north side of town.

In the spring of 1898 Grove, while on a business trip to Detroit, met the energetic Fred Seely, then a young, aspiring manager in the tablet department at Parke, Davis & Company. Grove invited Fred to visit him in Asheville, where Fred and Evelyn met over dinner that summer at the Grove residence.

That fall, less than three months after their first meeting, Fred asked E. W. Grove for permission to marry his daughter. Both father and daughter agreed and the wedding ceremony took place in St. Louis on October 24, 1898.

Fred Seely, age 27 and filled with ambition, had seen in E. W. Grove opportunities he could never have even imagined had he stayed with Parke, Davis & Company.

E. W. Grove, age 50 and in poor health, had seen in Fred Seely the opportunity to step away from the daily grind of running a major corporation -- without turning it over to someone outside his family.

And Edwin Grove, age 8, began to resent them both.

For the next six years young Edwin had to listen to his father extol the virtues of Fred Seely -- how Fred Seely had modernized their St. Louis manufacturing plant, how Fred Seely had reorganized their bookkeeping system, how Fred Seely had redesigned their labels, how Fred Seely was working on a revolutionary bottling machine, how Fred Seely had fired half of their traveling salesmen while nearly doubling annual revenues and how Fred Seely was going to manage the Paris Medicine Company so that Grove could retire to Asheville and spend more time with his family.

But E. W. Grove could never quite let go of the company he had built from a small Tennessee drug store into an international pharmaceutical giant. Fred Seely had sensed that early in his meteoric rise through the ranks of the Paris Medicine Company, but not young Edwin.

The squat, surly boy only saw that Fred Seely had taken away his beautiful older sister, that Fred Seely had assumed what rightfully should someday have been his place at the Paris Medicine Company and that overnight Fred Seely had become the son, the heir and the business partner E. W. Grove had always wanted -- but young Edwin would not be.

To compensate, Fred suspected, Grove had showered his teenage son with lavish gifts, including a new 1904 Maxwell. He enrolled Edwin in the best private schools in St. Louis and when Edwin, as was always the case, was expelled for his poor attitude, failing grades and, the last time, for bringing beer to school for his classmates, Grove hired the best private tutors, though none lasted long.

And when Fred, Evelyn and their two small children escaped to Atlanta in 1905 to re-start their own lives, Grove soon sent Edwin to live with them – and for Fred to reform. Fred laid down the rules, established curfews, monitored homework and put an insolent Edwin to work at the *Georgian*.

And Edwin hated him even more for it.

The day after he received his high school degree, having already been rejected by Georgia Tech, Edwin packed his bags and headed back to St. Louis, ready to make amends with his father and to prepare to claim his father's fortune.

And to bring down the one man he still hated -

Fred Seely.

E. W. Grove made it a point to profess to Evelyn that he would have helped Fred start a new company, a company of his own making, in either St. Louis or in Asheville, but that he could never forgive him for taking his only daughter and his grandchildren off to Atlanta. Had it not been for his love for his only daughter and his sense of responsibility for her children, his grandchildren, Grove would never have agreed to provide Seely with the financial backing he needed to start and run the *Atlanta Georgian*.

And Edwin, for all his troubles, was still his son, his only son and he soon filled the void in Grove's home and in his business left by Fred Seely's departure.

In 1909, as he neared the age of sixty, Grove had grown tired of the daily routine at the Paris Medicine Company and longed for a new challenge. He found it in the North Carolina mountains where for more than a decade he and his family had spent their summers, sipping lemonade on the front porch of their sprawling Liberty Street home, watching the neighborhood kids playing in their yards, taking walks beneath the lush oaks lining the streets. It was with growing reluctance each passing year that he had to close up the house at the end of summer and return to the sultry grime of the Pine Street warehouse district, where each day his workers mixed, bottled, packed and shipped off thousands of bottles of Grove's Tasteless Chill Tonic to drugstores across the country.

For Grove, the money had just become numbers on a weekly ledger sheet. The company practically ran itself and Edwin, who Grove knew wasn't smart enough to succeed on his own, could provide him with the opportunity to spend even more time in Asheville.

Besides, he reassured himself, general manager Frank Hammett was the one who was really in charge of the Paris Medicine Company and Frank would provide him with weekly reports on sales – and on Edwin, who now enjoyed Fred Seely's former office and title of vice-president.

And while E. W. Grove and Edwin would often argue over matters relating to the running of the Paris Medicine Company, on one thing they now agreed: it was time to get rid of Fred Seely.

By any means possible.

While Seely knew that E. W. Grove had a better sense of his precarious financial situation than anyone else, he also knew that his 68-year-old father-in-law did not want him to leave Asheville -- and in doing so depriving Grove of the joy of spending the final years of his life with his only daughter and grandchildren.

> *Grove,* he sensed, *wanted to strip him of the Grove Park Inn, leaving him dependent on his fledgling woodworking and weaving business to support his family.*

Grove would then turn the running of the hotel over to Edwin, would sell the Paris Medicine Company to free himself from any responsibilities in St. Louis and would begin providing Evelyn and their children with monthly checks -- an 'early inheritance' he might call it -- as a subtle reminder of Fred Seely's latest failure as a businessman, a father and a husband.

Knowing both E. W. and Edwin Grove would be at the Grove Park Inn to observe the festivities surrounding Ford and Edison had put even more pressure on Fred Seely. As the automobile entourage approached Asheville, Seely made it clear to his staff that every convenience of the hotel would be made available for Edison, Ford, Firestone and Burroughs, regardless of the request, the time of day or night, or the cost.

He had also given Edward Higgins, as his front desk manager, a long list of important guests, including those members of the press Seely deemed most influential, for whom there would be no charges due at the end of their stay.

The losses for the week would be staggering, but Seely knew he had to take the risk, for his financial future was on the line. Front page stories singing the hotel's praises across the country would silence the Groves, appease the bankers and refill his empty coffers.

But - the unexplained death of a young woman inside his hotel would send guests scurrying for the Southern Railway station.

As all of these thoughts pulsed through his mind, Fred Seely analyzed the possibilities. He was convinced no one could accidentally fall over one of the forty-inch balcony walls. As he was working on the plans for the fourth, fifth and sixth floor balcony walls, he had carefully calculated and tested their proposed height. If an average person stood sixty-eight to seventy-inches tall, he figured, then even when leaning over the wall more than half of their body weight would always remain below the top.

No one, he was sure, *could just slip and accidentally fall over the wall, especially not someone as petite as this young woman.*
She did not fall, at least not accidentally, he concluded.

So, what did that mean? -- that she had jumped
to her death?
But why?
Why would a beautiful, young woman commit suicide?
Why here? Why now?
It just did not make sense.
But if she had not jumped…. or fallen…?
Then - she would not have been alone….

Seely's head began to pound. No one else would think she had accidentally fallen either -- and suicide would seem inconceivable, especially for such a beautiful, young woman.

No, that wouldn't satisfy anyone....
There would be questions, there would be theories.
There would be rumors....

It would become a feeding frenzy for the reporters weary of documenting how Thomas Edison preferred his eggs or Henry Ford's latest political platitude on how to end the war in Europe.

They were bored, they were hungry, they wanted -- they needed -- a story that would sell newspapers.

In place of glowing reviews would come sensational headlines:

Murder at the Grove Park Inn?
Young Woman Victim of Savage Attack!
Hotel Killer On the Loose?

And it would signal the demise of everything Fred Seely had struggled to accomplish: his design and building of the hotel, the staff he had hand-selected and personally trained, his nearly-completed home atop Sunset Mountain and his hope for the future -- Biltmore Industries.

He knew, given his debt to the Asheville banks, that he could not recover from a scandal of this proportion, what with the press and the public speculating on how a young woman had died in the Palm Court.

And with no suspect and no witnesses, this story would not soon be forgotten.

Mysterious deaths seldom are.

Grove and Edwin would make sure of that.

If she had not fallen?

If she had not jumped?

Then, did that mean she had been pushed?

That she could have been murdered...?

Here?

At the Grove Park Inn?

Accident, suicide or murder, the result would be the same for him: E. W. Grove would petition one of the local judges to nullify his lease on the Grove Park Inn, citing the unexplained death of the young woman as evidence of Fred Seely's negligence in operating the hotel in the best interests of its owner.

And, like a row of dominoes, all that he had worked for would come crashing down. The banks would call in all of his loans, which, without any income from the hotel, he could not repay. He would lose his home, then Evelyn would take their children and move in with her parents. He would lose the Biltmore Industries workshops and all of his woodworkers and weavers would be let go.

Unless, of course, he went crawling to Grove, begging for help with the banks. Either way, his reputation would be ruined. And when word of his debts raced through the streets, he would lose the respect of the Asheville community, his friends, his family -- and of his wife.

"Mr. Seely...?" Robert asked timidly.

Seely nodded, still deep in thought.

He looked down at the silent young woman laying on the floor of the Chiles' room, noting with curious detachment how the color slowly drained from her cheeks.

Just who are you -- and what happened?

His stomach clenched.

And who is going to be looking for you --
a few minutes from now?

"Are you sure no one saw you, Robert?"

"I don't think so, Mr. Seely. I heard a door close way down the hall, but I didn't see no one."

Seely suspected he was right, for no one had called for help for the young woman.

No witnesses.

But he had to do something, and do it quickly. Seely thought for a moment before he spoke.

"Robert, this could look bad for you."

"But, Mr. Seely, I...."

"I know, Robert, I know you didn't have anything to do with this. But right now Sheriff Mitchell is downstairs, watching the movie, and he is going to be looking for someone to blame this on -- tonight -- and that could be you. You know about him, don't you?"

"Yes, sir. He arrested my brother, Louis."

Robert paused.

"Sheriff Mitchell don't like any Negroes. He said so to my mama the night he took Louis away."

"No, he doesn't, and that's why you have to get out of here. Right now."

"But -- where do I go?"

"Back to Sunset Hall. And don't worry. I'll take care of you. Right now we just need to get you away from here, so no one has any reason to suspect you."

Seely paused to collect his thoughts, then continued.

"I can delay the discovery of the body until you've left the hotel. That way no one will have any reason to connect you with her."

Robert nodded in agreement.

"Take the service elevator down to the time clock. Don't run. And, Robert, don't talk to anyone. Just be sure to punch out and go back down to Sunset Hall. If anyone asks, tell them you're sick and I sent you back to your room. Just stay there until I send for you. Understand?"

"Yes, sir."

"And talk to no one about this, Robert. Just do what I say and I'll take care of it for you."

"Yes, sir, Mr. Seely. And thank you."

Seely slowly opened the door and checked the Palm Court. He stepped out into the center of the atrium and, as he scanned the fourth, fifth and sixth floor balconies above him, slid one of the wicker rockers over the bloodstain in the carpet. *As long as no one moved it, the shadow would cover the stain.* Convinced the upper hallways were empty, he silently motioned for Robert to leave the room, then watched until the door of the service elevator closed behind him.

I can't leave her in the Chiles' room, he reasoned. *They'll be back any minute and Mrs. Chiles is likely to start screaming when she sees a dead body in her room.*

I have to get her out of there, but where? Every nearby room is taken. I can't put her in Edison's room or Burroughs'. Can't involve them. The storage room at the far end of the Palm Court?

No, someone is sure to call housekeeping tonight for an extra pillow or blanket or something from one of their trunks. I have to take her someplace safe, someplace to give me some time to think, someplace no one would stumble across her tonight. Not tonight....

He looked again at his watch. He now had less than ten minutes before the movie ended and his guests would be returning to their rooms. Staying close to the wall, he walked toward the opposite end of the Palm Court, where an unmarked oak door lead to the third floor storage room. Inside he knew he would find four canvas laundry carts, each standing ready for the morning shift that would report to their stations at precisely eight o'clock.

Each of the women would sit quietly on the third, fourth, fifth and six floors, ready in the event a guest would need them, but would not begin collecting soiled linens until nine. And even then only from those rooms from which the guests had left for breakfast, an early morning walk or a horseback ride on one of the seven trails leading through the maze of rhododendrons, hemlocks and leafy oaks covering Sunset Mountain.

Seely pulled the nearest cart from its numbered spot, confident the well-oiled rubber wheels would glide silently across the Palm Court to the Chiles' room and their unexpected guest. He grabbed from the shelf two carefully folded Scottish wool blankets, tossed them in the canvas cart and started back for the room. He listened for the sound of anyone leaving the movie before it ended, but could hear nothing.

Seely had paid Randolph Castleberry, manager of the Strand Theater on College Street, dearly for the right to show *Her Final Reckoning* for his own star-studded cast downstairs. Castleberry had planned on premiering the new release that Tuesday night, but Seely had persuaded him that delaying it one night would not cost him any business. An envelope of crisp ten-dollar bills had sealed the deal. Castleberry wouldn't trust anyone with the reels other than Seely, so despite everything he needed to do that morning, Seely had to drive to the downtown theater. As he stood in the lobby waiting for Castleberry, Seely had noted with silent approval the hand-lettered notice, "Balcony for Colored People."

Seely slipped back into room 347, pulling the cart behind him, taking care not to bump her head with it as he stepped over her body. He started to close the door, then decided to leave it slightly ajar in the event someone – hopefully not Mr. and Mrs. Chiles – came back before the movie ended. If anyone did come onto the third floor, he wanted to make sure he heard them before they heard him. He removed the two wool blankets and set them on the bed closest to her body.

He then knelt down and, slipping one hand beneath her knees and the other under her neck and shoulders, carefully lifted her up from the floor. His right hand slid under her thin, silk dress, rubbing up against her cool, soft skin. Unable to support her head, it hung lifeless, as the blood-stained towel slipped from his grasp and her long blond strands of red-streaked hair reached for the floor. Tucking her feet in first, he gently laid her down inside the canvas cart, sliding his left hand up beneath the wound in her skull, while with his right he carefully curled her legs so that she would fit in the bottom of the cart. He did not dare remove his hand from beneath her head without risking a blood stain on the bottom of the canvas cart – something his staff would be sure to report, fearful that if they did not, he would discover it during his next inspection.

He could not see the towel on the floor, but was able to feel it with his foot and drag it close enough for him to reach with his free hand. As he lifted up her head and slid the towel beneath it, he could not help but note how peaceful she looked, like a child taking a nap.

A door slammed somewhere down one of the upper halls. *Sixth floor,* he judged by the sound. Quickly he covered her with the two wool blankets from the bed, fluffing them up to appear as if they were covering a small pile of sheets and pillowcases, then opened the door and checked once again to make sure the Palm Court was still empty before leaving the room.

At the end of the Palm Court Seely pressed the call button for the service elevator Robert had just exited in the basement. Knowing it would take a minute before it made it back up to the third floor, Seely decided it would be best if he weren't seen standing next to the cart.

> *Besides,* he reminded himself, *he couldn't be sure one of his housekeepers or bellmen wouldn't be getting off the elevator.*

While he waited around the corner for the elevator to arrive, Seely found himself thinking back to his first night in Asheville, back in February of 1898, when he stayed at the Swannanoa Hotel on Main Street, listening until after midnight to the clanking of the elevator machinery down the hall. The following morning he was to meet with Mr. Grove to discuss plans for a new tablet-making factory in Asheville, a meeting that would alter the course of the remainder of his life.

The memory not only of their meeting, but of that sleepless night in the Swannanoa Hotel had never dimmed, so as he was planning the twin fireplaces for either end of the Great Hall, the idea occurred to Seely to design the fireplaces wide enough so that, in addition to a firebox capable of burning eight-foot logs, he could install elevators inside them as well.

When completed, each fireplace was more than forty feet wide, with a firebox large enough for a half dozen people to stand in. Each fireplace protruded from the wall more than eight feet, giving Seely room to install a guest elevator on the east side of the firebox, with the elevator doors out of sight to anyone warming themselves in front of the fire.

On the west side of the firebox in the north chimney, Seely had the workmen install an elevator only to be used by the hotel staff, for Seely never wanted his guests to share an elevator with one of the housekeepers pushing a cart of dirty bed linens. The staff elevator, however, bypassed the Great Hall, opening only in the basement.

And although Grove grumbled about the extra cost, with all three elevators and their machinery encased in concrete block and granite boulders, Seely could proudly state that no guest had ever complained of a sleepless night at the Grove Park Inn.

The elevator arrived and Seely used his key to unlock the oak door before sliding back the steel accordion grate. He grabbed the cart and wheeled it onto the elevator, closing the door behind him before releasing the brake. With a slight jolt, the elevator started its steady descent, sliding silently passed the Great Hall, where some of his guests were undoubtedly leaning against the other side of the rocks he was passing behind.

If they only knew....

At the bottom of the shaft Seely slowly opened the door and peered out into the narrow basement hallway. In the distance he could hear the indistinct voices of his housekeeping staff as they ironed and folded sheets and pillowcases. As he expected, the nearby bellman's room was empty, as each bellman on duty would be up in the Great Hall with Theodore, ready to assist the guests the moment the movie was over.

Seely stepped out into the hallway and pulled the cart behind him, then made a quick left turn down a slightly wider hallway, first passing by the door to the locker rooms near the swimming pool and then the tiled staircase leading up to the Great Hall.

At the end of the hallway stood two oak doors, one unmarked, the other with a small brass plaque inscribed, "Frederick L. Seely, President." He unlocked the door on the right and backed into his spacious office, pulling the canvas cart behind him. The six-foot tall grandfather clock made for him by the Roycrofters confirmed that the movie would be over in less than a minute. Seely checked to make sure the inner door connecting his office with that of his Miss Hatch was securely bolted.

With a final glance at the laundry cart, he turned off the light, locked his office door and bounded up the stairs leading to the Great Hall.

E. W. Grove with his grandson, Edwin W. Grove III, and son, Edwin W. Grove Jr.

Gertrude and E. W. Grove near their winter home in St. Petersburg, Florida.

Chapter 4

At the Grove Park Inn it is different from other hotels.
The ceiling of the Great Hall is over one foot thick, of solid concrete.
The ceilings of the bowling alley and billiard rooms beneath the Great
Hall are the same. All of our amusement rooms were built so that
guests could enjoy themselves until any hour practically without
restraint and without the noise penetrating to the sleeping rooms.

Frederick L. Seely, President
Grove Park Inn, Inc.
1918 Brochure

9:38pm
Tuesday
27 August 1918

Fred Seely slipped into the back of the darkened Great Hall just as his
guests were watching the last moments of *The Final Reckoning*. From
the beginning the plot had made him just a little uneasy. In it Pauline
Frederick played a Hungarian woman who marries a prince, only to
then have her former lover threaten to reveal their affair. He hoped
his guests would not find it too risque.

Pauline Frederick had been in the newspapers a great deal recently. Her marriage to actor Willard Mack was rumored to be on shaky grounds, as stories about Mack's drinking problem and difficulties with his overbearing mother-in-law seemed to be surfacing weekly.

As Pauline Frederick lay dying on the screen, begging forgiveness from her Prince Zilah, *played perfectly,* Seely thought, *by veteran actor John Miltern,* Seely's eyes gradually adjusted to the darkness. Every wicker chair and rocker seemed taken, as well as the stiff oak chairs brought in from the Plantation Dining Room for this special occasion.

Seely had personally selected the dining chairs from the 1912 Roycroft furniture catalog, thinking the black leather seats complimented the dark, fumed oak finish perfectly. But he had been stung by the steady stream of complaints from his diners over their lack of any arms. Seely hated to think of the cost, not to mention the inconvenience, of shipping the 400 chairs back to East Aurora just to have arms added to each one of them.

But now that he had the woodworkers settled into their new workshop across the road from the hotel, he had devised a plan. He was going to send Elbert Hubbard a sketch for a pair of short arms that, once he had approved a sample, he would have the Roycrofters make and ship to Asheville. He had calculated that he could pull twelve chairs at a time from the dining room, send them across the road to Biltmore Industries and have the woodworkers attach a pair of arms to each before sending them back to the dining room.

He made it a point to stop by the workshop every other day, even though some of the woodworkers were still sore at him over the abrupt departure of their foreman, George Arthur. The young, talented woodworker had first trained under the watchful eyes of

Charlotte Yale and Eleanor Vance, two Presbyterian missionaries from Chicago who had come to Asheville in 1901. Vance, a skilled woodcarver, had taken George Arthur under her wing and convinced Asheville's millionaire philanthropist George Vanderbilt to finance Biltmore Industries, a small manual arts school and cottage industry for the children of Vanderbilt's employees working on his 125,000 acre estate and in his 255-room mansion.

After Vanderbilt's sudden death in 1914, Fred Seely had watched and waited to see what his widow, Edith Vanderbilt, would do with Biltmore Industries, which had grown to include the weaving of homespun cloth on handmade looms. When it became apparent that the task of managing the Biltmore Estate and raising Cornelia, their rebellious teenage daughter, was affecting Edith Vanderbilt's management of the Industries, Fred Seely offered to purchase the business from her. She quickly agreed. Seely then negotiated a long-term lease from his father-in-law for several acres of wooded hillside adjacent to the Grove Park Inn. There, at his own considerable expense, he began construction of five English-style workshops for his woodworkers and weavers.

But problems soon arose with George Arthur, whom Seely felt was too lax with his woodworkers. Arthur fell behind on the daily logs Seely required, as well as weekly production reports and inventory accounts. Seely had reprimanded him sharply one day and the next morning George Arthur suddenly resigned. Regretfully, Seely accepted Arthur's resignation and replaced him with young Bob Stevens, who, although somewhat embarrassed over the circumstances of his promotion, had eagerly undertook the Grove Park Inn chair project.

As Seely's eyes adjusted to the darkness, the glow from the screen hanging over the south fireplace illuminated the forms of his honored guests seated near the front. Edison's broad, rounded shoulders identified him immediately, as did John Burrough's white mane and flowing beard, though it seemed to Seely that Burroughs might be asleep.

The tall, lanky Ford was also easy to spot, even when seated. Seely had been amazed at how athletic the tanned 55-year-old industrialist appeared, literally jumping down from his black Model T that afternoon before it had rolled to a stop in front of the hotel, enthusiastically greeting the crowd, shaking each of their outstretched hands.

His energy gave credence to the previous week's newspaper story of how, in a field in Virginia, he had pulled off his jacket, picked up a nearby scythe and challenged young Harvey Firestone Jr. to an oat cradling and sheaving contest. Unaccustomed to manual labor, the soft Harvey Firestone Jr. had fared poorly next to the wiry -- and fiercely competitive -- Henry Ford.

That evening young Harvey Firestone had declined Seely's offer of one of the comfortable wicker rockers near that of his father's, preferring, instead, to stand after the day's long ride down from Virginia. He now stood in the rear of the room, not far from Edwin Grove Jr. who, with his back to the screen, was whispering something to the bellman, Charles, as he tried to slip what Seely suspected was a ten dollar bill into the Negro's hand. Charles made no move to accept the money, but leaned over slightly to whisper a brief reply.

Edwin's flask had probably run dry, Seely surmised.

As he watched, Charles disappeared down the stairwell leading to the basement.

In all his forty-seven years, Fred Seely had never once taken a drink. Fresh out of pharmacy school, he had gone to work for

Parke, Davis & Company in Detroit, where one evening he watched in disgust as John Warren and William Kirney, two of his superintendents at the plant, had drunkenly ridiculed several of their fellow employees, including their own secretaries. The following morning their comments had spread throughout the office even before the two superintendents arrived at work -- and Seely saw how the mood in the office was never the same again.

Ten years later, in May of 1908, Seely had noted with satisfaction from his newspaper office in Atlanta the overwhelming approval of the prohibition statute by the voters of North Carolina. In Asheville, the 'drys' had whipped the 'wets' by a margin of 1067 votes to just 299, despite the area's long tradition of home-brewed moonshine.

The national movement to add prohibition to the country's constitution had been steadily gaining steam and North Carolina's ban on the production or sale of alcohol had eliminated the need for Seely to include a bar in the Grove Park Inn when he opened it in 1913.

The wording of state statute, however, did not prohibit his guests from bringing their own alcohol with them. Some brought so much they asked his waiters and bellmen to store it for them.

The problem, Seely soon discovered, was that since most of his guests stayed at the Grove Park Inn on an average of eight to fourteen days, their personal supply invariably ran out. Pressured by guests to find them some of their infamous local 'mountain dew,' his waiters and bellmen appealed to Seely for a solution.

A few, he had already noted, had been selling local moonshine to his guests for anywhere from $8 to $12 a quart. At first he had decided just to look the other way, but after some thought realized the potential problems this policy could court. At Fred Seely's request, his attorney, James Britt, had clarified the North Carolina statute for him.

As Britt explained, "I suggest that you should be careful not to put the hotel in the attitude or even the appearance of receiving, holding or serving the liquors for itself. Offenses against our liquor laws are not, of course, in the use of the liquors, but in the mode of supply. Your relation to your guests must be strictly that of serving for them, without charge, that which they have supplied for themselves."

But some of Seely's more vocal guests had made it clear they would have no problem obtaining alcohol from the local 'jug trade' if they were staying at the Manor Inn on Charlotte Street or downtown at the still elegant Battery Park Hotel, now run by Tench Coxe, president of the Battery Park Bank and close ally of Mayor Rankin.

Seely also knew from his informants that Asheville's chief of police, J. A. Lyerly, and county sheriff Emery Mitchell were both frequent dinner guests at the Battery Park Hotel, courtesy of Tench Coxe.

The three, Seely had noted as the movie was starting, *were now all sitting together in the Great Hall.*

Tench's father, Frank Coxe, had been one of the founders and principle stockholders in the original Asheville Country Club, whose clubhouse and golf course were now completely surrounded by land owned by E. W. Grove. Seely and Grove had positioned the hotel adjacent to the golf course, hoping to eventually acquire it from the stockholders, but each of Grove's offers had been rebuffed by the Coxe family. As Seely learned, the Coxe family had nearly as much money as E. W. Grove and resented the outside competition the proposed Grove Park Inn would represent for their aging Battery Park Hotel.

Frank Coxe, while still a young man, had inherited a coal field that he soon transformed into one of the largest coal manufacturing operations in Pennsylvania. But when the Civil War broke out, Frank Coxe left Pennsylvania to enlist in the Confederate army in his home state of North Carolina. Standing an impressive six-foot-four and weighing more than 250 pounds, Frank Coxe quickly rose to the rank of colonel.

When word reached him on the battlefield at Bull Run that the United States government was preparing to seize his family's coal fields in Pennsylvania, Frank Coxe hired a replacement to take his place in Kershaw's Brigade and headed north, slipping past sentries for both the South and the North in the dead of night.

But once Frank Coxe arrived in Pennsylvania, the Union Army attempted to draft him. Coxe countered by hiring a 17-year-old boy to fight in his place. The practice, while uncommon, was perfectly legal. Eventually officers from both the North and the South began to suspect him of being a spy, so Frank Coxe, fearing for his life, fled to Europe.

Upon his return after the war, Coxe discovered that each of his hired replacements had died on the same day in the same bloody battle. He was forever convinced, as he relished with each telling of the story, that the two men fighting for him had shot and killed each other.

"I am the only man ever killed twice -- who lived to talk about it," he boasted.

Colonel Coxe, as he preferred to be called after the war, soon built the family coal business into the largest in the country. He then founded several railroads before choosing to retire in Asheville. Impressed with both the people and the climate of the city, Colonel Frank Coxe decided Asheville needed an elegant downtown hotel.

Surrounded by manicured lawns and towering shade trees, the Battery Park Hotel opened to great fanfare in 1886.

Considered the finest hostelry in North Carolina, the sprawling Victorian hotel featured a fireplace in every room, Edison electric lighting and a water-driven elevator. Colonel Frank Coxe died in 1903 and left millions of dollars in real estate, stocks, bonds and property to his children. He had named his oldest son Tench, after the boy's grandfather who had fought in the Revolutionary War before serving as Assistant Secretary of the Treasury for President George Washington. Since his father's death, Tench Coxe had managed the family's extensive financial interests from his first floor office.

Like his father, Tench Coxe resented E. W. Grove's intrusion into Asheville, which he considered Coxe family territory, as well as the Asheville Country Club's golf course. But young Tench Coxe had underestimated his St. Louis opponent. When Coxe, the largest stockholder in the Asheville Country Club, had once again rejected E. W. Grove's latest offer to buy the golf course, which was badly in need of repairs, Grove took a different approach.

Grove summoned Fred Seely to his real estate office on Charlotte Street and, in a daring move, handed Seely a list of Asheville Country Club stockholders and a satchel full of cash. A Pinkerton detective hired by Grove had quietly determined which minority stockholders might be persuaded to sell their shares of stock. As Seely carefully explained to each one of them, the golf course would soon require extensive repairs -- all at the stockholders' expense. The course would have to be shut down for several months, depriving them of any income while the greens and fairways were being rebuilt and allowed to regrow.

The plan worked and before word could leak back to Tench Coxe, Seely had obtained for Grove enough stock to wrest voting control of the Asheville Country Club away from the Coxe family. At the next meeting the board of directors, which now included E. W. Grove as the majority stockholder, passed his motion to allow any guest at the Grove Park Inn to play alongside the members of the Asheville Country Club – for a nominal fee, along with an annual contribution by the Grove Park Inn toward the maintenance of the course.

As the Grove Park Inn grew in popularity – at the expense of the Battery Park Hotel - the breach between the two families widened even further. Given Tench Coxe's connections with Mayor Rankin, Chief Lyerly and Sheriff Mitchell, Fred Seely always had to tread carefully. Allowing any of his waiters or bellmen to provide alcohol without supervision to guests at the Grove Park Inn might easily provide Coxe with the opportunity to publicly embarrass Seely and the Grove Park Inn.

And while he could not imagine E. W. Grove ever siding with Tench Coxe, he could not underestimate the lengths Edwin Grove Jr. might go to revoke Seely's long-term lease on the hotel. The detective assigned to watch him reported that Edwin had recently begun having dinner at the Battery Park Hotel with Tench Coxe -- and Seely guessed the two weren't just discussing their golf games.

After several days of careful consideration, Fred Seely had mapped out a plan that would enable him to satisfy his guests at the hotel while minimizing his own personal risk. He approached Theodore, at age 32 his oldest and most trusted bellman, as the two men walked outside the hotel and down the path leading toward the livery stable. Seely selected his words carefully and deliberately.

"Theodore, we are going to have one and only one conversation about the subject of alcohol at our hotel. I am going to explain to you precisely how it is going to be handled and from this day forward you and only you are going to be responsible for it. If there is ever any problem, I expect you to solve it. If I ever hear of any problem, I will dismiss you on the spot and deny ever having spoken with you about the subject. Is that clear?"

"Yes, sir, Mr. Seely."

"Good. You will select a source who you can trust to deliver to you on a timely basis only the highest quality alcohol produced in this area. Only the best and the safest. I don't want anyone getting poisoned by some rot-gut moonshine, understood?"

Theodore nodded.

"All of your transactions and conversations with this person are to take place off the grounds and away from the Grove Park Inn. That individual is never to come to the Grove Park Inn -- or to know that you and I have had this conversation. You can use the baggage truck to bring the merchandise in boxes from your home to the hotel, but all deliveries must be made on Sundays between 10:00am and 1:00pm while I am at church with my family. Is that clear?"

Again, Theodore nodded. Seely continued.

"In the basement in the second storage room there is a closet used for cleaning supplies. I want you to move those supplies to another area of the basement, empty the closet and put your own lock on it. You and two other bellmen are to be the only persons with a key to this closet. Select those persons wisely, for your future will be dependent on them. Arrange your schedules so that one of them is to work those shifts when you are not here.

"Let the other bellmen and the waiters know that all inquiries regarding alcohol for any guest are to be brought to one of you. If anyone objects, if anyone continues to provide alcohol for our guests on their own, let them go. I will support you without question or discussion in that decision.

"All transactions and deliveries will be made inside the guest's room. No guests are to be taken to the basement and no alcohol is to be sold in the Great Hall, the Palm Court, the dining room or on any of the terraces. Bottles being delivered to a guest's room are to be kept out of sight in a small valise. Use any of those left behind in the storage room.

"I expect you and the other bellmen - and the waiters - to benefit financially from these transactions, but not to attempt to make excessive profits. If that should happen, if I receive any complaints from our guests, let the bellmen know they will be dismissed on the spot.

"If you are careful, if your men are not greedy, if you are trustworthy, Theodore, you and your men stand to benefit greatly from this arrangement. Understood?"

Theodore looked at Seely for the first time since they had left the hotel.

"I understand, Mr. Seely. I won't let you down."

"I know you won't, Theodore. That's why I selected you."

The arrangement had worked so smoothly that at times Seely wondered if anyone in the hotel was even requesting any moonshine from his bellmen. On occasion he would see either Theodore or Charles quietly making his way up to the guest rooms off the Palm Court with a small valise in hand. In each instance neither of the young men even acknowledged Seely's presence.

As Seely now watched from his customary spot in the Great Hall, Edwin waited a few minutes after Charles had left for the basement closet, then casually sauntered over to the stairway leading up to the Palm Court. Seely typically assigned Edwin to room 655, a corner room, where he was less likely to disturb any of the other guests with his late night poker buddies or one of the women he picked up in his car on Carolina Lane.

And Seely knew from past experience that when his brother-in-law sobered up and finally left, he would make no attempt to pay for any of his charges.

But what struck Seely at the moment, however, was how easy it had been for both Charles and Edwin to slip unnoticed out of the darkened room.

And how easy it would have been for anyone now in the room to have earlier slipped back into the Great Hall while the movie was still playing.

Anyone.

Seely knew, too, that Edwin was in no shape to climb six flights of stairs to meet Charles back in his room. He typically took the elevator, but Seely could see that Edwin had clearly taken the stairs leading to the third floor Palm Court.

But why?

Charles wouldn't risk losing his job getting caught making a delivery in the open Palm Court -- especially tonight, especially knowing his boss was watching him at this very moment.

Seely thought about the possibilities.

Edwin must have convinced the bellman that he was staying on the third floor tonight -- or had access to someone else's room there.

No, that didn't feel right.

There was something else going on.

Why now?

Why just before the movie was ending would Edwin
arrange for Charles to meet him in the Palm Court?
Was it just coincidence?
Or was Edwin expecting to find something there --
      like the body of a young woman?
A dead young woman.
With Charles conveniently there as his witness....

Seely struggled to recall if Edwin had been in the Great Hall when Robert summoned him to the Palm Court, but could not. In the rush to provide chairs for everyone and to make sure that his honored guests were comfortably seated, Seely hadn't had a chance to scan the 400 or more people crammed into the Great Hall before the lights were turned down.

Now, as he squinted his eyes, he could see a dozen or more people standing in the back of the room. Several were reporters that had followed the Ford camping party down from Pittsburgh, along with Harvey Firestone Jr., a few Asheville chauffeurs, mostly Negroes, a couple of his bellmen and a few women, including, he noted, 18-year-old Cornelia Vanderbilt.

Two hours earlier, just as the movie had begun, a brief but determined thunderstorm had rolled across the French Broad River valley, over the lush fairways of the Asheville Country Club golf course and up the slope of Sunset Mountain. Now, with the terrace doors propped open to capture the cool mountain tailwind, Seely realized that anyone standing or seated near the back of the Great Hall could have slipped in or out of the room without attracting anyone's attention.

Any of the people now in the room could have witnessed what had happened to the young woman -- *the dead young woman,* he reminded himself, *now hidden in his office* -- and could have easily returned to the Great Hall while Seely was dealing with Robert, the laundry cart and her body.

Anyone.

With a final flourish from Mr. Longhurst at the organ, the movie ended and Theodore switched on the lights inside the nine massive, hammered copper chandeliers hanging from their iron chains imbedded in the concrete ceiling. On cue, the waiters from the dining room began making their way through the crowd with baskets of fresh Henderson County red delicious apples, each one carefully inspected, washed, dried and wrapped in wax paper printed with Fred Seely's instructions for the proper disposal of the core. The practice, which had become a nightly Grove Park Inn tradition, had begun at the suggestion of E. W. Grove.

Born to a family of Tennessee sharecroppers, Grove had left home soon after his father returned from the Civil War. He headed for Memphis, where he enrolled in pharmacy school. Not long after he had finished his coursework, his father arranged for Grove to meet Dr. Samuel Caldwell, a Confederate battlefield surgeon from Paris, Tennessee. Dr. Caldwell had returned to Paris after the war, where he and a local banker, Albert Mitchum, had opened a small drug store. Grove went to work for the two men and eventually bought the store from them, renaming it Grove's Drug Store. There, in the back room, he developed his first in a series of pharmaceutical formulas that eventually made him, as he liked to joke, "the richest American in Paris."

Years later, after he had moved his business to St. Louis, Grove built the first public high school in Paris and for years afterwards provided the board of education with money specifically earmarked for fresh apples to be placed each day in wooden crates for the students. It was his way, he explained, of making sure no student would ever go hungry at school. One year the school board decided to forego the practice and, instead, applied the apple money toward teacher salaries. When word of the decision leaked back to Grove in St. Louis, the monthly check abruptly stopped coming. The board got the message and the apple crate was returned to the hallway.

The audience in the Great Hall rose almost in unison, amid a few groans from those seated in the uncompromising Roycroft chairs. As they began to break into smaller groups, Seely scanned the crowd, looking for anyone acting peculiar, anyone who seemed nervous, out of place, perhaps in a hurry to leave, anyone who might have been able to slip back into the Great Hall unnoticed.

Seely could hear the young Lynwood Jackson, called "L. B." by his friends, standing in the back with a group of men, including Hanes Moultrie, treasurer of the Bankers' Trust Insurance Company, and James Hare, a successful and popular stockbroker. Years earlier L. B.'s father had made a fortune patenting an automated bottle filling machine he had invented when he owned the Chero-Cola Bottling Works.

Seeing Jackson brought back bitter memories for Seely, who had come up with the same idea while working for Grove at the Paris Medicine Company factory in St. Louis. Nearly every night for a year Seely had labored on his machine, an intricate combination of belts, gears, plungers and conveyers he was convinced would make him as wealthy as his famous father-in-law.

As he struggled to work out a problem he was having getting the corking mechanism to adjust to the difference in height among the bottles -- a problem which caused the plunger to chip the rim of taller bottles, mixing shards of glass with the liquid -- Grove seemed intent on heaping even more work on him.

When Seely protested, explaining how his machine, when perfected, would eliminate the need for the eight women who washed, rinsed, filled and corked each bottle of Grove's Tasteless Chill Tonic by hand, Grove responded by sending him to Atlanta for several weeks to look into the possibility of opening a second plant there.

Although Seely had written back numerous times about the opportunities he felt Atlanta had to offer, Grove never seemed serious about leaving St. Louis. But Seely discovered in Atlanta his own opportunity to escape -- and soon began making plans to move his family further away from Grove. The bottling machine, that Seely had carefully tarped and stored in the basement of the Paris Medicine Company, was temporarily forgotten. When, years later, he inquired about it, he learned that Edwin had ordered it hauled off to the dump.

Seely pushed the memories out of his mind, forcing himself to catalog everyone he could see. *Young L. B. was definitely a possibility, although he certainly did not appear nervous or anxious to leave.*

Near L. B. Jackson stood Herbert Miles, a retired meat packing executive from Chicago who had moved to Asheville about the same time that Seely had come from Atlanta. Miles' wife, as Seely had learned, had been the sole heir to the second-richest man in New Hampshire. The couple lived in a 5,000 square-foot house on the southern slope of Sunset Mountain, not far from the Grove Park Inn. The brick home's traditional Georgian exterior provided few clues that the interior would be in the popular Arts & Crafts style, influenced, it seemed, by the controversial architect Frank Lloyd Wright, whom the Miles undoubtedly had read about in their Chicago papers.

Herbert Miles was talking with his architect Richard Sharp Smith, the handsome Englishman George Vanderbilt had brought to Asheville more than twenty years earlier to supervise construction of the Biltmore House. In 1911 Richard Sharp Smith had been among the scores of architects who submitted plans for Grove's proposed hotel -- and did not take kindly to his rejection by Fred Seely.

Smith had gone so far to request a personal interview with E. W. Grove, but Seely interceded, stating that Grove had turned all aspects of the hotel's design and construction over to him.

While the two men never discussed the matter again, Seely always felt that Smith suspected the truth: that with no architectural training or engineering expertise, Fred Seely could not have designed the Grove Park Inn without a heavy reliance on his and the many other proposals architects had submitted.

Fred Seely was well aware of Smith's work in Asheville and held it in high regard. He did hire his services for a few minor projects inside the Grove Park Inn. He had also recommended Smith to several of his friends, including, most notably, William Jennings Bryan, who had just commissioned Smith to design a summer home for him at the corner of Kimberly Avenue and Evelyn Place. Richard Sharp Smith had accepted Seely's invitation to attend the banquet and movie this evening, but showed no interest, Seely noted, in breaking away from Mr. and Mrs. Miles to thank Seely personally.

Not a possibility, Seely noted, as he also watched for Edwin Grove to reappear in the room.

Herbert Miles, along with attorney Junius Adams, Mayor Rankin and Solomon Lipinski, had reportedly been making plans to invest in a new downtown hotel to be called the George Vanderbilt. According to Seely's sources, the men had already contacted W. L. Stoddard, a New York architect who specialized in hotel design.

Seely had met Stoddard in 1912, when the architect came to Asheville in an unsuccessful attempt to secure the Grove Park Inn commission. The nine-story hotel was expected to contain nearly 200 rooms and would provide serious competition for both the nearby Battery Park Hotel and the Grove Park Inn.

Not far away, near one of the stone pillars, two spinster sisters, Miss Irene Hall and Miss Zilca Hall, both school teachers, had turned to talk with Harry Dunham and his wife, Ella, who waved at Seely when their eyes met. The Dunhams were anxious to sell Seely a new and larger pipe organ for the Great Hall, but he had no interest in talking business this evening.

No possibility any of them would have been with the girl.

Behind them he could see their chauffeur, Jonathan Henderson, breaking away from two other Negro drivers, Nathaniel Howard, the chauffeur for Edith Vanderbilt, and Arthur Greer, Junius Adams' driver, as they each waited for the signal to bring their cars down from the upper lot.

Could one of them have risked it? Risked being missed?

David Hildebrand, owner of the Asheville Supply and Foundry Company, had strolled over to the south fireplace, where he was showing Albert Malone, manager of the Manor Inn, the massive andirons his men had made for each of the fireplaces. Each andiron weighed more than 500 pounds and could support a stack of logs more than eight feet long. Hildebrand's blacksmiths had never made andirons as large as these – it took six men just to carry each one into the Great Hall – but he faithfully followed Seely's instructions and the drawing he had provided.

A list of the other people Seely could see in the room included some of Asheville's most important citizens and powerful businessmen: T. S. Morrison, president of the North Carolina

Electric Power Company and vice-president of Wachovia Bank and Trust; Laban Jenkins, president of the American National Bank, who had just built a large bungalow in Edgemont Park; Reverend L. B. Compton, superintendent of Faith Cottage, a rescue home for fallen women; and David Shaw, owner of the Richbourgh Motor Company, Buncombe county's distributor for Ford cars, were just a few who stood out in the milling crowd.

Seely also spotted Harry Finkelstein, a successful pawnbroker on Biltmore Avenue, as well as his attractive bookkeeper, Miss Rebecca Goldberg, whose looks alone provided grist for the Asheville society rumor mill. Edwin had joked over dinner one night in front of the Seely children "that he suspected Miss Goldberg had her hand in more than just Harry's till."

Seely waved at Jonathan Robinson and his wife, Sara. Robinson was one of Asheville's finest photographers and had taken a special interest in documenting the construction of the hotel. Seely had often seen him crawling on his hands and knees, pushing his Graflex camera ahead of him along the roof scaffolding to capture on film the workmen pouring the seamless layer of concrete. Lately, however, Robinson had been laid up with back problems. Rumor had it the photographer had cancer.

Charles Hites, news editor at *Asheville Citizen*, along with society editor Miss Dorothy Randolph and reporter Oswald Smith were huddled near the front desk, conferring with Robert Jones, the paper's president. Fred Seely always made it a point to phone Miss Randolph weekly, trying to keep the Inn's name in the paper as much as possible, providing her with the musical selections Mr. Longhurst would be performing each day, as well the names of any guest lecturers or performers he had procured.

There was one event tonight he would prefer remained out of Miss Randolph's column....

Seely didn't yet know Oswald Smith, but had heard that the young reporter was quite ambitious -- and eager to make a name for himself. Smith had been shadowing Henry Ford all day, hoping to be the one to lure Ford into announcing his intention to seek the presidency in 1920. Seely knew Oswald Smith wouldn't be the one to trap the wary Henry Ford – *but would undoubtedly pounce upon the opportunity to report in lurid details the unexplained death of a mysterious young woman inside the Grove Park Inn.*

Among those on the far side of the room, Seely spotted the distinguished Dr. Westray Battle, personal physician to Edith Vanderbilt and many other Asheville patrons of society.

A possibility?

Seely shook his head.

Not with Edith Vanderbilt here, too.

A highly sought-after widower, Dr. Battle wore his trademark white flannel summer suit and carried his rattan cane in a manner reminiscent of a British military officer. Known for his wit and dry sense of humor, the handsome and charming Dr. Battle had been rumored to have developed more than just a professional interest in Edith Vanderbilt after the death of her husband. When, two years earlier, Cornelia suffered an acute appendicitis attack, it was Dr. Battle who took charge of getting her into his automobile and driven down to Biltmore Hospital, where he personally selected Dr. James Lynch to perform the emergency surgery.

Seely turned and watched as the senior E. W. Grove slowly rose from his chair and scanned the room. *Always looking for Evelyn,* Seely noted. Grove was now sixty-eight and, though stout, carried his weight easily. He had refused to learn how to drive, preferring to walk almost everywhere he went in Asheville or, when the weather dictated, riding in the backseat of his gleaming Pierce Arrow, which Vincent kept spotless.

Grove generally arrived in North Carolina at the beginning of summer, just as the heat began to build in St. Louis. Twenty years earlier he had announced to the press that he would soon make Asheville his second home "on account of the health of his family and to enjoy a better climate than is found in St. Louis."

Leaving his wife, Gertrude, to fend for herself, Grove quickly made his way through the packed room toward Evelyn, who had watched the movie from a seat near the back of the room, close by in case Missy, the nurse watching two-year-old Fred Loring Seely Jr. asleep upstairs in their second floor suite, had needed to find her.

Seely could not help but smile as he watched Gertrude Grove struggle to push herself out of the front row wicker rocker she had claimed next to Thomas Edison and was now shoving people aside as she plowed her way toward Edith Vanderbilt, the elegant widow and queen of Biltmore.

Fred Seely harbored a secret fascination for the Vanderbilt family. George Vanderbilt, it seemed to Seely, had become even more famous after his death than he had been while alive. Stories, myths and rumors continued to circulate about his estate, his finances and his private life, stories which Fred Seely collected like others collect fine silver. His collection, though, had to remain hidden, ever since E. W. Grove chided him over dinner about his preoccupation with the reclusive millionaire.

Undeterred, Seely often wondered what it would have been like to have been born to a family so accustomed to wealth, to power and to privilege. And what he could have done had he, as the youngest of ten Vanderbilt children, been given a million dollars on his eighteenth birthday -- and then, upon the death a few years later of a father he never really knew, to have inherited an additional five million dollars, along with the annual income generated by a five million dollar trust fund.

Would he have done the same? -- escape from New York society to the remote North Carolina mountains, to have surrounded himself with more than a hundred thousand acres of land, to have built on the highest bluff overlooking his sprawling estate a 255-room limestone chateau, a house so large and so elaborately furnished that none in the entire country could be its equal, yet so remote that few outside his close circle of friends and family could ever see it, ever appreciate it, let alone penetrate its towering walls.

Was it true, as Edwin hinted, that George Vanderbilt had something to hide deep within his towering chateau, something his mother's circle of friends could not understand, would not deem acceptable?

What could have happened? What could have prompted the 28-year-old George Vanderbilt to leave his beloved New York City, the opera, the theatre, the galleries, the parties? To isolate himself amid 125,000 acres of forest, miles from Asheville, a sleepy mountain town he rarely even saw....

Edwin remained Seely's most reliable source of information regarding the unprintable tales of Biltmore. Seely had clipped and saved the newspaper reports four years earlier, in March of 1914, when 52-year-old George Vanderbilt suddenly died from complications after a recent surgery at a Washington hospital. Edwin, from his various drinking buddies, Seely surmised, came home with the lurid details to dangle in front of him -- how 14-year-old Cornelia had persuaded her mother to let her stay home from school to care for Vanderbilt, only to have to watch as her father, while reading the newspaper after lunch, clutched his heart and, with a loud groan, collapsed. In less than a minute, as Cornelia and Edith both screamed for help, George Vanderbilt died in front of them.

Seely had also learned that George Vanderbilt had first begun vacationing in Asheville in 1888. *Not long before E. W. Grove*, Seely calculated. Both men, though different from each other in every other respect, immediately began accumulating land. For Grove, it had amounted to 1,200 acres on the north side of the town. For Vanderbilt, it had been more like 125,000 acres, all south of Asheville.

The earliest purchases, Seely had heard, had been made in secret by Vanderbilt's attorney. One day, when a poor Negro farmer declined what all of his neighbors had considered a generous offer for his patch of worn-out ground, the frustrated attorney let slip just who was anxious to buy his farm.

The Negro farmer had chewed on that bit of information for a moment, then replied, "Why, I guess I would have no objection to having George Vanderbilt as a neighbor."

Even while his attorney was gathering ground, George Vanderbilt had approached Richard Morris Hunt, the Vanderbilt family architect, who then designed the 255-room mansion for the young bachelor. Hunt, however, was in poor health. In his place he sent his aspiring associate, Englishman Richard Sharp Smith, to live in a nearby farmhouse that Vanderbilt had purchased and remodeled to use during the six-year construction project.

Vanderbilt visited his embryonic estate quite often, staying with Smith at the farmhouse, playfully referred to as the "Brick House," where a full-time caretaker and Vanderbilt's personal servants attended to their needs. The two men could often be seen on horseback, both being accomplished riders, exploring the sprawling estate, selecting sites for farm buildings and cottages, and inspecting the work being done by the landscape crews under the direction of Frederick Law Olmsted. Smith must have appeared to some more like an English gentleman than a supervising architect, with his impeccable three-piece suits, silver watch fob, fashionable sideburns, mustache and rounded bowler derby.

The two bachelors soon found they had much in common, as both appreciated English and Continental cuisine, enjoyed hunting quail and riding horses on the estate, along with taking walks with their dogs. They each undoubtedly discovered an urban, more-worldly sophistication in each other's company than they typically found in Asheville's mountain natives.

Evenings were spent in the Brick House discussing the ever-evolving plans for the estate, often with prominent guests, family members and artists from New York City, as well as the principal players in the emerging Biltmore saga. On more than one occasion the after-dinner group gathered in the Brick House included Vanderbilt, Smith, landscape architect Frederick Law Olmsted, chief forester Gifford Pinchot and senior architect Richard Morris Hunt.

It was enough, Edwin Grove had suggested, *to make you wonder about Vanderbilt and Smith....*

For Vanderbilt, however, life changed dramatically after the month-long private party celebrating the completion of his house in 1895. After his family and friends had returned to New York, he found himself wandering alone through his sprawling palace, observing the carpenters and painters finishing his beloved library, while he personally supervised the cataloging of his collection of more than 20,000 books.

A few months later his mother died, prompting his return to New York for an extended stay. Much of his time there was spent sorting through his father's art collection, selecting pieces to be crated and shipped to Biltmore in preparation for leasing the Vanderbilt's Fifth Avenue landmark.

George Vanderbilt returned to Biltmore late in 1896, but something about him had changed. Over the past ten years, while he had focused on the acquisition of the estate and the design and building of his house, he had lost both his father and his beloved mother, had also attended the funeral of his mentor, Richard Morris Hunt, and had distanced himself from his family and friends in New York. He was 32 years old and unmarried; never having played the role of suitor, he had no prospects for marriage.

As his close friend and New York socialite Gifford Pinchot later recalled, "George was a lover of art and the great outdoors, a slim, simple and rather shy young man, too much and too long sheltered by female relatives, enormously rich, unmarried, but without racing stables or chorus girls in his cosmos."

That year, Seely theorized, *George Vanderbilt set out to make one more acquisition: an heir.*

He left Biltmore in 1897 and, accompanied by his friend Osgood Field, embarked upon a world tour, including several months traveling around Europe. In Paris he met 25-year-old Edith Stuyvesant Dresser, daughter of a decorated military general and a direct descendent of the colonial governor Peter Stuyvesant. She was a woman his mother would have approved. Rather than returning to America for what would have been one of the most heralded weddings of the decade, on June 1, 1898, the two were quietly married in a civil ceremony in a French town hall.

Just four months, Seely had noted as he pasted another set of newspaper clippings into his Vanderbilt notebook, *before he and Evelyn.*

The couple arrived at the Biltmore Estate on October 1st, greeted by throngs of estate workers, music and fireworks. Edith quickly assimilated herself into life at Biltmore, meeting the staff and settling into her new home. George returned to the management of the estate, meeting with various department supervisors, including his personal architect, Richard Sharp Smith.

Everyone thought Smith had fallen into a dream job.

Everyone, Edwin chuckled, *except Vanderbilt's new bride.*

While no one believed for a moment that Richard Sharp Smith had ever disappointed George Vanderbilt with any of his designs, his deadlines or his drawings, he was soon informed that his services as architect for the estate were no longer needed.

And their quaint "Brick House" was demolished.

Seely had learned the rest of the story himself: how Edith and George Vanderbilt had but one child, Cornelia, born in 1900, and that Richard Sharp Smith never worked for them again. He had gone on to become Asheville's most prolific architect, had married Isabelle Dameron, a young woman of Scottish descent who had worked for the Vanderbilts, and together they raised four children.

Not long after he and Evelyn had moved to Asheville from Atlanta, Fred Seely listened as a friend of the Vanderbilts recited a story regarding the famous couple. In April of 1912, Edith and George Vanderbilt, along with young Cornelia and Edith's sister, were nearing the end of their most recent trip to Europe. They had purchased first class tickets aboard the *Titanic*, but Edith's sister, just as they were scheduled to leave Southampton, had a premonition that the ship was going to sink.

She begged George and Edith not to board, until George, in frustration, finally left it up to his wife to decide. At first, Edith was determined they would not postpone their return to America, but finally, even as their trunks were being stowed, she gave in.

Irritated with her sister, Edith insisted that one of their servants make the trip aboard the *Titanic* to insure that their luggage arrived safely. She selected Frederick Wheeler, who became one of the 1,517 people who drowned on April 15th in the North Atlantic after the ship struck an iceberg.

It was said, Seely repeated as he told the story to Grove, *that Edith Vanderbilt never spoke of the incident again, and that she quietly provided for Frederick Wheeler's widow for the remainder of her life.*

E. W. Grove had never liked George Vanderbilt, calling him 'foppish' and 'a mama's boy.' Grove scoffed when Seely added Vanderbilt's name to the guest list for the official opening of the hotel, accurately predicting that George Vanderbilt would never lower himself to set foot in the Grove Park Inn.

The rejection, personally delivered by one of Vanderbilt's servants, had not upset Seely. The handwritten note on heavy parchment stationary lay on his desk for several days, prompting Seely to often wonder about the stories -- the soundproof party room, midnight swims in the basement pool, secret passages he and Smith had devised, exploits in the exercise room. Seely could not help imagining what might have gone on deep inside the Vanderbilt palace.

Edith Vanderbilt had been accompanied to the Grove Park Inn this evening by her now 18-year-old daughter, Cornelia -- heir to the entire Biltmore estate and her father's five million dollar trust fund. As he scanned the room, Seely caught sight of Cornelia outside on the darkened Sunset Terrace, her narrow face momentarily illuminated by the flair of a match lighting the cigarette in her lips.

Unfortunately, as the family's detractors chortled in private, along with a five million dollar trust fund, Cornelia Vanderbilt had also inherited her father's drawn, soulful face, sunken eyes, long neck and tall, awkward frame.

During the winter she attended private school in Washington, where her parents had purchased a home at 1612 K Street, just a few blocks north of the White House. She spent her summers in Asheville, riding on the estate and attending dances held at the Manor Inn, the Battery Park Hotel and, Seely knew, the Grove Park Inn.

Upon her father's death, many reporters had tabulated George Vanderbilt's assets as high as fifty million dollars, but Edith and Cornelia soon discovered the painful truth: the construction and maintenance of the family's palatial homes in Asheville, Washington, Bar Harbor and New York, plus a lifestyle which included lengthy annual trips to Europe, lavish parties, tutors and private schools, had drained the coffers nearly dry, at least by Vanderbilt standards. His total estate had been reduced to less than a million dollars, little more than $11,000 of which was available in stocks and bonds. Strapped for cash, George Vanderbilt had borrowed heavily against his life insurance policy and still carried a mortgage on their Washington residence.

Fortunately for Cornelia, under the terms of her grandfather's will, George Vanderbilt could only spend the income from his five million dollar trust fund, leaving the principle intact for Cornelia when she turned 25. In his own will, George Vanderbilt had bequeathed over a million dollars to family and friends, but at the time of his death had only enough assets to cover a small fraction of that amount.

So while the local press enjoyed calling Edith Vanderbilt 'the richest woman in North Carolina,' those close to her knew that title rightly belonged to her daughter. Edith's responsibility was making sure the estate remained solvent until it would be turned over to Cornelia in 1925.

Then, in July of 1916, a torrential rain spawned by two consecutive hurricanes pushed both the French Broad River and the Swannanoa River out of their banks. The Vanderbilt's prized manorial Biltmore Village, constructed for his more than 500 workers, soon laid under nineteen feet of turbulent water. Valuable farm buildings, homes, equipment, livestock and the estate's nursery were swept away. In all, at least 80 people died in the flood, including James Lipe, Edith Vanderbilt's estate manager, who drowned in a vain attempt to save three others.

While the Biltmore House remained safe on the bluff overlooking the two swollen rivers, more than a mile wide at their crest, Edith Vanderbilt waded in to help with the rescue efforts, offering her private car as a hearse for victims found in Biltmore Village.

Over the course of the next two years Edith Vanderbilt had been able to disguise her precarious financial situation, while quietly relieving herself of many of the burdens her late husband had accumulated.

Suddenly, across the room, Edwin Grove reappeared from the Palm Court stairwell, a suspicious bulge now evident to Seely in his left coat pocket.

> He had met Charles -- and somehow had bluffed or
> bullied the bellman into passing him a fresh bottle
> outside his room.

As Seely watched, Edwin calmly began making his way through the crowd toward the outdoor terrace where Cornelia Vanderbilt stood smoking a cigarette. If he noticed Seely watching him from beyond one of the stone pillars, Edwin gave no indication. His eyes were clearly focused on Cornelia Vanderbilt, whom Seely now recalled seeing with Edwin earlier in the evening, even before the movie had started.

Perhaps the transaction with Charles was simply fulfilling a boast he had made to Cornelia. And meeting in the Palm Court would have been faster and easier for Edwin.

Or was there more to it than that?

Had he really been expecting to find her body, to signal an alarm, to send Charles racing back down the stairs for Sheriff Mitchell, Chief Lyerly and the others?

And when she wasn't there, what then?

What would he do?

Charles quietly slipped out from behind the same doorway as Edwin had appeared and took his position near the bellstand. Nothing about him gave Seely any indication anything unusual had transpired.

No. Edwin didn't show Charles the blood stained rug - if he even knew to look for it under the wicker rocker.

Perhaps he had no idea.

Perhaps it was only about the whiskey.

Edwin leaned and whispered something in Cornelia's ear, as he deftly reached for her elbow and guided her toward the steps leading to the seclusion of the golf course.

View of the Grove Park Inn from the Asheville Country Club golf course.

The elevator hidden inside the south fireplace in the Great Hall.

Chapter 5

We consider that our bedrooms are for rest after a reasonable hour,
and we have the courage to enforce a discipline
that makes rest possible.
Every opportunity is afforded at the Grove Park Inn for a good time.
Dancing late, bowling, music and every reasonable amusement;
but we insist on every opportunity for guests to rest if they wish to.

Frederick L. Seely, President
Grove Park Inn, Inc.
1918 Brochure

9:50pm
Tuesday
27 August 1918

Standing together at the far side of the room was a group of promi-
nent Asheville businessmen, all of whom had been invited by Fred
Seely to the evening's events honoring Ford, Edison, Burroughs and
Firestone. As soon as the movie ended, they immediately clustered
around Junius G. Adams, legal and financial advisor to Edith and
Cornelia Vanderbilt.

Judge Adams, as he preferred to be called, like Tench Coxe, was a force to be reckoned with. Most people in Asheville, including Fred Seely, took care not to cross swords with the influential litigator. Like Seely, Junius Adams had strong ties to President Wilson's close advisors in Washington. For years, rumors had persisted that Adams was in line for a post in the Wilson administration, but Seely's friends in the capitol, most notably former Secretary of State William Jennings Bryan, thought nothing would come of it.

The rumors, Seely suspected, *most likely originated from Judge Adams himself.*

After the unexpected death of George Vanderbilt in 1914 and the disastrous Asheville flood two years later, Junius Adams had stepped in to serve as Edith Vanderbilt's personal attorney and financial advisor. Adams replaced Hamilton Twombly, George Vanderbilt's brother-in-law, who had tried -- unsuccessfully -- to stem the steady flow of money out of the Biltmore Estate.

Under Junius Adams' dictatorial hand, Edith Vanderbilt first sold more than 86,000 acres of land around Mt. Pisgah to the National Forest Preservation Commission for just five dollars an acre. Although the price was less than what George Vanderbilt had paid for it, the resulting $433,500 enabled her to preserve the house, grounds and staff.

Now, it was being reported about town, Judge Adams was pressuring Edith Vanderbilt to sell Biltmore Village, the manorial hamlet of stuccoed, half-timbered homes and shops her late husband had commissioned Richard Sharp Smith to construct for his estate workers and their families.

Seely heard that Judge Adams had held several informal talks at the Battery Park Hotel with George Stephens, a wealthy Charlotte banker who had vacationed in Asheville every year since 1898 and who had expressed an interest in relocating to the mountain city. George Stephens, however, had no intention of retiring. In addition to wanting to buy Biltmore Village from Edith Vanderbilt, he was rumored to have formed a partnership with Charles Webb to purchase the *Asheville Citizen*.

Seely had also heard that Junius Adams was recommending that Edith Vanderbilt carve off an additional 1,500 acres of land for an upscale residential building development. According to reports Seely had heard, a group of investors led by Junius Adams was planning to purchase the property from Edith Vanderbilt for $350,000, then subdivide it into three- to five-acre plots for a development to be called Biltmore Forest. Included in the plans were to be an 18-hole golf course designed by Donald Ross, a private country club and an exclusive clubhouse.

Initially, Mrs. Vanderbilt had been reluctant to part with any of the land adjacent to the grounds around the house, but an incident at the Asheville Country Club, where for years she had been a member, seemed to have changed her mind. According to local legend, Edith Vanderbilt, after finishing a game of tennis, had taken a seat in the dining area and lit up a cigarette. A new manager stepped over and politely reminded her that women were not allowed to smoke in the club's public areas. Mrs. Vanderbilt reportedly handed the manager her still lit cigarette, excused herself, then walked to a nearby phone, where she called Junius Adams at his law office.

"Mr. Adams," she reportedly said, "we're going to build a country club."

Seely, too, had originally hoped the female guests at the Grove Park Inn would only smoke in the Ladies' Parlor he had placed just off the Great Hall, but as the woman's suffrage movement grew in voice and in number, more and more women were brazenly lighting their cigarettes alongside the men in the Great Hall. Unlike the manager of the Asheville Country Club, who that day had lost forever the patronage of Edith Vanderbilt and her friends -- and would soon have to deal with a competing country club -- Seely had decided it was in his best interest not to enforce the rule too stringently. The empty Ladies' Parlor, he decided, could be converted into a Writing Room, thus enabling him to discourage guests from penning postcards and letters in their rooms, where some invariably spilled ink on his expensive French rugs.

Clustered around Junius Adams were several men whom Seely immediately recognized, including Thomas Wadley Raoul, owner of the Manor Inn and Albemarle Park, an eclectic grouping of quaint rental cottages on a well-manicured hillside above nearby Charlotte Street. Seely knew that E. W. Grove had long wanted to purchase from Raoul both the Manor Inn and Albemarle Park, which bordered the south edge of Grove's extensive holdings on Sunset Mountain.

If, as Seely suspected, Raoul had been selected by Adams to be one of the primary investors in Biltmore Forest, he might soon be ready to negotiate a selling price with Grove. The other two men Seely had met that evening just before the movie: Burnham S. Colburn, a retired banker from Detroit, and William Knight, a capitalist from St. Augustine, both of whom had come as guests of Junius Adams.

None seemed likely suspects....

"Did you hear what someone in Washington said the other day?" Judge Adams asked loudly enough for Seely to hear as he made his way toward the crowd pressed around Henry Ford.

"There are only seven men who will go through this war unscathed: Kaiser Wilhelm's six sons -- and Edsel Ford."

The men all laughed appreciatively. Seely glanced over and caught Raoul watching him for a reaction. Their eyes locked for a second, as Raoul shrugged his shoulders apologetically.

Though outsiders might consider them competitors for the Asheville tourist trade, Thomas Raoul and Fred Seely had recognized years earlier that they both could benefit by their joint efforts to improve the adjacent Asheville Country Club golf course. Since Raoul and Grove had emerged from the shake-up as its principle stockholders, guests at Raoul's nearby Manor Inn and the adjacent Grove Park Inn enjoyed discounted playing privileges at the golf course.

The course, first called the Swannanoa Hunt Club, had originally opened in 1894 with just five holes, but had evolved into a highly respected, 18-hole course designed by Donald Ross, the country's first and foremost golf course architect.

Raoul and Seely had labored together to convince the stockholders, including E. W. Grove and a sullen Tench Coxe, to provide $25,000 for the purchase of additional land from the Kimberly family necessary for the golf course's expansion, the cost of the architect's fees and reconstruction of the course. The result, they promised, would be the South's finest golf course outside of Pinehurst. "For someone who takes such a keen interest in the improvement of our golf course," Raoul once wrote Seely, "you certainly should consider taking up the game."

Raoul currently served as president of the Asheville Country Club and often ate lunch with Seely at the hotel, but Seely could not help but wonder if Raoul's new alliance with Junius Adams and his downtown political cronies would soon erode their friendship.

And what would Raoul think of what he had just done?
Would he have done the same?

With no obvious suspects, no one acting unusual, Seely paused in the middle of the Great Hall. He felt drawn back to his office, almost as if he needed to check on his guest, his unexpected guest -- *the only guest without a name* -- but he knew his absence from the room might later draw attention, unwanted attention to himself and his actions.

But if he had to stay, he might as well make Judge Adams pay for his remark -- by finding the only person the judge wouldn't want him with: Edith Vanderbilt.

As he approached, he noted with pride that she wore a tan skirt and jacket made from his hand-woven Biltmore Industries homespun, the single-breasted jacket buttoned at her tapered waist over a light blue silk blouse. Her fashionable hat was pinned to her long, brown hair, wrapped, as it always was in public, around the crown of her head. At forty-five, the widow of Biltmore need make no apology for her appearance, for she continued to turn heads wherever she went.

Spotting Fred Seely over Gertrude Grove's shoulder, Edith Vanderbilt shot him a silent plea for help. Mrs. Grove had already launched into a loud, detailed description of her most recent ailment, a partial obstruction of her lower bowel, which she theorized had been caused by scar tissue left from a surgery nearly twenty years earlier.

Seely recalled it clearly, for at the time Grove had preempted Fred and Evelyn's planned honeymoon that October, contending that only Evelyn could provide her stepmother with the care she would require after surgery. Grove had insisted that immediately following their St. Louis wedding, Fred and Evelyn would return by train to the Grove family home in Asheville, along with Gertrude and eight-year-old Edwin.

As soon as Mama Grove had been released from the hospital and settled into their master bedroom, complete with a sterling silver call bell on the mahogany nightstand, Grove conveniently felt compelled to leave for San Antonio to check on some of the jobbers working the territory for the Paris Medicine Company.

Seely duly reported to work each day at the dingy warehouse Grove had leased on the corner of South Main and Atkin Streets, overseeing production of Grove's Bromo-Quinine Cold Tablets. Each evening he locked up the shop, then walked up the hill to catch the streetcar outside the Social Smoke Shop at Pack Square for the return trip along Merrimon Avenue to his father-in-law's home.

There, after listening to Gertrude Grove's endless list of complaints about everything from the weather to her husband's continued absence, he and his new bride retreated to her second floor bedroom next to that of young Edwin. Their honeymoon had consisted of a single night at the Statler Hotel in St. Louis – compliments of Grove, who had been a regular client there for years. Their awkward fumblings in the dark and Seely's quick release left him feeling frustrated with himself. He had confessed his inexperience to her, but could not interpret her silence as approval -- or disappointment.

Their brief courtship, most of which had taken place during the summer of 1898 on her father's front porch, had not provided the opportunity for anything more than a lingering good night kiss. Grove had always insisted that they dine together as a family and Seely certainly could never have suggested that Evelyn come up to his room at the unsavory Swannanoa Hotel and its collection of rumpled traveling salesmen.

His plan to hire a horse and buggy for a Saturday afternoon ride in the country almost ended in disaster, as the horse bolted when some nearby boys started lighting firecrackers. Evelyn, who had never been comfortable around horses, was left shaking and terrified. It was all Seely could do to convince her not to walk back to the livery stable.

By the end of summer Evelyn had seemed ready to be married, although she never seemed as anxious as Seely to get out from beneath her father's roof. Their time together as a married couple in her childhood room did not prove to be much better than their wedding night at the Statler, as Evelyn always worried that Edwin would hear them. She consented to Fred's advances only when convinced everyone in the house was sound asleep, and then her only participation was to whisper in his ear to hurry, but to be quiet. After a few weeks it became easier not to ask.

He could not help but wonder if Edith Vanderbilt's
first nights with her new husband that same summer
had been as confusing for her.

"Mrs. Vanderbilt, did you bring your camera along tonight?" Seely asked teasingly as he stepped up beside the pair. He could feel Gertrude Grove bristle with indignation over the interruption.

"Why, no, Mr. Seely. My little Kodak doesn't compare with your cameras – and I knew there wouldn't be enough light in here for it. I'm sure your guests have tired by now of having their photographs taken. "

"You no doubt are right on both accounts, but if you would like to bring it along tomorrow to the luncheon, I'm sure we'll have ample opportunity to take some photographs out on the terrace. You'll be joining us, too, won't you, Mama Grove? Mr. Ford's personal chef is teaming up with our Mr. Moreno to create something special for us. I'm sure you won't be disappointed."

"I have a doctor's appointment in the morning, Fred, and I am sure he won't want me traipsing up here afterwards. Besides, unless Mr. Ford's chef can have some influence on him, your Mr. Moreno will be making something far too rich for my sensitive digestive system. Dr. Pritchard has insisted that...."

"Excuse me for interrupting, Mama Grove, but did you see that Dr. Westin is here this evening? That's him over by the front desk, in the dark suit. Evelyn's been seeing him and we're quite pleased with the progress she's making. Perhaps he could prescribe some medication for that persistent cough you've been dealing with. I understand he's considering opening a pulmonary clinic here in Asheville. I know he would enjoy the opportunity to meet you, for I'm sure he has heard a great deal about you."

"I would imagine so. Was he in town when we had the ground-breaking ceremony? It still irritates me that the newspaper failed to print a picture of me turning over the first shovel of dirt. Even with all we've done here, we're still considered outsiders, isn't that right, Edith?"

"Why, yes, I suppose so, although I'll assure you, Mrs. Grove, Asheville is far friendlier than Washington."

"You couldn't convince me of that. If it wasn't for the heat, I'd be on the train back to St. Louis tomorrow. But I had better go and meet Dr. Westin before he leaves. I hope we see each other again soon, Edith."

"I hope so, too, Mrs. Grove."

They watched as she swiveled and set her sights on the new doctor.

Dr. Ronald Westin had arrived in Asheville two years earlier, reportedly to explore the possibility of opening a pulmonary clinic to treat tubercular patients. He sought out Fred Seely almost immediately and over lunch in the Plantation Room outlined his plans to bring a number of potential investors up from Miami. Dr. Westin had also hinted that he might be able to persuade some major medical associations to hold their annual conventions at the Grove Park Inn.

Fred Seely had earlier instituted a policy of rejecting convention business, but the idea of hosting a group of prominent physicians and the residual business they could bring to the hotel intrigued him. Yet, as he listened to Westin that day, something about the doctor bothered him. And while he kept waiting to hear what Dr. Westin would expect in return for his referrals, no proposal was forthcoming.

When asked, Dr. Westin seemed purposely vague about his own background, so that afternoon Seely had called Sherman Burns, secretary of the William J. Burns International Detective Agency in New York, requesting a background report on the doctor. Burns later wired that Ronald Westin had a medical degree from Johns Hopkins University in psychiatry, but had also served an internship at the University of Miami in their pulmonary ward. Westin, who was fifty-five years old, had been married twice. The detective reported that Westin's neighbors were not sure if he and his second wife, who they believed to be several years younger than him, were still legally married.

Seely learned from his local sources that in the spring of 1917 Westin had signed a three month lease on an apartment at the Manor Inn, located halfway between the Grove Park Inn and downtown. Westin soon made good on his promise to bring a number of Miami businessmen to Asheville, always booking rooms for them at the Grove Park Inn directly through Fred Seely. After the first time, in which Westin brought two bankers and an attorney to Asheville for nearly a week, Seely made it a point to also set aside a room for Dr. Westin, at no charge.

Dr. Westin happened to be in the Grove Park Inn that prior February, when Evelyn, who had given birth to Fred Jr. on the 23rd of December (his father's 45th birthday), had a particularly rough night. In the weeks following the baby's birth, Evelyn had grown moody and disconsolate. She paid little attention to the other children, preferring, instead, to remain in her room at the hotel, where Fred had moved her and the baby down from their home, Overlook Castle, so that he could check on them both throughout the day.

The nurse reported that Evelyn had been crying most of that day and, other than during her breastfeeding times, had not asked to see the baby. That night Fred found his wife pacing the room relentlessly, sobbing uncontrollably. When he could not quiet her, he sent the nurse to find Dr. Westin. As Fred watched from the corner of the room, Dr. Westin calmed Evelyn in a low, soothing voice, coaxing her to sit with him on the couch. He stayed with her the remainder of the night, sending Fred to the pharmacy in the morning with a prescription for lithium citrate.

Upon his return to Asheville a few weeks later, Dr. Westin scheduled twice-weekly therapy sessions with Evelyn. As he explained to Seely, Evelyn was suffering from postpartum depression, which he felt he could treat with a combination of therapy and, when necessary, lithium. His concern was preventing her depression from developing into postpartum psychosis, characterized, he explained, by seeing things that weren't there, confusion, rapid mood swings and, worst of all, the potential of harming either herself or baby Fred.

Their therapy sessions were generally held in the Seely's second floor suite, but as the weather improved Dr. Westin often took Evelyn for long afternoon rides in his automobile. Fears of America's involvement in the war in Europe had severely shrunk the number of reservations that summer, enabling Seely to set aside a sixth floor room for Dr. Westin to use as needed, either on days when the older Seely children were in the hotel or when the weather prevented him from taking Evelyn out for a ride.

Seely never felt that Dr. Westin's monthly bill for her treatment reflected the amount of time he spent with her, so he never minded providing the doctor with a free room. Evelyn obviously enjoyed and benefited from their therapy sessions, which were now in their second year. Seely observed that Dr. Westin continued to divide his time between Miami and Asheville, although his plans for a new clinic did not seem to have progressed since he had arrived.

"I trust you enjoyed the movie, Mrs. Vanderbilt."

"I did, Mr. Seely, but I must say I was somewhat surprised at your selection. A bit daring for your typical Grove Park Inn crowd, wasn't it?"

"I feared as much, but with such little notice I really did not have any choice. It was either this or Ambassador Gerard's war picture, which I thought would be just too depressing for the occasion."

"You're probably right. You always think things through completely, Mr. Seely. And the hotel looks simply wonderful. Cornelia's up here quite often for your dances and has told me such complimentary things about it - and coming from an 18-year-old, that in itself is a compliment. But, tell me, how are our woodworkers and weavers getting along next door? I understand your new workshops are idyllic. Someone described them to me as 'quaint English cottages nestled amid the mountain pines.' It sounded so poetic."

"Very well, thank you. We've added five more looms and two additional colors: Midnight Violet and Chinese Red."

"That's wonderful." She hesitated slightly, then lowered her voice. "I was so disappointed to learn that young George Arthur has left. He showed so much promise -- and leadership. After Miss Vance and Miss Yale moved to Tryon, I wasn't sure what I was going to do, but he stepped right up and took charge and really held everything together, until..., well, I feel responsible for the troubles the two of you had. I should not have expected him to handle the negotiations between us. I was so worried that working over all of the numbers and the finances of the business would cause such a strain on our friendship that I neglected to think of how it would affect his relations with you afterwards, with you then becoming his employer. It was a mistake, my mistake and I wish to apologize to you for it. I feel I have cost you a wonderful manager, not to mention a skilled woodworker and carver."

"And if you had let me handle the negotiations," Junius Adams interjected, stepping into the conversation from behind Edith Vanderbilt, "Mr. Seely here would have had to pay double what he did for Biltmore Industries." He practically spit out his words. "You stole that one, Seely -- and you hammered poor George Arthur 'til he gave in to you. No wonder he couldn't work for you afterwards."

"Judge Adams," Edith Vanderbilt protested, "that is water over the dam. Mr. Seely had every right to offer what he thought it was worth and I accepted it gladly. No one else showed any interest in it and no one else certainly would have invested all that Mr. Seely has in the new workshops. Have you seen them?"

"No. Mr. Seely has not yet invited me over for a tour, but I'm expecting an invitation any day now."

"At your convenience, Mr. Adams. Our doors are always open wide for you."

Mrs. Vanderbilt smiled at Seely's subtle reference to Junius Adams' ample girth. "Perhaps you will accompany me over to Biltmore Industries tomorrow, Mr. Adams. After lunch?"

"With pleasure, Mrs. Vanderbilt. And, if I may, could I have a word with you now?" Adams looked at Seely. "In private?"

Mrs. Vanderbilt gave Seely a dour, playful smile, then sighed, "Yes, Mr. Adams. You may. Thank you, Mr. Seely, for a most memorable evening. I look forward to our luncheon tomorrow with your guests."

Seely watched with a tinge of jealousy he hadn't expected as Junius Adams, hand at her elbow, guided Edith Vanderbilt over toward his business partners.

He then took stock of the whereabouts of his special guests. As he expected, a crowd remained gathered around them, the largest pressed up against Henry Ford, looking even taller in his high, starched white collar above his tightly knotted tie, gray vest and jacket.

His wispy white hair and high forehead gave him more of the look of a statesman than an automobile manufacturer, Seely thought. *Perhaps he will end up in Congress, then what -- the White House? Ford might have a problem getting the politicians in Washington to adopt to his famous methods of efficiency, not that they couldn't use some streamlining....*

Unlike Ford, Thomas Edison looked miserable, unable to hear most of what was being said to him, nodding in deference and, Seely surmised, anxious to escape to his room on the Palm Court.

Seely headed for him first, noting on the way that John Burroughs and Harvey Firestone, clearly not the crowd favorites, had begun making their way toward the elevator. A few feet ahead of them Mrs. Chiles, with her husband in tow and a handkerchief over her mouth, had the same idea.

Perhaps Harold would get to meet John Burroughs after all, he thought.

Edison, in a loose bow tie and rumpled long jacket more fashionable twenty years earlier, smiled in appreciation as Seely approached. "Our guests have had a tiring day, folks, and I am sure you appreciate their need to get some well-deserved rest. May I show you the way to the elevator, Mr. Edison?"

Unsure how much of what he said could he heard by the 71-year-old inventor, Seely pointed toward the south elevator.

Edison turned and fell in step beside him, "Thank you, sir."

Seely handed Edison over to Frank Mull, the elevator operator, who made room for him alongside Burroughs and Firestone, plus Mr. and Mrs. Chiles. With three of the four campers now on their way to their rooms, the crowd around Henry Ford had increased in size. Both local and national reporters peppered the congressional candidate with questions about the successful advance of the French and British forces along the Hindenburg line, as well as reports of street fighting between American and Mexican forces in Nogales. But the crowd wanted to hear more of Ford's reaction to his nomination by the Democrats in Michigan as their candidate for the vacant senatorial seat.

Catching sight of Seely at the fringe of the crowd, Ford used the opportunity to deflect the reporters' persistent questions about the Michigan election and a possible bid for the White House in 1920.

"Our host, Mr. Seely," Ford announced to the crowd as he reached out and drew him forward by the shoulder, "has, I have been told, recently taken up the sport of horseback riding here in the mountains of North Carolina. Unfortunately, I have never developed an appreciation for those worthy steeds, but as someone once remarked, my aversion for horses may have subconsciously inspired me to pursue the development of the horseless carriage!"

As the crowd laughed, Ford leaned over and whispered, "May I have a few moments of your time before you retire for the evening? Perhaps in your office?"

Seely replied, "Certainly, Mr. Ford. I have just a few things to attend to first."

"Not a problem. Would, lets say, twenty minutes from now be convenient?"

Seely nodded, afraid saying anything else might draw attention to his plight. Ford immediately turned back to the reporters and his audience. "Thank you, gentlemen. And ladies. As I was saying, one day not long ago, as I was driving past a cemetery near my home I spotted a man digging the largest hole I had ever seen in a cemetery. Being a curious sort, I had to stop and inquire. 'What are you doing,' I asked, 'digging a hole for an entire family?'

'The grave digger paused, leaned on his shovel and looked up at me, 'No. Just one man.'

'Then, why such a huge hole?' I asked.

'Well, this fellow, he was a might bit queer. Seems he insisted that he be buried sitting inside his Ford automobile.'

Ford paused to let the visual image sink into his audience before continuing.

'Did he say why?' I asked.

'In fact, he did,' the grave digger continued, 'he said that his Ford had pulled him out of every other hole he had found himself in, so he reckoned it could pull him out of this one, too.' "

Seely stepped away as the crowd roared in approval, then pressed his back up against one of the six massive rock pillars supporting the concrete ceiling of the Great Hall. Instinctively, he looked up at the ceiling, judging where the young woman had lain, then looked over to where he had been standing.

I didn't hear a thing....

He thought back to the day when the workmen were shoveling twelve inches of concrete over the steel-reinforced forms. He recalled the men laughing over the amount of concrete he had them pouring into the hotel, yet, just as he had planned, little of it was now visible, as its gray, flat surface had been meticulously disguised by rocks, boulders, paint, stencils, tiles and rugs.

"The entire mountain could come crashing down," one of them remarked, "and this hotel would still be standing."

"It better be a money maker," another added, "cause they'll never figure out a way to tear it down." The men laughed. An Italian stonemason who, twenty years earlier, had ridden the train down from Cincinnati to work on George Vanderbilt's mansion chided the men, telling them how the foundation under the Biltmore House was nearly thirty feet deep and fifteen feet wide. "Ten million pounds of Indiana limestone we laid," he declared proudly, "and not one crack anywhere."

"I'll bet Vanderbilt paid you more back then than Grove is today, Sergio."

Not true, Seely thought. *Experienced stonemasons had been hard to come by.*

The Carolina mountain men were fine for hauling in wagon loads of rocks, building scaffolding and grunting boulders into place in this new six story mountain, but they had little experience mixing mortar to the perfect consistency, knowing which rock would fit before it was even picked up off the ground and judging how high the stone could be laid in a day before the mortar would have to harden or the section would come sliding down.

Seely had paid the common labors a dollar a day, fifty cents more if they brought a healthy mule. Carpenters had earned $2.50

for their ten hour shift and the stonemasons, like Sergio, were paid $3.50. They had stood in line each Saturday afternoon outside the wooden shanty propped up on stilts on the steep hillside near the entrance to the construction site. Inside, his foreman Oscar Mills, who always knew by first name every man and boy, Negro and white, working on the hotel, paid the workers in cash, securing from each one a personal promise to return the following Monday morning, letting those whom he or Seely had not been satisfied with know that they would not be needed.

Fred Seely had stood behind Oscar, watching the stacks of bills and silver coins dwindle as the line of men, the knees of their overalls patched or in tatters from the rough rocks, the fingers of their gloves worn through by ropes, rocks and chains, and the palms of their outstretched hands as smooth and as taunt as shoe leather from the hickory handles of the wheelbarrows.

As the crowd reluctantly began thinning, with the Asheville people making their way toward their waiting cars and guests toward the elevators at either end of the Great Hall, Seely continued to scan the crowd, wondering who in the room had come with the young woman in the pink dress, who would be lingering, looking for her right now....

Could someone have seen her fall?

Seen her jump?

He shook his head. He knew she did not fall and could not believe she could have had reason to jump.

Surely someone would have been with her.

But why not come forward? Why not yell for help?

Fred continued to scan the milling crowd.

Unless they didn't want help....

Unless it wasn't an accident....

Could someone have really pushed her over the wall....?

Did a murderer just walk out the door into the night?

Or up the stairs…?

But who?

And why?

Seely's head began to ache as he thought of the repercussions.

Not here. Not at the Grove Park Inn. And not now.

Not tonight.

Seely turned and bumped into Mrs. Anderson, wife of Colonel Clifford Anderson, a prominent Atlanta attorney and retired commander in the National Guard, as she stopped to open her purse.

"Excuse me, Mrs. Anderson," Seely apologized as he knelt down to pick up her small purse. "I am terribly sorry." He handed her the purse and motioned her ahead.

"Quite alright, Mr. Seely, but, please, go on. I'm sure you have far more important matters to attend to than me."

"No, not really. Just a bit distracted. I guess my eyes haven't completely adjusted to the light, but, thank you, I will."

Seely's heart began to pound in his chest.

Her purse.

She must have had a purse.

The girl's purse.

Where was it?

It wasn't next to her body, so where would it be?

A line had begun to form at each of the two elevators taking guests up to the rooms on the third floor Palm Court and the fourth, fifth and sixth floors above it. Guests on the short second floor wings would probably take the stairs, he reasoned, but everyone else – he hoped – would be waiting for an elevator.

He quickened his pace as he headed for the stairway.

Think about it, he told himself.

Her broken neck.

She must have been killed instantly.

She landed on the third floor, which means she must have fallen from the fifth or sixth floor.

The fourth floor might not have been high enough.

The fifth or sixth floor.

That's where her purse would be.

Perhaps no one had been up there yet.

Seely looked ahead at the line in front of the elevator. The first load had contained the Chiles, so it would be stopping at the third floor. Edison, Burroughs and Firestone were with them, as he had assigned all of them adjoining third floor rooms overlooking the golf course. The second load hadn't gone up yet, so perhaps he would have time.

Restraining his impulse to dash over to the stairs, he walked steadily across the Great Hall, passing the front desk to the steps leading to the upper floors.

"Mr. Seely!"

It was Edward Higgins from behind the front desk.

"If you have a moment? There is someone here who needs to talk with you."

Seely stopped at the foot of the stairs, as a half dozen heads turned at the sound of his name.

Not now, Higgins, he muttered to himself. *Not now!*

"Fred!" Someone else in the crowd called out. He tried to see who at the front desk needed to talk with him, but the crush of people around it made it impossible.

"Wonderful movie, Mr. Seely." He recognized Dr. Joseph Leidy, from Chicago, and his wife, Victoria.

"Thank you, Dr. Leidy. I'm glad you enjoyed it." He took another step toward the stairs.

"Mr. Seely!"

Edward's voice grew more shrill as he hurried from behind the front desk toward Seely.

Seely stepped up onto the first grey-tiled step, turned and calmly said, "Edward, I have to attend to Mr. Edison. I will be right back."

Before the desk manager -- or anyone else -- could protest, Fred Seely turned and started briskly up the stairs, leaving the din in the Great Hall behind him as he reached the landing and, finding himself alone, turned and took the stairs to the fifth floor two at a time.

Roycroft chairs, tray stands and lighting fixtures filled the Plantation Dining Room.

Chapter 6

*We prefer not to entertain children under ten years of age.
Not that we dislike children ourselves, but that we wish
to maintain a place where tired, busy people may get away
from excitement and all annoyances and rest their nerves.*

Frederick L. Seely, President
Grove Park Inn, Inc.
1918 Brochure

10:00pm
Tuesday
27 August 1918

The grey-tiled stairway leading from the ground floor of the Grove
Park Inn up to the second floor landing, where Fred and Evelyn's
four room suite occupied the far end of the short south wing, never
failed to remind Fred Seely of the tiled stairway that had lead to his
second floor office at the *Atlanta Georgian*.

No one spoke much of their seven years in Atlanta. Evelyn
had been homesick much of the time, pushed reluctantly into the
role of the wife of a newspaper publisher in a city she never enjoyed,
in a society she would never be accepted. Her days were totally con-
sumed by their children. Gertrude was not yet five, Louise was but
two, their son John Day Seely was a newborn -- and Evelyn would
soon be pregnant with James.

To make matters worse, her father, oblivious to the stress she was under, had in the summer of 1908 sent 18-year-old Edwin Jr. to live with them. Edwin had developed into a rebellious and disrespectful teenager that neither his father nor his mother could control. E. W. Grove was quick to point out that the spacious Peachtree Avenue home he had bought for Fred and Evelyn had enough room for all of them. Seely knew – as did both Evelyn and her father – that Fred could not afford to buy them a house as large as what his father-in-law had provided, so he reluctantly welcomed the resentful young Edwin into their home.

Seely's day typically began before six o'clock and he often stayed at the newspaper until well after the children had all gone to bed. The only way he could hope to exert any positive influence on Edwin was to put the young man to work at the newspaper, which Edwin hated -- and made no attempt to hide.

Whenever his thoughts turned to those early years at the newspaper, Fred Seely could not help but recall one particularly hot and muggy Friday in July of 1908. It had been just before noon, when he was studying the week's circulation figures Mr. Ringhausen had just dropped off. The numbers were good, too good.

Three years earlier E. W. Grove had convinced Seely to hire John Temple Graves as their editor at the *Atlanta Georgian*. Graves had worked at the other Atlanta newspapers and was well-known to the people of Atlanta, but Seely wondered if he would be able to exert any control over the outspoken editor. Graves had a history of battling with his superiors, but Grove was adamant that they needed an insider to have any chance of competing against the established Atlanta newspapers.

Readers had responded to John Temple Graves' editorials and his flair for sensational headlines. Seely had winced the first time he read "Men Are Blown Into Small Bits By Boiler Blast" and "Dead Infant in Sack Swinging from Tree Found in School Yard," but he could not deny the fact that Graves knew how to sell papers.

What he was totally unprepared for, however, was Graves' blatant call for the complete domination of the Negro race by the whites. Many people still held Graves personally responsible for the Atlanta race riot two years earlier, a deadly riot spawned by a series of lurid stories falsely claiming that three white women had been raped by roaming Negroes. Graves had advocated "reducing the Negro for his own protection and for his own welfare to the acceptance of a place of inferiority until such time as he can be separated from the white race and moved to another territory."

Regardless of how uncomfortable he sometimes felt, Fred Seely could not deny the growing popularity of his outspoken editor. Newsboys were selling papers as fast as they rolled off the press, especially Graves' special editions with his trademark lurid headlines.

But growing circulation figures meant more paper and more ink, far more than Seely had anticipated in the initial projections he had submitted to Grove. And, so far, advertisers had not come forward to help shoulder the cost.

Fred Seely was an outsider, a Northerner, a Yankee. The war had only been over for little more than forty years and evidence of the havoc General Sherman had unleashed on Atlanta still remained as a grim and bitter reminder of their defeat at the hands of the hated Yankees. Charred bridge timbers, warehouse walls pot-marked by artillery shells and ghostly bunkers still dotted the fringe of the city.

Old Confederate veterans, many without an arm or a leg, hobbled about downtown's Five Points, living off what they could beg from businessmen and cotton farmers who came to town. Resentment ran deep. There were those who still mourned the death of

John Wilkes Booth more than the president he had murdered, men who still drank a toast to Jefferson Davis and General Robert E. Lee, men whose fathers and brothers had been hastily buried in shallow craters near towns none had ever heard of, yet would never forget: Shiloh, Antietam, Bull Run, Gettysburg.

As Seely soon learned, one man – Captain James Warren English – now controlled Atlanta. Orphaned as a child, James English had learned the craft of a carriage maker from an uncle before enlisting in the Confederate Army. Though wounded five times, Captain English remained loyal to the cause, riding to the final meeting at Appomattox alongside General Lee. He returned to an Atlanta left a smoldering ruin by marauding Yankee troops.

Sensing opportunity, Captain English began buying prime parcels of real estate in the heart of the city. Then, when the inevitable rebuilding began, he established the Chattahoochee Brick Company and parlayed friendships with Georgia politicians into a contract by which his Chattahoochee Brick Company leased convict labor from the state prison for a few pennies an hour.

No one man was more responsible than Captain James English for transforming Atlanta's ravaged downtown -- an unruly conglomeration of taverns, railroad shanties and brothels -- into the metropolis that became Georgia's state capital -- and no one man had profited more from it. The ramrod straight Captain commanded town officials like he once commanded his troops, tearing down abandoned buildings, paving streets, shutting down gambling houses, even going so far as to have the Atlanta police empty the contents of one notorious gambling house into the street, where, as a warning to others, the pile of poker tables, roulette wheels, chairs and plush couches was set on fire.

At various times serving as both the city's mayor and police commissioner, Captain English and his cronies built the Atlanta Terminal Company, which serviced no fewer than six different railroad companies from points across the South and beyond. From atop his sixteen story skyscraper – the tallest in the city – at the corner of Marietta and Peachtree Streets, Captain English presided over not only his bank, the Fourth National Bank of Atlanta, but the city's financial district as well.

Fred Seely learned this and more in his first weeks as publisher of the *Atlanta Georgian*, the upstart newspaper naively intent on shouldering its way alongside the *Atlanta Journal* and the *Atlanta Constitution*, two well-established papers with strong political ties to Captain English and his appointees.

> *All it would take,* Seely reasoned, *would be one ad from English's Fourth National Bank to unlock the floodgates to a sea of advertisers.*

He and Evelyn had joined the First Presbyterian Church and watched as Captain English, his wife Emily, their six grown children and their young families strode into church each Sunday. Now nearly seventy and his mane turned white, the Captain's step never faltered. One Sunday, soon after the first issue of the *Georgian* had rolled off the press, Seely worked up the courage to introduce himself and Evelyn to Captain English and his wife. The captain, Seely noted, not only knew who he was, but seemed to have anticipated the meeting. Polite, charming, yet reserved, Captain English gracefully accepted their introduction, but stopped short of extending either a business or social invitation to the Seelys.

As he stood in his corner office that Friday afternoon in 1908, looking down at the bustling Whitehall Street below, Seely spotted

Frank Lochran standing across the street, suspiciously looking as if he were waiting for someone.

Lochran had once worked for Seely as an assistant pressman. His primary duty had been to periodically wipe the zinc plates clean with a rag dipped in a combination of mineral spirits and denatured alcohol to keep the recesses in the letters from filling with dried ink. Seely had never warmed to the 20-year-old, whom he had seen more than once smoking a cigarette on the loading dock while waiting for a load of paper to arrive. During his first week at the paper, Lochran had taught Edwin Grove a bawdy limerick, which Edwin impishly recited at the dinner table in front of their small children:

Peters Street for wagon yards,
Whitehall Street for stores,
Peachtree Street for dressy feet,
And Courtland Street for whores.

A few months earlier, Seely had been leaving the Piedmont Hotel, where he had hoped to secure an advertising contract with Hoke Smith -- owner of Atlanta's most elegant hotel and now a candidate for the governor's office -- when a small Negro newspaper boy, unaware of who Seely was, asked if he wanted to buy a copy of the *Georgian*.

Seely smiled, reached into his pocket for a shiny, new Liberty Head nickel and opened the rolled paper. His smile disappeared as he stared at the front page, where every "a" and "e" and "o" in the masthead were blots of smeared ink.

Seely called the newspaper boy back and quickly thumbed through each of his papers, his facing growing redder with each blurred masthead. Pushing the newspapers back into the arms of the bewildered boy, Seely practically ran the six blocks along Peachtree Street back to the newspaper, where he confronted Lochran as he was cleaning up the presses after the final run. Before Lochran could offer any explanation, an enraged Seely fired him on the spot, demanding, as he shoved the newspaper into his chest, that the young man leave the building that very minute or he would call the police.

Seely hadn't seen Lochran since that day and he guessed, as he watched him across the street, that Lochran was waiting for someone inside the *Georgian* building. But Lochran appeared to have no intention of crossing the street onto Fred Seely's turf. As he waited, Lochran lit up a cigarette and pretended to read the newspaper he had stuck in his back pocket. *The Constitution*, Seely noted. Seely didn't have to wait long to find out who Lochran was meeting, for within a few minutes he spotted Edwin Grove making his way over the streetcar rails to where Lochran stood.

Lochran offered Edwin a cigarette, which he declined with a glance over his shoulder up at the second floor office. Seely stepped back to avoid being seen, then, as he peered through a crack between the curtain and the wall, considered opening the window in hopes of hearing their conversation. The noise from the street, plus the risk of being seen opening the window, squelched the plan, so Seely could only watch as Lochran was obviously trying to convince Edwin of something. Edwin listened intently, then nodded, took out his wallet and handed Lochran some bills.

Whiskey, women or gambling, Seely muttered.

Edwin said something in return to Lochran, causing both young men to look at the new watches on their wrists – a recent fad Seely still felt was more suited to women than men.

Seely glanced over his shoulder at the Howard pendulum clock on the wall. It was a quarter until twelve. Seely left the office at

12:15pm each day, either driving up Peachtree Street to see Evelyn and the children at home or to take a potential client out to lunch. He suspected everyone in the entire office and plant knew his daily routine, including Edwin, who Seely was rotating through various departments in hopes of finding something that would interest the rebellious young man.

Everyone also knew that Edwin was the only son of E. W. Grove, Seely's silent partner and father-in-law. And while Seely implored his department heads to treat Edwin as they would any employee, none ever did. As a result, Edwin simply floated from department to department, never being asked to shoulder any real responsibility and never asking to. He was currently assisting Mr. Moore in the advertising department, but so far had only succeeded in burning up several tanks of gasoline and denting the fender of the new Maxwell his father had bought him on his last trip to Atlanta.

The two young men shook hands, then, with another glance up at Seely's office, Edwin trotted back across the street and disappeared from view. Twenty-five minutes later, at precisely 12:10, a single beep told Seely that Jeremy, one of their Negro delivery boys, had brought his car around from the garage at the far end of the printing plant. Seely picked up his hat from the oak hall tree standing beside his door, let Mrs. Davis know that he was leaving for lunch and headed down the stairs.

"Another hot one, Mr. Seely," Jeremy announced as he held the door of his shiny black Packard open for him.

"Thank you, Jeremy. It certainly is. When I get back will you check the water level in the radiator?" Jeremy nodded. "But be sure to let it cool off first. I don't want you blowing water all over the engine compartment."

"No, sir, Mr. Seely. I won't let that happen."

Seely nodded, checked his mirror and pulled out into the traffic on Whitehall Street heading north. Two blocks later, it would become Peachtree Street at Five Points, beneath the shadow of Captain English's bank. As soon as he was out of sight of the *Georgian*, however, Seely circled back on Pryor Street, then pulled into a vacant lot a hundred yards south of the *Georgian*. He eased his Packard just past a large wagon loaded with cotton bales until he could see the back of Edwin's car parked along Whitehall Street next to the building. As expected, Edwin appeared a few minutes later, jumped into his car and quickly headed toward Five Points.

Seely knew the conglomeration of streetcars at Five Points would slow Edwin down, so he didn't worry about losing sight of him. Seely opted to take Pryor back toward Five Points, keeping Edwin's car in sight between buildings as the young man continued north on Peachtree Street. At Houston, Edwin made a right hand turn and -- had he bothered to see if anyone was approaching from the south on Pryor Street -- could have easily spotted Seely's car. Seely ducked behind his steering wheel as Edwin flashed in front of him, then carefully followed a block behind as Edwin drove east on Houston Street.

Headed, Seely guessed, *for Courtland Street and his rendezvous with Frank Lochran.*

As his bawdy limerick professed, sections of Courtland Street provided men with their choice of either Negro or white prostitutes, any time of day or night. At the intersection of Houston and Courtland, Edwin Grove pulled to the curb and honked, prompting Frank Lochran to emerge from the doorway of a seedy apartment building carrying what appeared to Seely to be two rolled blankets and paper bags looking suspiciously like they contained liquor bottles.

Tossing the blanket into the back seat, Lochran hopped in and pointed north along Courtland. The two men continued up the street, which, considering the time of day and the oppressive heat, was relatively empty. A group of Negro men milled about a broken down delivery truck, while two working women, both white, stood on a raised stoop, scanning the cars that drove by for any potential customers.

Lochran seemed to have a destination in mind as he poked his head out the window and scanned barely visible house numbers. Suddenly he pointed ahead and Edwin slipped into an empty space at the granite curb. Lochran jumped out, leaving the car door open as he approached the door. He knocked loudly, then opened the door and disappeared from view. Seely had no choice but to pull his car over – directly behind the fractured delivery truck and its group of shade tree mechanics.

One of the girls on the step stood up hopefully, but Seely waved her away.

Barely eighteen, he thought.

Glumly, she sat back down, but not without hiking her dress and spreading her bare knees to give Seely a good look at what she had to offer. Embarrassed, he looked away, but felt his trousers tighten.

Ahead, Lochran reappeared on the sidewalk with two women in tow. The shorter of the two seemed about twenty-two, the taller a few years older.

Both were white, Seely noted, *and more attractive than he would have expected.*

Like the girl on the stoop, both wore skirts and blouses and had their hair cut short, as was the Atlanta fashion. The taller woman slipped into the back seat with Lochran, while the other plopped down next to Edwin and pulled the door closed.

As he followed a block behind, Seely watched Edwin speed up Courtland Street, cross Ponce de Leon Avenue and head north past Atkins Park, E. W. Grove's new housing development on the far north side of Atlanta.

He now knew where Edwin was going.

Beyond Atkins Park was a wooded section of rolling hills that Grove also owned, but had not yet developed. Oscar Mills, Grove's construction superintendent, and his crew had recently cut a road into the property, where they had built a machine shed for their grader and other equipment.

Seely knew the property well, as he had walked it several times with both E. W. Grove and Oscar, as they marked the location of future roads and building lots.

What he didn't know was how Edwin had found out that Grove had pulled Oscar and his men off the project just last week, sending them over to Fortified Hills, yet another of his developments around Atlanta, to work on the curbing there. Seely watched as Edwin's car disappeared in a cloud of dust as he pulled into the unmarked access road. Knowing he couldn't follow Edwin down the narrow road without being spotted, Seely parked his car a hundred yards to the west, where an overgrown logging road also lead deep into the property.

Seely knew the road Edwin had taken would lead him northeast to where the machine shed stood, then turned sharply west along a steep ravine, following the same former logging trail Seely had entered from the opposite end. Seely guessed that Edwin and Lochran wouldn't risk getting caught behind the machine shed by Oscar or one of his men. He figured they would continue west until they would be out of sight of anyone who might be sent out to the shed for some equipment.

As he topped the last gentle rise and headed down toward the ravine, Seely listened for the sound of Edwin's car approaching from the opposite direction, but could hear nothing other than the jays in the pine bows overhead announcing the arrival of an intruder.

Perhaps I was wrong.

At the point where the logging road dropped sharply down-hill, then turned to run alongside the ravine back toward the machine shed, Seely left the trail and climbed up an embankment overlooking the logging road and the ravine. To his right and several feet below him, Seely could see a pile of boulders that marked the spot where Oscar's grader had stopped widening the deserted logging road. Directly beneath the embankment where he stood, the narrow logging road had grown up in rhododendron and young oak and pine trees. No match for Oscar's steam-powered grader, but they would prevent anyone from driving an automobile any deeper into the woods.

At that moment Seely could hear the approach of Edwin's Maxwell slowly making its way over the hard clay ruts left by the grader. By the time it rounded the last turn and came to a stop a few feet from the boulders, Seely had lain down behind a large fallen pine tree through which he could clearly see the car and the logging road just a few yards below him. The glare of the mid-day sun on the windshield made it impossible for him to see what was happening inside the car, but from the sounds of laughter rolling out of the open windows, the four had been enjoying the contents of Lochran's paper bags.

After about five minutes, the back door swung open and Lochran stumbled out, announcing, "I gotta take a piss."

As he stood with his pants open facing the ravine, the other three emerged from the smoke-filled car. Edwin steadied himself on the fender, holding what appeared to be a whiskey bottle in one hand, while each of the women cradled a blanket in their arms. The taller and older of the two grabbed Lochran as he was finishing.

"Come on, honey. Let me shake that thing for you."

Laughing, the two of them stumbled off together down the logging trail beneath Seely, disappearing into a rhododendron thicket several yards to his left.

"Eddie and I are going to stay here, Marge," the younger woman yelled after them, but they didn't bother to respond.

"Come on," she said to Edwin, "Help me spread this thing out. I don't want to get any poison ivy on my tush."

Edwin walked unevenly around the boulders to where she had begun spreading the blanket out on a patch of level ground, directly below and just a few yards from where Seely hid. Though the air was still, the young woman placed her shoes on two of the corners, her purse on a third.

"Put your shoes over here," she directed Edwin, who had made his way to the blanket. "Here, Babs," he said, handing her the bottle, now nearly empty, "Hold this for me, will ya?"

"You sure didn't leave much for me," Babs pouted, finishing off what was left of the whiskey. She turned and flung the empty bottle into the ravine, nearly stumbling in after it. Edwin grabbed her around the waist to keep her from falling and she turned, laughing, to face him.

While Seely watched, they each began fumbling with the other's buttons, but she finished first, tugging his open shirt out of his trousers, then dropping her arms while he struggled with her last button.

She laughed and pulled open her blouse, revealing two large, teardrop-shaped breasts. Edwin immediately took one in each hand, kneading them beneath his fingers, then leaned down to kiss each of her dark nipples. Babs slipped her right hand beneath his outstretched arms and began rubbing his crotch, then dropped to her knees and unbuttoned his trousers, pulling them and his shorts down to his knees. Seely could hear Edwin groan in pleasure as she took him in her mouth and slowly began bobbing up and down.

While she did, Seely could see her reach for her purse and pull out a condom. He watched with strange admiration how seamlessly she brought Edwin to a full erection, slipped a condom on him and rolled onto her back, gently pulling him down atop her as she spread her legs, pulled up her dress and guided him into her.

Poised on his knees and palms, Edwin began thrusting into her, the white cheeks of his ass caught in the glare of the sun.

She pulled her blouse open again and lifted one loose breast up to his lips. Her hips quickly match the cadence of his and in less than a minute or two Edwin began to groan loudly, his face now buried between her shoulder and her neck, as he finished with three heaving thrusts, each accompanied with a howl that sounded almost as if he were in pain.

Babs rolled Edwin over onto his back as Frank Lochran called from somewhere in the rhododendron thicket. "Hey, Edwin! Ready to switch?"

A few seconds later Marge, the older of the two women, though she certainly looked no more than twenty-eight to Seely, emerged from the woods, carrying a bottle and her purse while smoothing down her dress and fussing with her hair. Like Babs, her blouse remained open, her two smaller, pert breasts barely concealed by the thin fabric. While the women switched places, Edwin reached down and pulled off his wet condom, flinging it into the weeds along the edge of the ravine, then finished pulling off his trousers and shorts. Marge handed him a bottle, which Edwin took a long swig from while resting on one elbow.

For an eighteen-year-old, Seely thought, *Edwin certainly had developed a taste for whiskey.*

Marge set her purse aside and went to work on Edwin's limp member, skillfully bringing it back to a full erection with her hands and mouth. As she did, she reached over and slid a condom out of her purse, unwrapped it and prepared to slip it on, but Edwin, pulling her hand away, had other ideas.

"Not this time," he muttered as he grabbed her shoulder with his left hand and roughly shoved her onto her back.

"Hey," Marge protested from beneath him, "what do think you're doing?"

Edwin pinned her right wrist to the blanket while he spread her legs apart with his knees and scooted forward to enter her.

"No way, mister," Marge insisted. "Put it on or get the hell off of me."

Edwin stopped, pushed himself up on his extended left arm, then, to Seely's amazement, suddenly slapped the woman across the left side of her face. The sound sickened Seely.

"You asshole," she spat at him, a trickle of blood appearing at the corner of her mouth.

Edwin raised his right hand to hit her again. "No, don't!" she pleaded, lifting her arm to block the blow, "Its, its okay. Just don't hit me, okay? It's alright. Whatever you want, Eddie. Whatever you want."

Edwin paused, his hand still poised above his head as he considered whether or not to hit her again. Marge carefully lowered her arm from over her face, sliding it down between them until she grasped him in her hand and began stroking.

"Its okay, Eddie," she cooed. "There… like it that way?"

Seely watched as Edwin's white ass scooted forward and slowly began rhythmically thrusting between her open legs. Marge reached up and pulled his right hand down to her breast, rubbing it over her raised nipple.

Edwin complied as he increased the speed of his thrusting. As he did, Marge wrapped her left leg over the back of his, then grasped both sides of his ass with her hands, pulling him deep inside her. Then, with a deft move, she shifted her weight to one side, used her shoulder to push Edwin in the opposite direction and in one practiced movement rolled Edwin onto his back with her atop him.

Before Edwin could react, she sat up and began slowly raising and lowering herself on him. "Take a look, Eddie," she whispered as she raised the hem of her dress for him to watch what she was doing. "You like that, baby? Nice and slow, in and out. Just for you, Eddie. Just the way you like it."

Edwin's head dropped back to the ground as he extended his arms and began clutching and releasing the edges of the blanket in syncopation with the rise and fall of her body on his. As he watched, Seely could see Edwin's hips rising to meet each of her downward thrusts as he neared his climax.

Marge could sense it, too, as she dropped her dress and placed each hand over his waist as she raised and lowered herself. Edwin began to moan in pleasure, lifting his pelvis until only his heels and his shoulders touched the ground beneath the plaid blanket.

But just as Seely expected to hear Edwin come a second time, Marge suddenly slid off him, reached down with her right hand to grasp his swollen penis and began sucking on it. Edwin made a low guttural sound, but seemed paralyzed as she furiously pumped it. Then, she lifted her head a few inches, pulled it out of her mouth and pointed it up toward his chest as she continued to expertly pump it with her right hand. A few seconds later large globs of warm, white semen shot across his pale, hairless chest.

Edwin let out a long, deep moan and collapsed, his muscles spent, his eyes closed against the glare of the mid-day sun. Marge slowed the pace of her strokes, coaxing the last of his cum out onto his stomach, as she reached over and pulled her purse closer.

Seely watched spellbound from his vantage point above them as Marge pulled something from her purse, something she seemed to be showing Edwin. Seely couldn't make out what it was until he heard a distinctive, metallic click and saw the shiny four-inch steel blade flash from the palm of her hand.

The sound snapped Edwin out of his slumber, but before he could react he felt the sharp point of the switchblade against the soft flesh on the underside of his chin. His eyes opened wide to see Marge's face just inches above his.

"Did you like that, Eddie?" Her voice no longer cooed like morning doves on a window ledge. She pressed the point deeper into the folds of fat beneath his chin, her voice low, raspy, insistent. "Did you like that, Eddie?"

Afraid to nod, Edwin blinked his eyes several times.

"Good. I thought so."

Marge looked down at the white globs on Edwin's chest. With the point of the knife still pressed under his chin, she began running a finger through them.

"You really like your jizum, don't you, Eddie? Like to spread it around. Like to share it with everybody." She paused. "Well, Eddie, maybe you'd like a taste of your own medicine." She scooped up a white glob of semen on her index finger and carefully carried it up to his mouth.

"Open wide, Eddie. I got a little present for you."

Edwin slowly opened his lips and Marge turned her finger over, letting the heavy, white fluid run to the end of her fingertip where it hung momentarily before dropping onto Edwin's tongue. "That's a good boy, Eddie," she said, scooping up another glob and wiping it across his lips, "You take your medicine like a good mama's boy."

Marge slid her left hand down over Edwin's stomach, pushed his shriveled, limp penis aside and cuddled his testicles in her palm. "Now listen to me, Eddie-boy," she instructed him, lifting his head backwards with the tip of her knife. "Listen real good. If you ever, ever hit me -- or any of my girls -- again," she pressed the knife until Edwin squeaked in pain, "I'll cut your nuts off."

With that, she pulled the knife back and squeezed his testicles together tightly in her clenched fist. Edwin's knees jerked to his chest, as he screamed out in pain.

"Hey!" Lochran yelled from the woods. "What's going on over there?"

"Everything's fine, Frankie," Marge answered calmly, as she stood up and began buttoning her blouse, while Edwin rocked back and forth in pain, groaning as he clutched his swelling testicles. "You guys about done in there?"

"I think so," Babs answered breathlessly. "How about you?"

"All finished."

Marge looked down as Edwin rolled over onto his hands and knees and began puking in the grass. She closed her switchblade and slipped it back into her purse.

"I'll meet you back at the car."

That night, for the first time in weeks, Evelyn relented to Seely's advances, but as he closed his eyes and struggled to stay focused atop her listless body, all he could envision was the woman in the woods, slowly raising and lowering herself, her pointed breasts glistening in the sun, beads of sweat clinging to her nipples as he gazed up at her.

The Palm Court, as seen from the 4th floor.

Chapter 7

We do, however, make one request and insist very positively upon
compliance with it: that guests refrain from unnecessary noise
in their rooms after 10:30pm. All public and amusement rooms
are open without restriction regarding hours, and the Management
will do all in its power to contribute to the comfort
and amusement of guests in those rooms.

Frederick L. Seely, President
Grove Park Inn, Inc.
1918 Brochure

10:00pm
Tuesday
27 August 1918

Fred Seely sprinted up the first and second flight of stairs, ducking past the open doorway leading to the third floor Palm Court, where he could hear the voices of Harold Chiles and John Burroughs as the first group of passengers stood chatting just outside the elevator. Frank Mull had already closed the door and was returning to the Great Hall for his second load of guests.

Seely grabbed the brass handrail and pulled himself up the stairs three at a time. Convinced that the young woman had to have fallen at least from the fifth floor to have died nearly instantly, Seely by-passed the fourth floor and lunged up toward the fifth, praying that no one had reached it before him.

Looking down from the fifth floor balcony to where, just minutes earlier, she had lain on the concrete floor of the third floor Palm Court, Seely began making his way around the parapet wall toward where he judged she would have been standing. He ducked back as Mr. and Mrs. Chiles, along with Burroughs, Edison and Harvey Firestone Sr. walked across the Palm Court toward their third floor rooms, their voices rising up toward the open skylight.

Staying close to the guest room doors, Seely reached the spot directly above where the girl had landed and began searching for her purse.

It was empty. There was no purse in sight and nothing seemed out of order. At that moment the second elevator -- the one at the opposite end of the Palm Court -- stopped at the fifth floor. Seely could hear the operator, Paul Johnson, pulling back the accordion iron grate in preparation for opening the oak door leading onto the fifth floor.

While his guests might think it curious that the general manager of the hotel would be alone on the fifth floor at this time of night, he could easily concoct a believable story: a guest needed assistance with a lock or a concern over the position of the skylight after the storm. But if a scandal did erupt, Seely did not want to put himself in a position which might arouse even the slightest bit of suspicion, especially with what he -- and Robert -- knew about the body of a young woman now hidden in a laundry cart in his office.

And he knew the Groves would love to pounce on any
opportunity to have him arrested....

Standing just a few feet from Paul Johnson's elevator, Seely saw that he could not flee undetected back to the south staircase from which he had come. Instead, he drew in a breath and forced himself to rush toward the elevator, dashing past it and into the empty stairwell just as Johnson opened the door and his guests alighted.

Seely sprinted up the empty stairs to the sixth floor, hoping that Paul Johnson would not also be bringing any guests in his elevator to the top floor. As he approached the spot where he suspected the young woman would have last been standing, Seely could already see that there was no purse in sight -- just a small drink table and one of the standing oak and copper ashtrays. He carefully peered over the wall to the Palm Court forty feet below, checking to see if the purse had somehow landed behind one of the wicker tables or rockers, where he might have missed it in his rush to pull her body into the Chiles' room.

Nothing seemed out of place -- other than the lone
wicker rocker covering the crimson stain --
and he could see no sign of a purse.

As he stepped back from the balcony wall, he could hear the sounds of even more voices drifting up from the floors beneath him, as guests began exiting the elevators and stairwells and heading to their rooms. He also could hear the barely perceivable sound of the elevator stopping at the sixth floor, just a few feet away.

He was trapped, with no escape. There was no way he could make it off the sixth floor without being seen.

And being spotted running toward either stairway
would only make it look worse.

Straightening his tie and smoothing his vest, slightly rumpled from his dash up the stairs, Seely prepared to greet whoever came from the elevator. As he glanced down at his carefully creased pants, something caught his eye a few feet further away from where he had been expecting to find her purse. It was a cigarette butt, along with a second one six feet beyond it.

"Why, Mr. Seely, is there anywhere in this hotel you can't be found?" It was Mrs. Burleson, along with her husband, Melvin, and his business partner, Luther Hargus.

All three were from Florida, he recalled.

St. Petersburg.

"You must be tucking each of your guests in at night, eh, man? Or maybe just someone special?" Hargus chided. The two men laughed loudly as they jostled each other, spilling out of the small elevator, each a bit tipsy, or so it seemed.

Seely smiled as he took a few steps toward the cigarette butts.

"That thunderstorm came up quickly," he explained, "so I thought I had better check on the skylights."

"Well," continued Mrs. Burleson, ignoring Luther's remarks, "it certainly will be cool enough to sleep with the windows closed tonight – and that's something that never happens in August back in St. Petersburg."

"She's trying to get me to stay another week, Mr. Seely! Any chance you could make me a deal?"

"That just might be possible, Mr. Burleson," Seely replied as the three approached him.

"By Jove, that's the spirit, Seely. Everything's negotiable! That's the way business ought to be run in this country, Luther. These wartime measures of Wilson's have put a crimp in everyone's business. Rations, price controls, war tax. Just like a Democrat to stick their noses into our business. Who knows better how to run your hotel, Seely – you or some bureaucrat in Washington?"

"I suspect some of them would find it challenging," Seely replied, "just as you or I might were we in their shoes, sir. But the bottom line is that we all have to find our own way of helping to win the war."

"You know, he's right, Melvin," chided Luther in a feeble attempt to appear serious. "What would you rather do: give up a little sugar -- that you surely don't need -- or enlist in the army? Did you read where the War Department is going to let men between forty-five and fifty-five start signing up next month? Are you ready to turn in your putter for a Springfield rifle?"

The men laughed.

"Hey, Fred -- excuse me -- Mister Seely," Luther Hargus turned back toward him, his voice becoming rancid. "I heard tonight that your brother-in-law asked you to pull some strings to keep him out of the war. Is that true? Somebody said you were up in Washington just a few weeks ago - and I see Edwin's still hanging around, so, what's the dope?"

"Yeh, trying to drink away his old man's fortune."

"There's not enough moonshine in all of North Carolina for him to do that," Hargus snorted derisively at his partner.

"He always manages to find someone to help him."

"Like you?"

"More like someone wearing a skirt." The men laughed. "At least not for very long," Hargus added, doubling over at his own joke.

"Edwin's always liked the ladies," Burleson explained to his wife, then turning back to Luther Hargus, "and he isn't one to let a wife get in the way."

"Or a husband!" Hargus howled.

"You men are such gossips! Listen to them, Mr. Seely. You'd think they were a couple of little old ladies at a quilting bee."

Seely chuckled nervously, anxious to avoid Luther Hargus' question about Edwin and the draft board. At 28, Edwin was a prime candidate for any branch of the service -- and Seely would love nothing better than to see him shipped oversees and slung in a muddy French trench with mortars whistling over his head.

As for his political connections, Seely had first met Woodrow Wilson in 1903, when he was visiting Princeton. Later, as publisher of the *Atlanta Georgian*, he had publicly endorsed Wilson's candidacy both for governor of New Jersey in 1910 and for president in 1912.

But Seely's close friendship with former Secretary of State William Jennings Bryan, who in 1915 had resigned in protest over President Wilson's pro-war policies, had made it difficult for Seely to convince his political friends that he still supported the president. Seely knew that asking those same individuals to keep his worthless brother-in-law out of the war would destroy his hard-earned credibility with them.

He could not understand why Grove had never bothered to cultivate any friendships with politicians in either St. Louis or the Missouri statehouse. When he needed their help, Grove always turned to Seely, who had learned the value of friendships with those in positions of power.

Grove and other pharmaceutical manufacturers had always been accustomed to having complete control over their ingredients, which often secretly included morphine, cocaine and mercury. When confronted, they declared that they were more qualified than any government agency to determine safe amounts for the American public.

Publicly, E. W. Grove had supported the first Pure Food and Drug Act of 1906, but only because not doing so would make it look as if the Paris Medicine Company had something to hide. Privately, he derided the politicians who demanded full disclosure of his ingredients, including those who had become friends of his son-in-law.

Seely would have loved to flatly refuse Edwin's request for help getting a deferment. Were the truth known, he would have called the St. Louis draft board himself to come get Edwin, but he was being pressured by Grove, pestered by Edwin's mother, Gertrude, and pleaded with by Evelyn.

In an effort to keep a fragile peace within the family, Seely had arranged for Edwin to meet with Missouri Senator William Stone and George Williams, their family attorney in St. Louis, knowing full well that neither of these men would find any reason to recommend a deferment for Edwin.

When it appeared that Edwin was about to be drafted, Evelyn stopped speaking to him and moved from their bedroom into the nursery. Seely put up with her silence for a week, then grudgingly arranged for Edwin to travel to Washington to meet with his friend Josephus Daniels of Raleigh.

Like Seely, Daniels was a former newspaper publisher, but Daniels had left a successful newspaper career to enter politics. Never a candidate himself, he had risen to become the head of the Democratic Party in North Carolina. In 1912 Daniels managed Wilson's successful campaign for the White House and had been rewarded with the post of Secretary of the Navy.

Washington insiders credited Josephus Daniels with convincing William Jennings Bryan not to run for president a fourth time, suggesting that a cabinet post would await him if the Democratic party remained unified and Wilson took the White House.

Daniel's plan was to name Bryan as Secretary of State, in previous administrations a largely ceremonial position. Bryan had agreed, as did a reluctant Woodrow Wilson, who harbored serious reservations about how the bombastic orator would fit with Wilson's more reticent style. Unlike Wilson, Bryan loved the campaign trail, with its unbridled opportunities to do the two things he loved the most: standing behind a podium and sitting at a banquet table.

It was Bryan who had introduced Fred Seely to Josephus Daniels at a fund-raising dinner hosted by Seely in Atlanta, one which E. W. Grove -- despite Seely's repeated requests -- had shown no interest in attending. Seely and Daniels had remained friends thereafter, with Seely making it a point to invite Daniels and his wife, Addie, to the Grove Park Inn several times. When the Secretary of the Navy was too busy to get away, Seely often traveled to Washington to meet with him there. In 1913, after the Inn had been completed, Seely and Daniels even talked about going together to buy the *Washington Herald*, but the deal never materialized.

In May of 1917, just after America had entered the war, the forty-six year old Seely had written to his friend:

It just occurred to me that possibly there might be some secret mission I could carry out for you or some strain from which I could relieve you in a capacity where the Government makes no allowance. I would, of course, do what I could without pay and without recognition.

Of course, as you know, the war situation makes it pretty worrisome for me with the hotel business I have been fighting so hard to establish, and I cannot be away continuously. But I want to do my duty to my country and to a friend that I love and trust as I do you.

I don't know just what I could do, but I happen to have had a lot of experience, and I know values. In addition, I have a personal acquaintance with and the confidence of such men as Mr. Ford and Mr. Schwab and deal with a lot of the men with whom you have to deal with. If there happens to turn up anything you think I could do better than anyone else, I will try to do it.

It is not my desire to be in the front, for I think you know that my duties here at the hotel are pretty heavy and that I am anxious to keep the wheels here turning.

Seely had heard nothing back from Josephus Daniels and assumed his letter had never reached the secretary's desk. Neither ever mentioned it to the other.

No deferment had been forthcoming for Edwin, leading Seely to suspect that he had kept the St. Louis draft board at bay either by exaggerating his new relationship with the Secretary of the Navy or by making good use of his father's ample supply of cash.

Regardless, the resentment of both Edwin and his father toward Seely's refusal to appeal directly to President Wilson himself had grown steadily with each day that the war dragged on. Evelyn continued to ask him about it, prodded, no doubt, by her father, her stepmother and her half-brother.

The announcement on the front page of Monday's newspaper of the death of 24-year-old Lieutenant Lawrence Loughran, the son of a prominent Asheville family, intensified her pleading. Seely had read the reports thoroughly, as he knew the Loughran family, even though they were Catholic. Larry was their youngest of three sons. All three Loughran boys had enlisted and two were now serving in France. Larry had requested the aviation branch and had been assigned to a Royal British air squadron, where he had received special training as an aviator scout. He had arrived at the front just four weeks prior to his death.

According to local newspaper reports, Loughran had been piloting one of four British fighter planes shot down by German aircraft in a single morning's air battle.

As he read the newspaper article, Seely could not help but shake his head at the irony: a bright, college-educated young man of twenty-four with a sterling future ahead of him is killed in France, while Edwin, a drunken leech, uses his father's money and his brother-in-law's connections to stay out of the service so that he can do what? – *drink, drag prostitutes back to the hotel and cheat on his pregnant wife.*

"Well, I'm sure Mr. Seely has more important things to do than stand here and listen to you two gossip. Get to your room, Luther. You men have an early tee time tomorrow."

Snapping to attention and presenting her with an exaggerated salute, Luther replied, "Yes, sir." As he marched off toward his room, he shot back at Seely, "Better get on your staff, Mr. Hotel President. There's a couple of cigarette butts on the floor."

Shaking her head, Mrs. Burleson grabbed her husband by the arm and pulled him down the hall after a staggering Luther Hargus. "Good night, Mr. Seely," she called back.

"Good night, Mrs. Burleson."

Seely watched as the men fumbled with their keys, then disappeared into their adjoining rooms.

Poor Mrs. Burleson, he mumbled.

Anxious to distance himself from the sixth floor and the guests who were making their way back to their rooms, Seely quickly leaned over and picked up the first cigarette butt.

Camel.

It had only been smoked halfway down when the ember had been squashed. The tip of the cigarette was still damp with saliva, confirming what Seely had expected, *that it had not lain there for long.* He knew that Dellie Buckner would have walked the Palm Court hallways between eight and nine o'clock, picking up glasses, straightening the wicker furniture and wiping out the heavy Roycroft ashtrays, just as she did every weekday evening. Dellie wouldn't have missed two cigarette butts on the floor, for, with three small boys to raise by herself, she wouldn't do anything to risk losing her job.

With his left hand Seely reached for his handkerchief to wrap up the cigarette, momentarily forgetting that he had left it pressed against the wound in the girl's head. Annoyed with himself, Seely carefully slipped the cigarette butt into his coat pocket, then stepped forward and picked up the second one. It felt slightly different from the first.

A different brand, he surmised.

A quick inspection revealed the name – *Oasis* – still legible, though this one was shorter than the first. But what caught his attention was the red-stained tip.

Lipstick.

So, you came up here for a cigarette….

But - where's your purse?

He dropped the second cigarette into his other coat pocket, not sure why he kept them separate from one another. Making sure he hadn't missed anything else, he headed toward the stairs. He needed to get back to his office, quickly, but the sounds of voices coming up the stairwell made him realize how impossible that now was. The Great Hall would still be packed with guests and visitors, as well as photographers and reporters.

He had seen John Robinson vying for a photograph of Henry Ford in front of the fireplace and imagined Herb Pelton was there as well, along with photographers from the *Citizen* and the *Herald.*

Pelton, easily identified around Asheville by his ever-present bow tie and white shirt, specialized in panoramic photography, but supported himself largely through postcards, which he and his partner printed and sold to the tourist trade.

Pelton had just recently dissolved that partnership and Seely had hoped that Pelton would take a young itinerant photographer by the name of George Masa under wing. Seely had been providing Masa with some work as a bellman and as a woodcarver at Biltmore Industries, but it was obvious Masa, a Japanese native, was not happy doing either. Seely had seen George earlier in the evening, taking pictures from the terrace, talking with the entourage of national reporters and photographers who followed the Ford, Firestone and Edison parade into Asheville. Most of them would still be lingering in the Great Hall, hoping for a quote or photograph to send back to New York or Washington.

Knowing it would be empty, Seely pressed the sixth floor call button for the service elevator, then stepped back to collect his thoughts.

Two cigarettes.

One with lipstick – Oasis. The other a Camel.

Two people.

One man, one woman?

No purse. No suicide note.

He let the possibilities rise to the surface.

Probably not a suicide or an accident....

Unless, he debated with himself, *she was sitting on*
top of the wall and fell backwards.

He argued back.

But who would be foolish enough to sit atop a narrow
wall forty feet in the air?

Unless they were both drunk....

And if she did fall, why wouldn't the second person call out for help?

Seely glanced back just to make sure he hadn't missed something.

No glasses, no bottles, no flask left behind.

No smell of spilt alcohol near the cigarettes.

None on her breath.

Seely shook his head. *What breath?*

Maybe they had been drinking in one of the rooms and came out here to smoke a cigarette.

Robert said he had heard a door close somewhere.

But which room?

Seely scanned the hallway along the balcony wall.

There were eight rooms along this corridor, two being occupied by the Burlesons and Luther Hargus, Dr. Westin was at the far end, in 641. Edwin at the other - 655.

Why would either of them walk that far to smoke a cigarette?

Why not right outside their room?

Why walk down by room 647?

Seely paused.

Luther Hargus was in room 649.

Luther pointed the cigarette butts out to him.

Surely Hargus wouldn't have done that if one of them had been his, would he?

But if Hargus had been there when she fell, had been on the sixth floor, then he would have known by now, simply by the lack of any commotion, simply by glancing down at the third floor Palm Court as he got off the elevator, that her body had been moved.

And he would have guessed that Seely, just by being right there, right then, had found – and had moved – her body.

Had Hargus been taunting him?

Had Hargus been the one?

The service elevator arrived. For the second time that evening Seely stepped in, closed the door behind him, along with the steel accordion grate, and set the lever to the Lower Level.

As the elevator quietly slipped passed each of the guest room floors, Seely faced the truth:

If someone had been with her when she fell – or had been pushed – if someone had then leaned over the sixth floor wall and watched her die, then that person had most likely been standing in the darkness of the Great Hall a few minutes later, not wanting to be missed, waiting for someone to find the body.

Waiting for the shout, the alarm, the throwing on of the lights in the darkened room, the mad rush up the stairs led by Sheriff Mitchell, the confusion in the Great Hall and the Palm Court....

That person might also have watched as Fred Seely, after spotting the small light in his office by the front desk, suddenly left the Great Hall and disappeared up the stairs toward the Palm Court.

Alone.

And when, a few minutes later, no alarm was sounded, no call came for either a doctor or the sheriff, that person would have guessed that Fred Seely had moved her body, that Fred Seely had decided not to tell anyone, that Fred Seely had made the decision to hide her body somewhere in the hotel.

The elevator shuttered to a stop at the bottom of the shaft.

The second person.

A Camel smoker.

No lipstick.

Was he a witness - or a murderer?

Fred stood with his hand on the steel grate.

And what is that person going to do?

More important, he shot back at himself,

what are you going to do?

Guests enjoying the Old Hickory rocking chairs on the front terrace.

Chapter 8

*The Grove Park Inn is not a sanitarium, a hospital or a health resort,
but it is operated on the highest plane that a home-like resort hotel
can be operated. It is a resting place for people who are not sick,
who want good food well-cooked and digestible, with luxurious,
though sanitary surroundings. Persons with any form of tubercular
trouble will not be received at the Inn.*

Frederick L. Seely, President
Grove Park Inn, Inc.
1918 Brochure

10:15pm
Tuesday
27 August 1918

Since the opening banquet on July 12, 1913, Fred Seely had made it
clear that the Grove Park Inn had been designed for -- and would
cater to -- tired businessmen.

And they had responded.

Businessmen, capitalists, politicians, entertainers, heirs to
industrial fortunes, they left behind their jobs, their staffs and often
their families for a few days -- or weeks -- of rest and relaxation.

But, as Fred Seely discovered, these men of wealth and power soon tired of simply staring at the scenery, regardless of the panoramic views of the distant Blue Ridge Mountains. These were men of action, men who desired more than a wicker rocker and a copy of *National Geographic.*

And while Seely provided them with the opportunity for a swim in the indoor pool, a round of golf, a few frames of bowling or a horseback ride up Sunset Mountain, for some, he discovered, meeting their needs was more of a challenge.

For some of his clients, coming to the Grove Park Inn meant the opportunity to also enjoy some of the local brew and to spend some discretionary time with an obliging young lady.

And they expected Fred Seely to provide them with both.

Early each morning Fred Seely would sit at his ebonized Roycroft desk and study the list of reservations Miss Hatch had prepared for him, making notations in the margin for Edward Higgins, who reported to the front desk promptly at seven. Fred Seely always assigned his most favored guests a room on the third floor, opening onto the Palm Court and overlooking the golf course and the Blue Ridge Mountains to the west. Preparations often included dismantling and removing a pair of double beds in an adjoining room and replacing them and the nightstands with a couch and comfortable chairs, creating a two room suite out of a pair of bedrooms.

Several of his guests had soon become regulars, on whom Seely kept a detailed file of their personal preferences. He knew their favorite foods, any medical issues, the names of their children, whether they played tennis, swam in the indoor pool or enjoyed riding, even which waiter and table they preferred.

He also knew the name of their hometown newspaper, which, if they were scheduled to stay at the Grove Park Inn for more than three days, Seely arranged to have waiting for them each day on their assigned table.

Once the largest sleeping rooms on either side of the third floor Palm Court had been filled, Fred Seely began assigning guests to the slightly smaller rooms in either the north or the south wings. A few of these had shared bathrooms, which he held back in the event a guest insisted on bringing children and their nurse. Seely permitted Negro nurses to sleep in the guest rooms along with the children, but did not allow them to walk about the hallways unless they were accompanied by their charges. Chauffeurs, Negro and white, were assigned a room in Sunset Hall, the staff dormitory, under the supervision of Mrs. Hughes.

At the 1912 groundbreaking ceremony, Seely had announced to an *Asheville Citizen* reporter that the 150-room hotel would be completed in just twelve months, but he missed his deadline by twelve days. On the night of the inaugural banquet, several of the rooms on the sixth floor remained unfinished, prompting Seely to establish the practice of first assigning the rooms on the third, fourth and fifth floors. Even after the painters had finally left, the rugs had been unrolled and the last of the furniture installed – two beds, two nightstands, a mirrored vanity and chair, a writing desk and chair, a tall chest of drawers and a rocking chair, all modeled in the Arts & Crafts style after Roycroft designs – Seely continued to assign the rooms on the lower floors first, but for a different reason.

Single men, he discovered, as well as some husbands traveling without their wives, were more apt to indulge in practices which might prove embarrassing to his other guests. Seely found it less worrisome to assign these men to rooms on the sixth floor, where their indiscretions might remain undetected – at least to the general public.

Daily housekeeping reports on each room provided Seely with detailed information on which guests had organized late night poker games and how many empty jars of moonshine they had left behind. He also kept track of which men awoke the following morning with one of the local ladies of the night asleep beside him. In most instances, the men and their escorts had arrived back at the hotel late enough that the other guests had already retired.

Seely's bellmen knew from experience to watch for the arrival of any inebriated guests and their escorts, and to quickly guide them to the elevator for the trip up to the sixth floor. His housekeepers, too, knew what was expected of them the following morning. Those assigned to the sixth floor often were called upon to help one of the late-night arrivals find her clothes among the strewn bed sheets (often with a groggy – and naked - famous client still entangled in them), zip up a sparkling dress and find her way out of the hotel. Seely had made it clear that none of these ladies of the night were to exit through the Great Hall. The housekeepers led them to the service elevator, took them to the basement level and sat them in a wooden chair by the employee entrance to wait for a cab.

For Fred Seely, however, one of his most embarrassing incidents occurred only days after the hotel had opened. The North Carolina Press Association had agreed to hold their annual convention at the Grove Park Inn and their organizer requested that Seely arrange for two of the local prostitutes to come to his room after their banquet. He was a publisher of great influence whose patronage Fred Seely had sought – and whose support and endorsement he desperately needed if he hoped to make the Grove Park Inn a financial success.

The publisher knew his group would be paying the highest rates of any hotel in Asheville and made it clear that they could find both rooms and an 'accommodating' management at the Battery Park Hotel. He proved to be only the first in a long list of powerful men accustomed to giving orders -- and having those orders carried out, regardless of the cost or inconvenience. As Seely soon learned, many even went so far as to specify their preference: white or Negro (a favorite among the northern politicians), thin or heavy, large or small breasts, blond or brunette, classy or country. The list seemed to Seely longer than any of his dining menus.

That first time, in July of 1913, Fred Seely didn't know what to do or who to ask, and, at Theodore's recommendation, ended up driving himself down to Carolina Lane, where he unsuccessfully scanned the crowded street for likely prospects. At the end of the last block he pulled his Packard against the curb and rested his head in frustration on the steering wheel.

A light tapping of a fingernail on his windshield jerked his head back so violently he heard his neck pop. A young, gum-chewing girl, her breasts swinging freely beneath her beaded dress, smiled as she leaned in his passenger window. He could not believe that someone so young, so pretty could be offering herself to him.

How long had it been? Weeks? A month?

"Nice car," she purred as she ran her fingertips along the leather upholstery. "Want to take me for a ride?"

Resisting the urge to press the gas pedal to the floor and race back to the hotel, Seely nodded, unable to speak. The girl opened the door and popped into the seat, pulling the door closed and letting her dress slide slightly above her knees. Seely could see that she wore no stockings.

"I'm Sophie," she giggled, as she slipped off her shoes and tucked her feet under her bottom, letting her knees, now pointed directly at him, slide slightly apart.

"I'm...."

Seely left the sentence unfinished, suddenly aware that people on the street were staring at him, his gleaming Packard and the young girl sitting next to him.

I'm an idiot.

Before she could again speak, he rapidly explained why he had picked her up, leaving out any reference to who he was, simply stating that he needed two girls to come to the Grove Park Inn on Thursday night.

"The Grove Park Inn?" she asked hesitantly.

"Have you heard of it?"

Sophie laughed. "Of course, I've heard of it, silly. Only, well, that place is pretty fancy. I think maybe you'd better talk with Madame Swann."

"Madame Swann?"

"Yeh, she handles all the hotels and nice boarding houses in town."

"Okay," he said slowly, "so how do I get in touch with this Madame Swann?"

"Don't worry. I'll tell her," Sophie replied as she began to get out of the car.

"But you don't know my name."

Sophie laughed. "She will." She leaned back through the window and raised her eyebrows suggestively. "Sure that's all?"

Seely jammed the gas pedal to the floor.

The following afternoon Miss Hatch stepped to his door and announced that he had call. "A Madame Swann," she added with a note of disapproval.

Seely closed the door between their two offices, then picked up the receiver.

"Mr. Seely?" The voice had a distinct French accent, though fading, as though it had been years since she had seen the Eiffel Tower – *if ever*, he thought. "I am Madame Swann. I understand we might have some business to conduct."

"I'm not sure what you mean."

"That's quite alright, Mr. Seely. I understand completely. Discretion is one of my many virtues."

"I see," Seely replied.

"Perhaps, Mr. Seely, we should meet and have a discussion. Somewhere other than the Grove Park Inn. Someplace more discreet? Say, my office, four o'clock tomorrow? I'm at 112 Carolina Lane, second floor."

The following day Fred Seely walked up the marble staircase inside a well-kept brick office building on Carolina Lane. Madame Swann's office was at the end of an expansive hallway, just beyond the offices of an attorney, a real estate company and a tailor. The frosted glass door was neatly lettered:

M. Swann

Asheville - Atlanta - Charlotte

Please Knock.

A young, attractive receptionist let him in. "Can I get you a cup of coffee, Mr. Seely?" she asked before he had a chance to introduce himself.

"No, I'm fine, but thank you."

"If you change your mind, just let me know. Madame Swann should be off the phone any minute now."

Seely took a seat in a comfortable leather chair and surveyed the small, but sophisticated outer room. Prints of Paris street scenes hung on the wall, a large Persian carpet covered all but the perimeter of the white-tiled floor and the end table next to him offered the latest editions of V*anity Fair, Photoplay* and *House Beautiful.*

Before he could decide whether or not to open one of the magazines, a tall, elegant woman he guessed to be no more than forty years old opened the inner door and walked toward him.

"Mr. Seely, I do apologize," she exclaimed with what he perceived to be legitimate emotion. "I had no intention of staying on the phone so long."

She turned to her receptionist. "Margaret, would you please hold my calls until Mr. Seely and I are finished?" Margaret nodded. "Come, Mr. Seely, it is such a pleasure to meet you at last."

Seely and Madame Swann exchanged pleasantries regarding the July weather, the construction and opening of the hotel, and his time spent in Atlanta, where, as it turned out, Madame Swann had a home and office. At the appropriate time, however, Madame Swann deftly began making her pitch for an exclusive arrangement with the Grove Park Inn. Seely listened intently, agreed with her on every point, then interjected. "But I don't want any of your girls hanging out in the Great Hall – or parading around in skimpy clothing. This is strictly a first-class hotel."

Madame Swann smiled, then stood and motioned him over to a bay window overlooking the street. "Tell me, Mr. Seely, how many of my girls do you see down there?"

Seely looked up and down the Carolina Lane, then pointed at a young woman leaning against a lamppost, smoking a cigarette. "There."

"Not one of mine."

"Over there?" He pointed at another obvious prostitute strutting down Carolina Lane.

"Not mine, either."

"That one?"

"No."

"So, the answer is none?"

Madame Swann looked at him and, without so much as a glance out the window, answered, "Three."

"Three? Where?"

Madame Swann pointed toward a young woman adjusting a mannequin in a ladies' apparel store across the street. "That's Lossie."

"The one working in the clothing store? But doesn't the owner know?"

Madame Swann smiled. "I'm the owner."

Seely was impressed. "And the other two?"

"The woman in the light green dress who appears to be shopping -- that's Jennie -- and the young woman selling flowers from the cart, Joy."

As if on cue, the woman who had been studying one of the dresses in the clothing store turned and waved at Madame Swann and Fred Seely. Madame Swann waved back, then returned to her desk, motioning Fred to take his seat. "We have a simple system. When a client calls, I raise the blind and, depending on which of my girls he wants, I set a particular vase, small statue or flower arrangement on the window sill. They each know their own signal."

"Very impressive, Madame Swann. I trust you don't have any problems with the police?"

"Lets just say I'm a good businesswoman, Mr. Seely. Not much different from you, really. We both have clients with special needs and we take care of them. And when we do a good job, we both profit accordingly, wouldn't you agree?"

"You present a convincing case, Madame, but I'm still a little concerned about one of them getting out of a cab and walking into the hotel alone, looking for one of our guests."

"You're fortunate, Mr. Seely. Your friend Mr. Coxe and I had the same situation over at the Battery Park Hotel, so we've already worked out a solution. You see, I don't send any of my girls out alone. They generally arrive with Victor, who also manages my store across the street. Unless Victor is already scheduled, in which case another equally suitable gentleman will appear.

"One of the gentlemen will escort whomever you request to the Grove Park Inn and they will arrive looking like any couple who might be coming up for dinner or for your evening's entertainment. Victor will have been given the room number of the client, who he will call from your public telephone.

"The three of them will meet, Victor will make the introductions, they might stroll around the lobby or out onto the terrace for a few minutes, so as not to draw attention to themselves, then eventually Victor will lead them down one of the hallways, where he will handle the finances and set up a time for her to meet him back in the lobby. If she is even a minute late, he will go to the room and make sure everything is alright. Or, in case there's been a change in plans, to collect an additional fee."

From that day forward, Fred Seely never had to drive down Carolina Lane again. When one of his guests came to him with a special request, he simply placed a call to Madame Swann. The women, generally accompanied by Victor, arrived in one of her cars (she had four, he later learned, as well as similar arrangements with the Battery Park Hotel, the Kennilworth Inn and the Swannanoa Hotel) and, as promised, blended in naturally with the other guests. While he suspected the women often carried a flask in their purses, they never appeared drunk.

He enjoyed watching the little ballet Madame Swann's ladies and Victor performed each time they arrived at the hotel, smiling at the bellmen, nodding to the other guests, engaging in polite chit-chat about the weather, politics or the day's news.

He even had his favorite – Jenny, the window shopper. She appeared a few years older than the others and had a sensual maturity that appealed to him.

> *She was someone,* he sensed, *who brought her own level of confidence – and experience – to bed, someone who could make it an evening never to forget.*

His instincts must not have been wrong, for more than one of his regulars specifically requested Jenny whenever they were staying at the hotel. She always made it a point to smile at him when they passed in the Great Hall, unlike Victor, who simply nodded in deference before taking a seat near the terrace to read until the appointed time.

Fred Seely also noted that he never saw Madame Swann at the Grove Park Inn with Victor. Like himself, as she had pointed out, she was a business owner and she ran it like a professional. As her business at the Grove Park Inn prospered, she offered to pay Seely a referral fee, designed, he presumed, to ward off any competition. He had declined, preferring to remain financially -- and legally -- detached from any of her transactions.

"Well, then, Mr. Seely," she replied, "in that case let me say that anytime you wish, you can have one 'on the house.' My treat."

Luther Hargus's taunts about Edwin and the two cigarettes were still ringing in his ears as Fred Seely stepped off the service elevator in the basement of the Grove Park Inn and walked slowly toward his office. The customary murmur of voices from down the hall had quieted, as all of his housekeeping staff had left for the night, either to their homes in Asheville or to Sunset Hall, the three story stucco dormitory Grove and Seely had constructed two hundred yards below the north end of the hotel, adjacent to the stables.

Sunset Hall had been supervised since it opened in the fall of 1913 by Mrs. Hughes, whose husband had been killed in a terrible sawmill accident. Seely provided her with a small apartment directly behind the sign-in desk, which was staffed by either Lyda Jordan or Jessie Couch when she wasn't on duty.

As they planned the dormitory, Seely had designated the first floor of Sunset Hall for the male employees: Negroes down the right hall, the white males down the left. The second floor was reserved for the women: Negroes down the right hall, the white women down the left. The smaller third floor was generally empty, except for times when guests brought chauffeurs or nurses they did not want staying in the hotel.

Each room was furnished with a bed, an inexpensive dresser, a washstand and a chair. Seely had overheard enough conversations coming from the housekeeping rooms in the basement of the hotel to suspect that late night trysts were taking place in the empty rooms on the third floor, most recently between Dallas Benson, a handsome young Negro plasterer working for Seely on the new workshop at Biltmore Industries, and Jessie Couch, one of the maids who also helped Mrs. Hughes at the desk. Seely knew that Jessie had access to all the room keys.

One Sunday afternoon Seely had strolled down the hill on the pretense of inspecting the rooms in Sunset Hall. After picking up the master key from Mrs. Hughes, Seely climbed the stairs to the third floor. He went directly to the last room on the Negro side, the one least likely to be assigned, and unlocked the door. Getting down on his knees to feel between the wire mesh springs and the bottom of the thin mattress, he found precisely what he expected -- three un-wrapped condoms. He considered for a moment taking them, imag-ining the panic Benson would feel when, at a critical moment, with Jessie Couch lying there with her cotton print dress pulled up above her brown waist and her panties down around one ankle, he reached under the mattress and discovered his condoms were gone.

But the idea of Dallas Benson and Jessie Couch, both good employees, having sex in Sunset Hall didn't really bother Seely, so long as it didn't involve any of the white staff. And the thought of Jessie becoming pregnant – and Seely losing a good employee – brought his empty hand out from beneath the bed.

At least somebody is getting some sex, he thought.

As he closed the door and walked back toward his office, he recalled something his friend Elbert Hubbard had said while they were out riding horses. "The only man who looks under a bed," the sage of Roycroft observed, "is someone who has been there."

Seely stepped inside his office, then turned and both locked and bolted the door behind him before switching on the light and bringing himself to look at the laundry cart beside his desk.

Somehow he had thought she might be gone.

The idea of being alone in his office with a dead body didn't really bother him, even though he had never seen a corpse outside a casket. It was more as if she were his guest, albeit, an unwanted guest, one he was responsible for. He gently pulled the wool blanket back from her face, then froze as her light blue eyes stared up at him.

Not even death, he mused, *could steal her beauty.*

The blood had stopped flowing from her wound and he was relieved to see that none of it had seeped into the canvas fabric.

So beautiful, he thought, as he arranged her hair to cover the crimson strands. He ran the backs of his fingers along her cool cheek, not yet totally convinced she would not suddenly speak to him.

Such a waste, such a terrible waste….

The steady tick of the Roycroft clock filled the silence of the room, jolting him from his reverie. He needed a plan.

> *The person who Higgins said needed so desperately to*
> *speak to him, who could that have been?*
> *Someone who came with her tonight?*
> *A friend?*
> *Could they be speaking to Sheriff Mitchell? Right now?*
> *Or Junius Adams? Or Grove himself?*
> *It didn't matter. The question each would ask would*
> *be the same – where's Fred Seely?*

And it wouldn't be long before they came here looking for him. Higgins knew he had gone up the stairs, but no one had seen him take the service elevator back down to his office. They might be looking for him upstairs first. That would give him a few minutes more time.

> *Robert.*
> *He should be in his room at Sunset Hall, waiting for*
> *instructions, but how long would he wait?*
> *Would he panic?*
> *Would he start walking home, hoping for a ride out*
> *to Avery's Creek?*
> *What should he do about Robert?*

He reached into his pockets and felt the cigarettes.

> *The second person. The only one who saw her fall.*
> *A man? A woman?*
> *If it was an accident, why didn't they stay?*
> *Why didn't they call for help?*

Why didn't anyone come running?
Robert....

He would have been the nearest to them, the only one not inside one of the rooms. Making his rounds, checking the hallways around the Palm Court.

He would have heard her scream. But he didn't....

It began to sink in.

She did not scream.

Who falls three stories and doesn't scream?

Seely looked down at her, curled up inside the canvas cart.

Someone who's not conscious. Passed out.

No smell of alcohol. Drugged?

The wound on the back of her head.

Maybe it happened before she hit the floor.

Maybe on the sixth floor...?

Two people. An argument.

The hastily dropped cigarettes.

Unfinished.

But what would he have hit her with?

A gun? A club?

Seely almost laughed at himself.

No one walks around the Grove Park Inn with a gun in their belt. Or a club.

No, it had to be something already there.

A bottle? Wouldn't it have broken?

He didn't see any glass, no smell of spilt alcohol.

Think!

Something else, something already there....

Like the ashtray. The Roycroft ashtray.

Solid oak with a heavy copper bowl.

Probably thirty inches tall and shaped like a club.
Maybe the cigarettes on the floor had been in the bowl
and fell out when he picked it up - and hit her with it?
Was his imagination running away with this?
But it explains so much - why no scream, why no
alarm, no shout for help.
Why no second person coming forward....
The second person. A murderer?
But if he wanted it to look like an accident or a
suicide, why not leave her purse - either on the
sixth floor or calmly drop it down next to her?
Why take it? Why risk getting caught with it?

Seely knew he had to talk to Robert, to tell Robert what to do and what to say. He had to get to Robert before anyone else did, before Robert said too much. But Robert still thought her body was up on the third floor, that Seely was delaying letting anyone know about her death until after Robert had left the hotel.

He could deal with Robert, but what about the second
person?
Would he have left? Slipped out with the crowd
headed back down the mountain to Asheville?
Possibly, but he would have waited until the movie
had ended to avoid drawing attention to himself by leaving
early. He would have waited, perhaps in his room, perhaps in
the back of the Great Hall, hidden by the crowd.
Either way, he would have quickly figured out that no
one had sounded an alarm, no one had sent the sheriff
running for the stairs. Given this unexpected turn, he might
have stayed behind, curious to see what was about to unfold.

*Curious to see what Seely was going to do -- with a
dead woman in a hotel packed with famous
guests and newspaper reporters.*

Along with the chief of police and the county sheriff.

The thought froze Seely.

*What would happen if the man with her was talking
to Sheriff Mitchell right now?*

Seely reached out for the desk to steady himself.

But, really, what could he say?

*That he had seen a dead woman in the Palm Court at
nine-fifteen that night, but that he had waited nearly an hour
to report it – and now the body was gone?*

The blood stain on the carpet would confirm part of his story, except for why he had waited so long to report it -- and where the
body was now. Sheriff Mitchell wouldn't take kindly to that. He liked
quick conclusions with no loose strings. Anyone coming forward
with a story that had more questions than answers was going to find
himself on a short leash with Sheriff Mitchell holding the other end.

*No, he wouldn't be talking. Not yet. Not until he knew what
had happened to the body. And right now all he knew, all he suspected,
was that Fred Seely had found the body and had moved it before anyone else came upon the scene.*

*But he didn't know where – although right now that wouldn't
be hard to figure out,* Fred mused, *considering there was a bulging
laundry cart sitting in the middle of his office.*

*If Fred took care of Robert – and hid the girl's body for just a
while longer – then there was nothing the second person could tell,
nothing he could prove, that wouldn't also make him a key suspect.*

But first he had to deal with Henry Ford, who would be
knocking on his office door any minute now.

E. W. Grove, Henry Ford and Fred Seely together on August 27, 1918.

Chapter 9

*"What will you do if you are nominated
by both Democrats and Republicans?" he was asked.
The noted automobile maker, the inventor of the Ford tractor,
bright-eyed, brown-skinned from his life in the open, far from such
questions, vigorous and animated, laughed like a boy.
"Why, I will pitch a penny to settle it."*

The Asheville Citizen
August 28, 1918

10:20pm
Tuesday
27 August 1918

Fred Seely walked over to the far corner of his office and, taking a key from his pocket, unlocked a door leading to his private darkroom.

He had first become interested in photography on his trip to Java in 1900, when he and Evelyn had combined their delayed honeymoon with a business trip for the Paris Medicine Company. He would have preferred to have taken Evelyn to England, but Grove, anxious to eliminate their reliance on the large pharmaceutical supply houses, offered to pay for an around-the-world cruise if Seely and Evelyn would go to Java to negotiate a quinine contract with the Dutch plantation owners.

The future of the Paris Medicine Company depended on a steady, affordable supply of quinine, refined from the bark of the cinchona tree into a crystal known as cinchonidine. In 1899 a severe shortage of quinine crystals had threatened the future of several pharmaceutical firms and supply houses, which for the first time in memory had been forced to bid against one another at public auctions in London and Amsterdam.

Grove's investigation had determined that over-harvesting had nearly eliminated the cinchona tree in South America, leaving the small, overlooked island country of Java as the principle source of the tree's bark.

Fred and Evelyn had left St. Louis by train on the 22nd of October, then sailed from San Francisco the 6th of November. They had made love their first night on the ship, but before they could again, Evelyn developed morning sickness. She suspected she was pregnant -- and they wouldn't be returning home for six months. She was miserable and Seely was wracked with guilt.

Seely and Evelyn spent nearly two months in Java, where they discovered she was the only white woman on the entire island. Making matters even more difficult, only two other people on the island could speak English. As a honeymoon, the trip was a disaster, but Seely was able to negotiate a long-term contract securing for the Paris Medicine Company enough cinchonidine to produce Grove's Tasteless Chill Tonic for years to come.

Seely had documented their entire trip with his first camera, a Kodak Brownie #1, which had just been introduced eight months earlier in February of 1900. His interest in photography continued after their return, but it was not until he and Grove founded the *Atlanta Georgian* in 1905 that Seely had the opportunity to set up and experiment in his own darkroom.

Eight years later, while designing the arrangement of the offices in the Grove Park Inn, he took the opportunity to build a darkroom off his basement office. Measuring nearly eight feet wide and more than ten feet deep, he had outfitted it with the best equipment available: processing tanks, chemicals, trays, timer and enlarger, everything neatly and systematically arranged along both long walls. The center aisle remained clear and provided Seely with ample room to roll in the laundry cart.

As he was carefully tucking the two wool blankets over and around her body, he heard a knock at the door.

With a glance back at the cart, Seely hurried out of the darkroom, locking the door behind him. He strode across the room, drew back the bolt and opened the door.

"Worried about burglars?" Ford chided him as he brushed passed Seely.

He had been here once before, three years earlier, drumming up support for his ill-fated Peace Ship. Against the advice of E. W. Grove, who had always considered Ford a naive opportunist, Seely had accepted Henry Ford's invitation to sail aboard the *Oscar II*. They left New York in December of 1915 with Fred Seely as one of the two hundred unofficial 'ambassadors of peace' bound for Europe. But without the support or endorsement of either President Wilson or congress, Henry Ford's Peace Ship floundered under mismanagement and public ridicule.

Embarrassed by the fiasco aboard the *Oscar II*, Henry Ford deserted his delegates in Norway. Later, claiming to have been ill, Ford sailed back unannounced in the middle of the night, leaving Seely and the others to fend for themselves. The two men never spoke of the matter again. It had been a public relations nightmare for the wealthy automobile manufacturer, plus an early setback, many of the political observers reckoned, in his goal of running the country from the White House in 1920.

Seely watched as Ford silently studied the room's furnishings and artwork as carefully as an auditor taking inventory, sizing up the assets of its occupant. Seely had never felt completely at ease in Henry Ford's presence. He always felt he had to choose his words carefully, fearing something he said would be misinterpreted, perhaps later repeated, out of context.

It was nearly 10:30pm, yet Ford, as always, looked as trim and tidy as he had several hours earlier. His high, starched collar showed not a drop of sweat, not a stain to reflect the day's activities. His face, like that of a former athlete, had retained its narrow profile, prominent cheekbones, angular jaw. Seely instinctively ran his hand along his own neck, embarrassed at the thought that Ford might have spotted the soft roll of flesh which had formed around his own collar. Ford's eyes, slightly sunken, continued to survey the room until they landed on Seely. A thin, wry smile appeared.

A smile, it seemed to Seely, *that always gave the impression that Ford knew something of importance, something secretive, but that he had not yet decided if you were worthy of his confidence.*

As he watched Ford circling the room, Seely speculated as to what matter of great importance demanded a late-night appointment.

Something to do with William Jennings Bryan, perhaps, or Ford's candidacy? The Michigan senatorial campaign? Perhaps advice on Wilson, whom Ford had shown little respect for since the president had rebuked his request for support of the Peace Ship.

Ford knew of his close ties to both President Wilson and Bryan -- and Seely had supported Ford's Peace Ship unconditionally -- perhaps Ford was thinking ahead to his campaign.... Could he be considering him for his staff? Perhaps to head his campaign in the South....?

Seely had the front pages of two newspapers framed and hanging in his office: the *Asheville Citizen's* coverage of the hotel's opening banquet and the *New York Times* report on the sinking of the *Lusitania* in 1915. Ford stepped forward to study the *Times.* Their mutual friend, Elbert Hubbard, along his wife, the outspoken feminist Alice Moore Hubbard, had been aboard the *Lusitania* on the morning of May 7th when, just eight miles short of the Irish coastline, a lone German submarine, limping back to port with just one remaining torpedo, found the luxury liner in its cross-hairs. As the startled passengers watched helplessly from the starboard decks, the submarine's last torpedo cut a deadly path across the calm sea, rocking them violently as it exploded upon contact with the ocean liner.

A few seconds later, a second explosion ripped another gaping hole in the *Lusitania's* hull.

The two blasts had disabled the ship's rudder, but her engines continued to spin the giant propellers. Though sinking, the *Lusitania* forged head, forcing even more water into the lower compartments at a rate faster than anyone could have expected.

Two miles further toward shore, having left a trail of floundering bodies, broken deck chairs and capsized lifeboats in her wake, the *Lusitania* finally slowed, stopped and toppled over, sinking in three hundred feet of black, freezing water.

It had been just eighteen minutes since the torpedo struck.

Of the 48 lifeboats on board, only six managed to remain afloat after the last of the *Lusitania's* four smokestacks disappeared beneath the water. Nearly 1,200 bodies, more than 100 of them children, either sank to the bottom with the *Lusitania* or would wash ashore the following days.

"You know, Fred, if it hadn't been for President Wilson, our friend Hubbard would still be alive."

"How's that?"

"Remember back in 1911 and 1912, when the rascal was taking such great delight in shocking the prim and proper ladies of East Aurora with his off-color jokes – you know, the one he printed in *The Philistine* about the spinster and the knothole?"

"I don't think I saw that one, but I remember all the trouble it caused him."

"You mean all the trouble he caused himself. The man had a knack for trouble. I was there -- at his hotel at Roycroft a few years earlier -- and I declare the man simply looked for ways to stir up trouble. Wasn't enough that he spawned an illegitimate daughter, then hid her away for nearly ten years. He had to go and start printing dirty jokes in his magazine.

"Well, they brought him up on five charges of obscenity. Only one stuck, but the judge took away his passport as part of the sentence. Who knows why?

"Anyway, when he decided to pay the Kaiser a visit, Hubbard couldn't buy a ticket without a passport. And the only way he could get his passport back was to get the verdict set aside -- with a presidential pardon, which your friend Mr. Wilson gave him -- just in time for Hubbard and his wife to be able to get tickets aboard the *Lusitania.*"

"I had no idea…."

"Not many people did. I'm not sure why Wilson even bothered with it. Should have been Bryan's jurisdiction, as Secretary of State, but Bryan hated Hubbard. The evangelist versus the agnostic. Who knows? Maybe Wilson did it just to irk Bryan."

"I did know about that. Bryan wrote me that he could never accept Hubbard's hostility toward Christianity and the Christian church – and I don't think he felt Hubbard had done the right thing in divorcing his wife so that he could marry Alice Moore."

Ford continued to study the framed newspaper.

> *It must have to do with his campaign. Michigan in the fall. Two years in the Senate, then the White House.*
> *With me delivering the Southern states for him....*

Seely continued. "Its ironic that just a few years earlier Hubbard had written a piece for *The Philistine* about the sinking of the *Titanic* and the Strausses."

"Owners of Macy's?"

"That's right. He told the story of how when the Strausses realized there wouldn't be any room for them aboard the lifeboats, they turned and headed back to their stateroom, arm-in-arm, to await their fate."

"One of your Vanderbilts was on board as well, wasn't he?" Ford asked.

"Alfred. A nephew of George Vanderbilt of Biltmore. George Vanderbilt's widow was here this evening. I'm sure she would love to meet you tomorrow at the luncheon."

"Is she still a Vanderbilt – or has she remarried?

"Still a Vanderbilt, though I don't know for how much longer. She and her daughter spend most of their time in Washington. Its been four years now since he died. Complications after surgery on his appendix."

Ford nodded, thinking for a moment. "This Alfred, aboard the *Lusitania*, he was the playboy, right?"

Seely shrugged. "If you believe all that you read in the papers. Seems his first wife caught him in his private railway car in bed with the wife of a Cuban diplomat. That little indiscretion cost him ten million in the divorce – and to top it off the diplomat's wife ended up killing herself when he left her. A couple of years later Alfred got caught again, this time with the wife of a prominent doctor in Baltimore. She was the daughter of Captain Emerson – the man who invented Bromo-Seltzer – so I don't know who paid off the doctor, but the two of them did get married."

"Perhaps he got what was coming to him."

"Perhaps."

"Was his wife along?"

"No. She stayed behind – with their two sons. He was going over to check on some of his horses."

Ford shook his head. "Lucky for her. How much did he leave behind?"

"His father -- Cornelius II -- had left him $42 million, but Alfred had run it down to about half that when he died. According to the New York papers, she got $8 million and the rest went to his sons, one by the first wife, two from the second."

"Like I said, he probably got what was coming."

"Well, it sounds like he died more admirably than he lived. According to several people who made it off the ship, Vanderbilt took off his own life vest and wrapped it around a mother and her baby. They made it out safely, but Vanderbilt's body was never found."

"Same was true for the Hubbards, right?"

"They never found their bodies, no."

Ford turned back to the newspaper. "Quite a list of people

who went down with Hubbard, too. Charlie Frohman, going over to London to see his new play, along with Charlie Klein and the pianist, Charles Knight."

"What do you think about the story about Percy Lane?"

"The London art collector?"

"They say he had been in the states buying up some expensive paintings – lots of Impressionists, plus a Rubens – and that he had them all sealed in watertight lead containers."

"How deep is it there?"

"I heard about three hundred feet."

Ford shrugged. "Interesting. I guess it would all depend on where they were in the ship."

"And where the second explosion came from?"

Seely expected Ford would have an opinion on the source of the controversial second explosion.

"From all accounts there was but one torpedo. They could see it coming from the deck. Wasn't the boilers, for the engines kept running right up to the end. The Germans, of course, claim it was illegal gunpowder Wilson was sending to the Brits."

"Do you think so?"

Ford thought for a moment. "Wilson had an election coming up, and he was betting his political future on one campaign slogan – 'He kept us out of war.' So, it would have been a big risk and I'm not so sure he would have taken it."

"But he didn't keep us out of the war."

"That's the thing. I think Wilson knew war with Germany was inevitable, but he thought he could control it. But first he had to get re-elected."

"Which didn't turn out to be as easy as many people thought...."

Ford smiled.

> *He's checking me out, seeing what I know, how I could
> help. He knows the Northern industrialists, the labor
> leaders, but he needs help in the South. In Atlanta.
> And Miami. My help....*

"If you really want to know what was on board the *Lusitania*,
talk to Dudley."

"Malone?"

"The one and only – Dudley Field Malone. Have you met
him?"

"I know of him, but, no, our paths have never crossed."

"I don't suppose Dudley would ever come to Asheville. He's
a New Yorker, through and through. His father was a Tammany Hall
Irishman. They say old man Malone single-handedly kept Bryan out
of the White House in '96.

"Dudley was raised on New York politics and hitched his
wagon to Wilson back when he was at Princeton. Became his campaign manager for governor in 1910 and primed him for the presidency in '12. How that Irish Catholic boy could deliver all those New
York Jew votes for Wilson, I'll never know, but he did. And Wilson
never forgot him. Gave him the biggest plum job in all of New York –
Under-Secretary of State in charge of the Customs Office. And Dudley needed it."

> *Under-Secretary of State. Like Malone. But not New
> York. Evelyn would never like New York. It would
> have to be in Washington. Ford would understand....*

"How so?"

"He was broke most of the time. Spent everything he made as
a lawyer on booze and women. Couldn't resist either."

"Doesn't sound like someone Wilson would cater to."

"Typically, no. But politics make strange bedfellows. They each needed what the other had. And since Dudley wanted to stay in New York – and Wilson didn't really want him chasing skirts around the White House – the Customs House job was a perfect reward."

"And since the *Lusitania* sailed from New York...."

"Dudley had to verify the manifest."

"And there were some munitions on board, right? Listed on the manifest?"

Ford nodded. "Rifle shells. Remington .303's. Four million rounds." Seely looked surprised. "Sounds like a lot, but its not. And from what Dudley told me, they were perfectly legal – and they wouldn't explode, which is why they were listed on the manifest, plain as day, for anyone to read."

"So, if not the rifle shells, what caused the second explosion?"

"Like I said, you'd have to ask Dudley." Ford paused. "And if you do, ask him about the cheese...."

"The cheese?"

"There's been some whispering, something about an unusual number of crates of cheese listed on the manifest. Rumors about cheese no one ordered."

"But why would Malone...."

"Dudley's always been pro-British. He thought we should be supporting them from the beginning. Big on the war-preparedness plan. He lobbied to get the first military camp in the state of New York -- at Plattsburg. Of course, he never got around to enlisting himself, but that's Dudley for you."

"But he knew about the German submarines."

"Dudley claims he never thought the *Lusitania* would be attacked. She was a passenger ship, the fastest on record – and she was supposed to have two British destroyers flanking her as she approached Ireland."

"What happened to them?"

"Depends on who you ask. Some say they got lost in the fog that morning. Others say they were never supposed to find the *Lusitania*, at least not until the Germans had. While they never let on publicly, the British needed us, but they knew Wilson wouldn't declare war on Germany without provocation."

"Which the sinking of a neutral ship would provide – a neutral ship with Americans on board."

"That was the thought."

"So, where's Malone now? I know he resigned last year over the suffrage issue."

Ford shook his head. "The man was thinking with his pecker. Threw away his entire political career for a piece of tail. One day he's in Washington for a meeting and he goes to hear the trial of Alice Paul and the suffragettes they arrested for picketing in front of the White House."

Ford paused before continuing.

"Now, you've got to understand that back in 1915 – not that long after the *Lusitania* – when Wilson was running for re-election, they figured it would all come down to California. Whoever won California would win the White House. So, they sent Dudley out to convince all the women in California that if they campaigned for Wilson, he would come out in favor of a federal amendment giving women the right to vote."

"But I thought Wilson had made it clear he thought suffrage should be decided by each state?"

"He did – until it looked like he might not get re-elected."

"So Malone delivers California – just like he did New York in

1912 – and waits for Wilson to act?"

"Which, so far, he hasn't. Dudley felt like he crawled out on a limb for Wilson -- and Wilson cut it off behind him."

"Who was the woman?"

"Doris Stevens. One of Alice Paul's group. Leave it to Dudley to sniff out the only one who isn't a lesbian. Dudley volunteered to represent the women in their next trial and found out from the prosecutor that orders were coming directly from the White House. He confronted Wilson, wasn't satisfied with what he heard and went to the press with his letter of resignation. Wilson had no choice but to accept it."

"So what's Malone doing now?"

"When he isn't representing the women – free of charge – he's sleeping with Stevens. His political career is over, so he probably figures the publicity will bring him some new clients, which, the way Dudley spends money, he'll need – fast."

Seely stole a glance at the clock, wondering how long he would have to wait before Ford divulged the reason for his late night visit.

Perhaps a message to be delivered to President Wilson? Or Bryan? Would he ask me to be his contact with Wilson and Bryan? To get their endorsement? Could I convince the President to support Henry Ford? Invite Wilson to the Grove Park Inn. Ask him here....

As if on cue, Ford turned back to him.

"I was wondering if you could do a favor for me, Fred."

Must have to do with Bryan.... Or the President.... His campaign staff..... Was he going to ask me to head his campaign?

Would they move to Washington?

And afterwards.... certainly not a cabinet post, but an under-secretary? An ambassadorship -- to a smaller country?

"When we were here last my wife was taken with those hickory rockers you have out on your terrace, you know, the ones with the cane seats."

The rockers? What's he talking about?

Seely replied, "The Old Hickory rockers. Yes, I know the ones you mean."

"I think she would like a dozen or so of them. Do you think you could get in touch with your man there and order some for her? Shipped to Dearborn?"

Seely struggled to listen.

The stinking rockers!

That was his 'big' favor?

"I would be glad to do so. Those were a special weave they made for us. I wasn't happy with the ones in their catalog, so I asked them to make the splints a little narrower. Makes them more comfortable. Would she prefer the tall back or the hoop back style?"

"Better order a dozen of each, just to be sure."

"I'll take care of it tomorrow."

Ford walked toward the door, then paused with his hand on the knob.

"Say, Fred, couldn't help but notice old man Weicker and his wife are staying here tonight. I didn't think you were catering to Jews down here."

"Times are tough, Henry. Their money spends the same as everyone else's."

Ford shook his head in disgust. "You're being naïve, Fred."

He took a step toward Seely. "Do you want to know who really started this war? The Jew bankers, that's who. They're the ones who are going to benefit the most from it. They're the profiteers and you want to know why? Because they'll sell to both sides. They'll let us beat our brains out over some petty European squabble so they can step in later and take over."

Ford stepped closer to Seely. "And they're doing it, step by step. Who do you think controls the railroads today, Fred? The Jews. And the supply of sugar? The Jews. And the woolen industry? Yep, it's the Jews. And in some parts of this country the tongues of businessmen are tied because for years they have lived by the unwritten law that Jews must never be singled out as Jews. And I'll tell you, Fred, its that silence that is going to open the door for Jewish world imperialism."

An awkward silence hovered over the two men.

The stinking rockers.

Seely thought for a second.

"I'll make you a deal, Henry. I'll ask the Weickers to leave if you're ready to go upstairs and announce to the reporters that you're no longer going to sell cars to Jews."

A scowl flitted across his face, then Ford slowly smiled.

"Better watch out, Fred. Someday I just might make you eat those words."

Ford turned and strode out the door, not bothering to close it.

Asshole.

(front) William Jennings Bryan and Fred L. Seely;
(back) Mary Baird Bryan, Evelyn Grove Seely and an unidentified friend.

Chapter 10

We dress all our waiters in freshly laundered white suits,
with the sleeves buttoned around the wrist –
not dragging in your food.
Every waiter is placed in line in lecture each day
and finally inspected as to his personal cleanliness,
even to the examination of his fingernails.

Our employees wear rubber heels and maids are provided
comfortable chairs in their respective corridors, where they report
for service at 8:00am, but they sit and read until 9:00am,
being where guests can call them.

Frederick L. Seely, President
Grove Park Inn, Inc.
1918 Brochure

10:30pm
Tuesday
27 August 1918

As he stood in the doorway of his Lower Level office, listening to
Henry Ford's footsteps fade away as the automobile manufacturer
climbed the narrow tile staircase up to the pack of hungry reporters
prowling the Great Hall, Fred Seely knew what he had to do.

He quietly closed the thick oak door, then turned the black oval knob on the iron dead-bolt, to which he had the only two keys. One he kept tucked in his vest pocket; the other was locked in the hidden wall safe in his small office behind the front desk in the Great Hall.

He double-checked the sliding bolt on the door leading to Miss Hatch's adjoining office. She was home in bed, safely tucked into her little bungalow on Edgemont Road, just a quarter mile below the hotel. The former schoolteacher had come to Seely soon after the Inn had opened, explaining – not asking – why Seely needed her to help keep his affairs in order. The tall, prim woman was not to be dissuaded and Seely had immediately liked that quality in her.

No one in his life, he was sure, *was more loyal to him than Miss Hatch.*

No one.

Nothing he had ever said in her presence, none of the letters he had dictated to her, none of the conversations she had overheard from her office had ever made their way back to Seely. She walked to work each weekday morning, with her tidy sack lunch tucked into her needlepoint satchel, arriving at her gleaming oak desk at precisely eight o'clock.

Seely had instructed James Evans, one of the hotel's two chauffeurs, that should it ever be raining, snowing or colder than forty-five degrees, he was to be sitting in the hotel's Packard at 7:45am outside her house.

Nothing was ever mentioned of the arrangement, other than her simple "Thank you, Mr. Seely" as she hung her raincoat in the closet.

Their day always began with two brief exchanges: he would hand her the notes he had made in a shorthand code only she had learned to decipher, notes she would immediately translate into memos for the various department heads with changes Mr. Seely wanted made.

This morning he had left two for Albert Barnett, one of his assistant managers:

Mr. Barnett:

I wish you would go in the telephone booth and smell the telephone where a guest has to talk over it. The odor yesterday was so bad that I can't believe it has been washed for a year. It is that horrible smell that comes from saliva thrown into the telephone from an unhealthy person. This is another of the small things that could be attended to by someone beside myself and I think it ought to be attended to regularly.

F. L. Seely

Mr. Barnett:

I notice the two elevator men continue to slam the doors, particularly early in the morning. This annoyance simply must be stopped and if you can't get good results out of the two men you have, I wish you would replace them with others. I am firmly of the opinion, however, that with more disciplining these men would be better than any you could get.

F. L. Seely

She would hand to him one, sometimes two envelopes. The first would be the night report from Edward Crook, the hotel security officer Seely had hired. ("Interesting name," Miss Hatch had once commented with her wry smile, "for a security officer.")

The second envelop, when his services were required, came from a Pinkerton detective.

Under his agreement with the Pinkerton agency, Seely was not supposed to know who any of the detectives were that he had hired, but he had spotted one of the more recent ones his second day on the job. At first Seely said nothing, then decided that was ridiculous. As he walked passed the detective, who was pretending to be admiring a Roseville vase at the News Stand, he silently handed him one of his business cards with the scribbled notation "My office, ten minutes."

The Grove Park Inn, Seely explained, *simply is not a hotel where strangers could loiter for long without being noticed by him or one of his alert bellmen.* Seely made it clear that in the future, should any particular subject to which he had been assigned be inside the hotel, the detective would wait in his car until the individual had departed.

Last week Seely had requested that Pinkerton's send him a young Negro male detective to infiltrate the staff of colored waiters who worked in the hotel dining room. The detective, whose name was Berkley Long, or so he told Seely, met Seely the first night at the streetcar stop just below the entrance to the Grove Park Inn.

Seely pulled up at 10:30pm and motioned for Long to get in. They drove up Old Toll Road to the top of Sunset Mountain where Seely had explained how he wanted Long to apply for a job at the hotel as a waiter and to report to Seely what was going on in the basement rooms.

His first report the following day included the following:

At 9:00am I boarded a streetcar and went to the Grove Park Inn to apply for a job. When I arrived I saw Charley Sisney in the baggage room.

He told me to come in. I told him I was looking for a job, as a waiter. I had a few minutes to talk with him and he said he had only been at the Grove Park Inn nine or ten months, but had worked at the Battery Park Hotel fifteen years, and quit there to come to the Grove Park Inn, and he did not know whether he would stay here long or not; that he could get more money at another place, but did not say where.

He asked me to go down in the colored staff dining room and he would show the headwaiter to me and I might get a job. We went to the dining room, but the headwaiter had not come down. Charley said he was in a hurry, and told me to sit down and wait until the waiters came down and I could see the headwaiter.

The waiters began to arrive about 10 a.m. One of them asked me who I was waiting for, and I told him the headwaiter, and he told me to come in their dressing room, that he would be down in a few minutes, so I went in. The boys were playing poker, betting from fifty cents to two dollars, and two of the men were playing craps.

A big, fat, dark man came down from upstairs with a little whiskey in a half pint bottle and drank it and lit a cigar. He had straight dark hair and was heavy built. The headwaiter - Fred Bluford - did not come down until 11:10 a.m. and I applied to him for a job. He said he was filled up right now, but if I would give him my name and address, just as soon as he could he would let me know. I told him if he would put me to work I would give him ten dollars, but he said he did not sell anybody a job, that Mr. Seely would fire him if he found out. Fred said that all he does is to ask a man to do his work, and that is all he wants.

*I left and went back to the baggage room and was told Charley Sisney
had gone to town. I went to the streetcar line and while standing there
waiting for the car Charley passed by leaving the hotel in a Cadillac
Sedan with three white men. He was sitting in the front with the driver.
I boarded a streetcar at 11:25 a.m. and went down to Eagle Street for
lunch.*

That afternoon Seely sent for Fred Bluford, his headwaiter,
and told him he wanted him to add one more Negro waiter to the
staff. If Bluford suspected that Seely knew about his interview with
Berkley Long that morning, he gave no indication. The next morning Seely saw Long in the hotel dining room, but said nothing.

Later in the day Miss Hatch gave him a plain white envelope
with his name printed neatly in the center. Seely read that day's report from his undercover detective and filed it in the locked cabinet
in the corner of his office. He waited twelve days, so as not to draw
attention to Berkley Long, then systematically began dismissing
those waiters who had been drinking on the job, gambling and complaining about their superiors. The last one he fired was the detective
Berkley Long.

Convinced Henry Ford would not return, Seely opened the
door to his darkroom and gently pulled the canvas cart back into
his office. He reached down with his right hand and slid the blanket off her head, not sure how he would react. Still, she appeared to
be sleeping, at peace with the world, her legs bent at the knees, her
feet tucked beneath her bottom, her arms crossed over her chest,
the pink ribbon holding her bodice partially closed looped over her
long, delicate fingers.

He lifted the blanket out of the cart, folded it carefully and
set it on his chair. Stepping over to the leather couch against the wall

– a couch he had slept on many nights when he couldn't find reason enough to go home – he adjusted the pillows at one end, covering the top one with a small, clean washcloth from his private bathroom. Then, drawing a deep breath, he leaned over the cart and slowly began easing his hands, then his wrists, and finally his forearms under her body.

He could feel her muscles just beginning to stiffen. *It had been less than two hours since she died,* he calculated. He recalled from his chemistry class that rigor mortis typically set in two to four hours after death, when the lactic acid in the muscles began to bind the cells together. The process would be complete in six to twelve hours, after which the body would remain rigid for three days before the decomposition of the cells would cause it to again go limp.

His own back muscles strained under her weight and the awkward angle he had to assume as he raised her out of the cart, cradled in his arms. Her head, without any support, fell back unnaturally, pulling her mouth open. Fred looked away and hurried toward the couch, easing her head down upon the washcloth he had placed on the pillow. He reversed his earlier procedure, sliding his arms and hands out from beneath her body, now resting on the couch.

Moving quickly – and listening for footsteps in the corridor - he arranged her feet, her legs and her arms into a sleeping position, then smoothed out the folds in her dress. He carefully lifted her head a few inches off the pillow so that he could straighten her hair and adjust the angle of her pale, white neck. He gently closed her eyelids and supported her chin with the seam of the pillow. He tucked the edges of the washcloth under a thick strand of blond hair, then stepped back to view her.

As he did, he suddenly recalled where he had seen her.

Last night - in the Plantation Dining Room.
With Dr. Westin.
Ron Westin....

Seely typically dined at home late on Monday nights, eating a cold plate left for him by their cook. Evelyn had a regular afternoon session with Dr. Westin each Monday, which sometimes stretched into the evening. Afterwards she generally went straight to bed and was asleep by the time Fred finished eating.

Yesterday morning, however, Dr. Westin's secretary had called Miss Hatch to cancel his afternoon session with Evelyn. When they spoke at noon, Evelyn seemed rather depressed, so Fred had asked her to have dinner with him that evening at the hotel. He had hoped a quiet meal without the children would improve her spirits -- and would give him a chance to observe how prepared his dining room staff was the night before the arrival of Henry Ford's group.

Distracted by all of the preparations, Seely had paid little attention to the other diners -- or to Evelyn, who seemed lost in her own thoughts. He had to leave the table twice while they were eating, once to chastise a waiter for wearing a soiled uniform, the other to confer with Mr. Moreno in the kitchen to make sure the shrimp for the pre-movie banquet was being properly chilled.

He recalled, though, Evelyn asking him if he knew the woman dining at the far corner of the room with Dr. Westin. He remembered looking over at their table, where Westin had a young woman locked in one of his deep, intense gazes while, Seely calculated, the smooth talking doctor was charming her with stories of his medical miracles and plans for his revolutionary new clinic.

Now, as he studied her face, he was sure she had been Dr. Westin's dinner guest last night.

"*And,*" he wondered aloud, "*Were you his dessert -- up in room 641?*"

After dinner Evelyn had complained of a headache and asked Fred to call the house to let the children's nurse know she was going to spend the night at the hotel. Silently relieved to know he wouldn't have to drive her back home -- and could return to his office to review the room assignments for Tuesday night once he had walked her back to their second floor suite -- Fred was glad to oblige. When he finally came to bed just past midnight, Evelyn was sound asleep.

Suddenly, the telephone on his desk rang. Seely jumped as if he had nearly stepped on a coiled copperhead. He stared at it, not sure what to do. It continued to ring, even louder, it seemed. He worried that someone in the hallway might hear it. For a moment he considered putting the blanket over it, muffling its incessant ringing, but was afraid he would knock the receiver off the cradle.

Finally, it stopped.

> *Higgins at the front desk,* he assumed.
> *Who else would dare call his office this late?*
> *And even Higgins knew that he would have to have*
> *a good reason to call now.*

"Someone needs to talk with you," Higgins had said.

"*Someone looking for you,*" he whispered to her lying on the couch.

For a moment he felt as if the two of them were hiding out together. In a few minutes, though, Higgins would have the bellmen out looking for him. And Henry Ford, undoubtedly still in the Great Hall with a dozen reporters gathered around him, would probably send them scurrying down the stairs to his office.

> *And I still don't know who you are.*
> *But I will....*

Seely stepped back into the darkroom and pulled one of his prized cameras -- a German-made Ica Halloh equipped with a Dominar lens that made 8" x 10" negatives -- down off the second shelf on the left hand side. He began with a picture of her from across the room, full length. Through the viewfinder she looked as if she were asleep on his couch.

His couch.

Seely stepped closer, filling the entire frame with just her body, minimizing anything else. He would have to remember to destroy that first negative.

Nothing on the wall, nothing on the floor, not even the arms of the couch should be identifiable, he reckoned.

Nothing about the pillows would distinguish them from any others. And he could always get rid of them.

He snapped a second series of photographs, moving side to side to change the view slightly each time.

He stepped even closer, toward her feet, changing the angle as he concentrated on her facial features. Her high cheekbones, slender nose. A faint dimple in her chin.

Scandinavian descent. Especially with the blond hair.

He found that by kneeling he could avoid any blood-streaked strands of hair, most of which he had carefully tucked behind her head. He worried, though, that the close-ups of her face might look suspicious, what with the color all drained away.

Stepping over to the doorway, he switched off the ceiling light, leaving the glow from his desk lamp as the only light in the room. This made focusing more difficult, but he was sure the shadows would disguise the fact that she was not alive.

Pretty sure.

Thinking it would make her look more convincing, he set the camera down, unfolded the blanket and carefully draped it over her feet, legs, torso and shoulders, tucking it around her chin, as if she had been chilly just before she fell asleep. He shot several more photos of this pose, reminding himself to dispose of the blanket later. And the pillows.

A set of footsteps came dancing down the tile staircase outside his door. Fast. Light. Only the balls of their feet touching each tread.

Someone who knew the steepness of the stairs well. Certainly not a guest.

The barber had left even before the movie started. The bowling alleys and swimming pool were closed. The changing rooms were unlocked, but there were restrooms closer to the Great Hall than the ones in there.

Had to be one of the bellmen. Adam Hall or Jonathan Martin, perhaps. Both white, athletic.

Adam was leaving next week to go to college at Chapel Hill. Jonathan's father was a paper salesmen, a ne'er do well who spent too much time at the Social Smoke Shop on Pack Square, playing cards in the back room with the high rollers from Charlotte who always seemed to have a flask to pass around the table, yet who seldom drank themselves.

A firm rapping on the heavy oak door. "Mr. Seely?"

Jonathan Martin. A solid young man Seely felt he could trust, but not with this. Higgins wasn't long for the front desk and Seely had his eye on Jonathan as a replacement. He was every bit as bright and as ambitious as Adam, but born to the wrong family, at least as far as going to college was concerned.

But Seely could do things with Jonathan. He could teach him more here than they could at Chapel Hill. He didn't need a college degree, just like Seely hadn't needed one – and look what he had done: risen to be a department head at a major pharmaceutical manufacturing company, had been granted a patent, had founded a successful newspaper and was president of a nationally-recognized hotel, plus the owner of his own weaving and woodworking business.

Jonathan could go far with what Seely had to show him – and the contacts he could make through friends of his, like Theodore Hitzler, president of the Fifth Avenue Bank in Manhattan; Samuel Van Sant, the former governor of Minnesota; and Arthur Davis, president of the Aluminum Company of America in Pittsburg.

Yes, a bright young man like Jonathan could go far, farther than he had. Farther than Asheville.

"Mr. Seely?" Jonathan rapped his knuckles against the brittle, yellow varnish. "Are you there?"

Seely stared down at the thin streak of light running the width of the door. He sensed Jonathan was at that moment stepping back to do the same, wondering, he guessed, if he should press the issue.

Would he ever imagine, Seely mulled, *that I was in here with a beautiful young woman lying on my couch?*

Then he smiled and nearly said out loud, *Who's dead?*

Jonathan's rubber-soled shoes softly padded their way down the hallway toward the changing room. *Higgins had the bellmen out looking for him.* The next knock on the door might be that of Henry Ford, along with whoever had wanted to talk to him – and a dozen curious reporters.

"And just who might that be?" he asked lightly of his guest on the couch.

"A friend of yours? Perhaps your date for the evening?"

His stomach tightened.

"Your parents? – along with Sheriff Mitchell?"

The thought of this girl's parents looking for her, looking for her here, at the Grove Park Inn, at his hotel, the thought that upstairs, right now, people were gathering, listening to her parents explain how they hadn't seen their daughter since the movie started, listening to Sheriff Mitchell and Chief Lyerly question them. Her parents – people no different from him, a father of five children, one of them – *Gertrude* – just a few years younger than her – *Gertrude* – she had wanted to come to the movie with her mother, but Seely hadn't let her.

> *Gertrude.*

> *It could have been her lying in the Palm Court....*

"What have I done?" He closed his eyes and shook his head.

"Why didn't I just leave you where I found you?"

But he knew why, or so he thought. Perhaps it wasn't too late. Perhaps he should just go upstairs and call Sheriff Mitchell aside and explain to him what had happened, how he and Robert had discovered the girl's body and brought it here so as not to upset all the guests.

Mitchell would be pissed, he would yell and swear and threaten to arrest Seely for moving her body. Seely wouldn't deny it. He would just apologize and tell him exactly what had happened. Show him the blood stain under the wicker rocker, the laundry cart, the staff elevator. He could put her back in the cart first. Not mention anything about the photographs.

The press would feast on it. His guests would leave in droves, flamed by rumors of a murderer stalking the halls of the hotel. Business would plummet. Grove would get his lease nullified and the banks would begin calling in his loans.

But if he could convince them to give him some time, he could repay them in full once all of the looms at Biltmore Industries were up and running. A local scandal might cost him the Grove Park Inn, but in all likelihood his homespun customers around the country wouldn't even hear – or care – about it.

I could survive it, he argued.

And he wouldn't have to say anything about the two cigarette butts in his suit pockets. *But - Luther Hargus might.* And Hargus would make sure the sheriff knew he had been up on the sixth floor tonight. Listening to Hargus tell the story, it would sound like Seely might have been up there removing any evidence that would link him to the girl.

But no one would think him a suspect. He had been in the Great Hall during the entire movie. At least until Robert called him.

But a half dozen of his own staff, he realized, *along with several guests standing in the back of the room, had seen him leave the Great Hall and disappear up the stairs.*

And none of them knew the girl was already dead.

If Sheriff Mitchell didn't think of it, Seely was sure Edwin would be whispering it in his ear: perhaps Fred was meeting the girl, a girl no one seemed to know. Evelyn had complained that Fred was spending all his time at the hotel, perhaps the young woman had something to do with that, then a lovers' quarrel, a fall, perhaps a push, knowing everyone was at the movie, what better reason to move the body....

But Robert would collaborate his story. Robert knew what had happened. And even though he was colored, Sheriff Mitchell would have to listen to him, would have to realize that neither Robert nor he had anything to do with the girl's death. They had just found the body.

And, yes, in a moment of panic, they had moved her, but only to avoid upsetting any of the guests.

That's all.

Seely would need to have Robert here when he spoke with Sheriff Mitchell. He would have to have Robert here to dispel any thoughts of Seely having anything to do with the girl while she was alive – or with her death.

He stepped back to the door and listened for the sound of anyone in the hallway. Convinced it was empty, he picked up the phone and called Mrs. Hughes at the desk in Sunset Hall. He glanced at the clock. It was nearly ten-forty. She undoubtedly had gone to bed. On the third ring Mrs. Hughes, her voice sounding heavy, answered the phone.

"Mrs. Hughes, this is Mr. Seely."

"Yes, Mr. Seely." She cleared her throat. "What can I do for you?"

"I need to talk with Robert. Can you go up to his room and have him come down to the phone?"

"I, I would, Mr. Seely," she stammered, "but I, I can't. I mean, Robert's not there."

"What do you mean, not there?" Seely demanded, his throat tightening.

"I was going to tell you in the morning, what with it being so late and all," she offered apologetically. "I just didn't think you would want to be disturbed tonight, what with all your famous guests up there."

"Tell me what, Mrs. Hughes?"

"Well, Robert came back here around 9:30, said he wasn't feeling well. Yes, here it is in the log." He could hear her flipping open the employee logbook. "He came back at 9:28. He signed in and went to his room."

"But he's not there now?"

"No," she slowly answered, "he came back down a little later and wanted to know if he could use the phone. Said he needed to call his mama. Naturally, I let him."

"What did he say to her?"

"Why, I don't rightly know, Mr. Seely. I didn't listen. I went back to my room,"

"So, what happened?"

"Well, I did hear him hang up the phone and go back up the stairs, so I came back out and checked to make sure everything was all right. There wasn't nobody around, so I went back to my room and laid down. I must have dozed off, for a little while later I heard a truck pull around the side of the building, then I could hear someone running down the stairs. I looked outside and saw Robert. He went around the truck and got in the other side. Then they took off."

Seely thought for a moment.

"Mrs. Hughes, would you take a look at the schedule book and see when Robert's due back on?"

She paused.

"Mrs. Hughes, are you still there?"

"Yes, Mr. Seely, I am."

"Well, could you look at the schedule book for me?"

"I don't think Robert's coming back, Mr. Seely."

Seely sucked in his breath, held it momentarily, then let it slide out.

"Why not, Mrs. Hughes?"

"Well, when I saw him leave he had his bag with him." She paused again, "And he left you a note."

A note.

Seely closed his eyes tightly.

Something in writing. About the girl?

Robert, you idiot….

He steadied himself against the desk. "Is it in an envelope?"

"No, Mr. Seely. He just wrote it on a piece of paper and left it on the desk, under the telephone."

"Did you read it, Mrs. Hughes?"

"I, I did, Mr. Seely, but before I knew it was for you."

"Has anyone else seen it?"

"No, I don't think so. It couldn't have been out there very long. I don't think anyone else came or went."

"Where's the note now, Mrs. Hughes?"

"Right here, with me."

"Is anyone there with you?"

"No, no one."

"Then, would you read it to me, please? Quietly."

"Yes, sir. Here it is:

Dear Mr. Seely –

I am very sorry I have to leave like this, but knowd you would understand. Please give ten dollars from my next check to Lyda Jordan. Send the rest to my mama.

Robert

Neither of them spoke.

"Mr. Seely?"

"Yes, Mrs. Hughes?"

"That's it. That's all there was."

"Thank you, Mrs. Hughes." Seely thought for a moment. "Mrs. Hughes, are you still there?"

"Yes, Mr. Seely, I am."

"Mrs. Hughes, why do you think Robert wanted me to give ten dollars of his to Lyda Jordon?"

"Why, I don't know, Mr. Seely. Would you like to ask her?"

"She's there?"

"Why, yes, I mean, she was. She went back to her room a few minutes ago, but she was here, watching the front desk for me. Now that you mention it, she probably saw Robert when he was leaving."

"Could you get her for me? I would like to talk with her."

"Yes, Mr. Seely. It'll just take me a minute."

Seely winced as she dropped the receiver on the hard wooden counter, then listened as her footsteps receded down the hallway.

Robert was gone.

Gone.

But -- maybe he just went home.

Maybe he's not even on the schedule for tomorrow. He could have been taking his clothes home for his mama to wash.

Seely shook his head as he stared at the young woman on his couch.

Not with the note.

He was gone -- but perhaps not far....

"Mr. Seely?"

"Yes, Mrs. Hughes."

"I have her here." Seely waited.

"Hello?" The Negro girl's voice was timid, but not sleepy. Seely guessed she hadn't been to bed yet.

~ Bruce E. Johnson ~

"Lyda?"

"Yes, Mr. Seely?" Mrs. Hughes had obviously told her who was on the phone.

"Lyda, did you see Robert tonight?"

Again, a few seconds of silence.

"Lyda?"

"Yes, Mr. Seely, I did see him."

"What did he say to you, Lyda?"

"Not much, really. Just that he was leaving."

"Leaving for the night?"

"I don't think so. I think longer than that."

"Did he borrow some money from you? Ten dollars?"

"Yes, sir. It was all I had."

"Where was he going, Lyda? – And Lyda, I'll make sure you get your ten dollars back. First thing in the morning. Don't you worry about that."

"Thank you, Mr. Seely. Robert said you would."

"So, where was he going?"

"He didn't really say." Her voice sounded like she had more to say herself.

"But you have an idea, Lyda?"

"Its just, well…."

"Yes?" Seely struggled to hide his impatience. He glanced toward the door.

"Well, he left with his brother."

"And does his brother live around here?"

As he spoke, Seely was thinking. *One of Sheriff Mitchell's deputies could pick Robert up, bring him back to the hotel, where Robert could explain how he found the girl's body on the third floor, while Seely was still down in the Great Hall.*

197

That would take care of eliminating him as a suspect. And Seely could vouch for Robert. Then he would just have to deal with having moved the body....

"Not really."

Seely's plan vanished.

"Where do you think they went, Lyda?"

A long silence, then she spoke.

"The Dark Corner."

Seely groaned.

The Dark Corner.

Greenville County, South Carolina.

Everyone within five hundred miles had heard stories about the Dark Corner, a dense, forested valley straddling the border between North and South Carolina in terrain so steep that parts of it had never seen the light of the sun in 300 million years. Surrounded by mountains so rugged and rocky that not even a mule could climb in or out. Ringed by tangles of rhododendron thickets so dense even an experienced mountain man could get so disoriented he might never emerge.

The Dark Corner.

A haven for outlaws and moonshiners. The only place in North or South Carolina where your crime was more important than your color. And Robert's brother had a truck. A moonshine runner.

Edwin had told them stories about the Dark Corner over dinner at his father's home on Liberty Street. In one, a headstrong deputy from Spartanburg had chased a fugitive into the Dark Corner, determined to bring him out at any cost. As he drove his car down through the narrow road that lead into the depths of the valley, he ignored the shotgun blasts along the ridge warning those ahead that an intruder was approaching.

The deputy was never seen again.

Another time, Edwin went on, a team of seven revenue agents was sent out from Charlotte to the Dark Corner with orders to break up an illegal moonshine operation believed to be furnishing eighty percent of the moonshine sold in western North Carolina. They met one Monday morning with the sheriff of Greenville County, who tried to convince them to stay out of the Dark Corner.

The agents reportedly laughed at him, showing off their arsenal of weapons in the trunks of their cars. As ordered, the sheriff led them to the road leading to the valley, but refused to go any further. Ignoring their taunts, the sheriff returned to his office and the revenue agents began their raid, tearing down the road with their guns loaded and ready.

Three days later, the sheriff received a call from a farmer on the opposite side of Greenville County. There was a car abandoned alongside the road not far from his house. The sheriff drove out to investigate and found one of the two cars belonging to the seven revenue agents from Charlotte.

In a straight, neat row across the dash of the car were seven silver badges – each with a bullet hole through the center.

Seely wasn't sure how much embellishing Edwin had done to the story, but he had heard enough to know that if Robert's brother was hiding out in the Dark Corner, no one was going to bring Robert back to Asheville. He hung up the phone.

He was now a suspect in a crime no one even knew had been committed. A few minutes ago he had been ready to confess to disturbing a crime scene. How severe could the punishment for that have been? But without Robert to back him up, he wasn't going to avoid being a suspect.

Perhaps the only suspect.

The Coxe and the Grove families hated each other, but now they could join hands – around his neck.

Tench Coxe funneled enough money into each of Sheriff Mitchell's re-election campaigns to eliminate any opposition from either party – and for that he was sure Sheriff Mitchell was always ready to repay a favor. Charging Fred Seely with the murder of a beautiful young woman, who, perhaps, had threatened to reveal their affair to his wife, would satisfy both Edwin Grove and Tench Coxe. It would also improve Mitchell's standing with the citizens of Buncombe County, some of whom had begun complaining among themselves of the strong-arm tactics he and his deputies practiced, especially on the young, colored men who hung out on Eagle Street.

Unsolved crimes make people nervous, he explained to each new deputy, *which is why we don't have any.*

Seely turned and studied the girl's serene face once again.

So beautiful, even death could not defile you.

Yet someone had stolen from her the precious gift of life, someone had pushed her over the top of the sixth floor wall, someone who then watched her fall nearly forty feet, someone whose face may have been the last thing she saw as her head slammed into the concrete floor.

He swore he would find the person who had stolen her life - and was about to ruin his.

An eye for an eye....

*The Sunset Hall dormitory on the Grove Park Inn grounds
where many employees stayed.*

Foreman Oscar Mills watches men tighten joints on water pipes in the basement.

Chapter 11

Water is piped to us seventeen miles, directly from the slopes
of Mount Mitchell, nearly seven thousand feet in altitude.
The plumbing material is the finest that has ever been placed
in any hotel in the world. The soil pipe was hydraulically tested
and then galvanized. The hot water pipe, 18,000 pounds in weight,
is solid brass. The steam pipes are of genuine, lap-welded,
wrought iron.

Frederick L. Seely, President
Grove Park Inn, Inc.
1918 Brochure

10:50pm
Tuesday
27 August 1918

If there was one thing that Fred Seely knew at this precise moment
in time it was this: the sooner he distanced himself from this girl's
body, the safer he was going to be.

Right now no one else – no one other than Robert and whoever had been smoking a cigarette with her on the sixth floor balcony
earlier that night – even knew that the young woman was dead.

By now Robert was halfway to South Carolina with his moonshine-running brother, knowing full well – and Seely couldn't argue with him – that just by being a young black man alone with a blond white girl – *a very beautiful and very dead, white girl* – would make him the prime suspect.

And while Robert may have trusted him, Seely sensed that Robert wasn't about to put his life in his employer's hands.

White hands.

For all Robert knew, Seely and Sheriff Mitchell could be standing next to the girl's body in the Palm Court, waiting for his deputies to drag Robert back from Sunset Hall, where Seely had sent him to hide.

No wonder he had run....

And whoever had been smoking the second cigarette on the sixth floor -- *the person who an hour ago had watched her fall, her thin pink dress billowing around her* -- that person had apparently not yet come forward, for whatever reason.

And might never, Seely thought as he stood in his office.

But that individual, he argued, *could also have figured out that the only person in the hotel with any reason to move the girl's body, to hide it or even just delay the discovery of her death was Fred Seely.*

Even if he didn't know why. Even if he didn't know just how precarious Seely's finances were at the moment. That revenues for the first half of the year were down more than $30,000. That his bankers were growing more impatient by the day. That his future hinged on the national publicity Henry Ford, Thomas Edison, Harvey Firestone and John Burroughs were going to bring him in this week's papers -- papers he had already ordered in advance from Washington, Chicago, Miami, Boston, Pittsburg and New York -- papers that would have front page photographs of the group standing in front of the

Grove Park Inn, with quotes about their stay, their meals, the Great Hall and the hotel's staff, plus long, detailed articles describing the building of the mammoth hotel. Seely had already envisioned where he would display the framed newspapers in the Great Hall and had begun designing new ads he would complete with quotes from the most influential reporters.

But what if, in a moment of remorse, the person who had been on the sixth floor with the young woman decided to come forward with details of the accident?

What would happen then?

But -- what if he wasn't so remorseful?

What if he had something to hide? What if the girl hadn't fallen, that it hadn't been an accident?

What if he suddenly realized that there was now someone else he could shift the blame to?

That someone being me....

What then?

He might pull Sheriff Mitchell aside, might mention something about having seen Fred Seely disappear -- while the movie was still playing -- up the stairs leading to the Palm Court. Might then have asked Chief Lyerly if anyone else had heard a soft thud near the end of the movie.

Placing me at the scene would be easy enough to do.

Just a casual observation, one tossed lightly into the conversation, like a hand-knotted fly cast over a swirling eddy in a trout stream.

Then -- let the sheriff set the hook.

Deliberate, yet distant enough to not draw attention to himself. He could then slip away, melting into the crowd during the commotion that was sure to ensue, as search parties were formed to comb the entire hotel. Strolling, perhaps, back up to the sixth floor to retrieve the only evidence that might eliminate Fred Seely as a suspect – the second cigarette butt.

Anyone who knew Fred Seely even casually knew his abhorrence of cigarettes. No one for a moment would believe that Fred Seely could have been on the sixth floor of the Palm Court during the final minutes of the movie -- smoking a cigarette.

Fred instinctively ran his hands along the outside of his suit jacket's pockets, feeling two small lumps.

You certainly took care of that loose string for him.

That's when it hit him.

A murderer could easily become a witness –
against him.
And there would be nothing Seely could do,
not without Robert, to disprove it.
Not with her body here on the couch in his office.
Not with Luther Hargus ready to testify he saw Fred
Seely next to two cigarette butts - that had
then disappeared.

Seely felt as if he had just set one foot in a trap that had not yet sprung. Sweat began to bead on his brow. His collar grew tight around his neck. He could hear the clock ticking behind him.

Stay calm.

He might still escape, but only if he acted quickly.

The bellmen were out looking for him now, perhaps along with Sheriff Mitchell, checking the lounges, terraces and hallways. It would only be a matter of minutes before someone else came knocking at his door. His absence was soon going to be suspicious.

But they didn't know the young woman was dead,
just that she was missing.

And Sheriff Mitchell wouldn't get too upset about a young woman slipping off into the night. She wouldn't be the first to take a walk down across the golf course holding hands with a young suitor. He might send his deputies out looking for her, just to appease whoever was upset over her disappearance, but he would not inconvenience some of the most powerful men in Asheville by herding everyone back into the Great Hall and ordering the hotel doors locked and guarded.

Unless someone had already spotted the blood stained carpet under the rocking chair.
And had shown it to Sheriff Mitchell....

Regardless what might be happening in the Great Hall, Fred knew he had to make an appearance, he had to step in and take charge. He couldn't be found quivering in his office, unsure what to do. He had to take action.

The Grove Park Inn was his hotel.
And he was not about to give it up easily.

If they did come now, if they did find him in his office, he figured his meeting with Ford would provide him with a reason for being here rather than the Great Hall -- Ford would vouch for that -- where he imagined Sheriff Mitchell was now interviewing either the friends or the parents of the young woman lying on his couch.

But if her body was still here, it wouldn't matter who he had been meeting.
His business, his career, his life would be over.
All taken from him in just one evening, one evening that was supposed to have been the most important in years.

He still believed his office had been the only place he could have safely taken her, but now he realized he had to move her again.

He couldn't risk waiting until 3:00am and carting her up to the Palm Court, hoping to put her back where he found her without someone catching him. Even if none of his guests happened to come out of their room, his own staff, including Mr. Crook, his house detective, had been trained to detect any suspicious movements or behavior, especially in the middle of the night, especially with a hotel full of famous guests. The sound of the service elevator at three o'clock in the morning would bring someone out to investigate. Seely had dismissed too many workers for lesser infractions for him to think anyone on his staff would dare let the service elevator leave the lower level in the middle of the night without finding out by whom – and why.

Though he wasn't ready to admit it, Seely had known from the moment he saw her lying on the floor of the Palm Court what he might have to do.

He turned and walked back into the darkroom, where he opened the door to one of the maple cabinets attached to the back wall. He carefully set aside several boxes of photographic chemicals until he reached one that he had glued to a false back panel. He pulled the box forward to reveal a spring-loaded, wrought iron bolt recessed into the wall. Sliding it to his left, he could feel a section of the wall move a fraction of an inch on its well-oiled hinges. He then closed the cabinet door, stepped back and pulled open a three foot wide section of the wall.

Reaching up into a dark cavity in the ceiling, he switched on a string of bare light bulbs stretching over forty yards of rough dirt floor.

The dimly lit cavern was the unfinished basement crawl space directly beneath the Great Hall. Six, huge, cylindrical concrete shafts, like six silent sentries rising out of bedrock, passed through the gray cement ceiling where they became the six rock-encased pillars in the lobby, their stones monogrammed with Fred Seely's motivational quotations.

At either end of the cavernous crawl space the rough block and stone foundations for the two massive fireplaces squatted on the ground, the area around them littered with rocks, bricks, steel rein-forcing bar, broken bottles, lunch pails and discarded tools, silent reminders of the men who had labored here under Seely's command five years earlier.

Water, steam and waste pipes crisscrossed the terrain, some suspended by straps from the low, concrete ceiling, now cloaked in wispy spider webs, others partially buried in open trenches. The room was cool, moist, yet not wet. Spindly crickets scurried for cover beneath the wide, rough-sawn poplar planks strewn about the room, green planks, now cupped and twisted, planks which had come from E. W. Grove's sawmill located on timberland he owned in neighbor-ing Madison County.

The room seemed in total disarray, a stark and unsettling contrast to the spotless grey tile floors and freshly-vacuumed French carpets just a few feet above him. To anyone who knew Fred Seely, the area seemed totally out of character.

But it was exactly as he had planned.

To anyone peering inside it, the crawl space seemed not only uninviting, it looked dangerous. Eerie. Almost haunted. Nothing about it would draw anyone in. Nothing in sight gave any indication it had ever been visited since the workmen finished tightening the last pipe in July of 1913.

Several of the light bulbs were burnt out. A few were shat-tered, their jagged edges exposed below the brass sockets, shards of sharp glass left lying in the dirt below. Each one had been carefully broken by Seely, who didn't want anyone to even wonder if the crawl space was being used for anything other than emergency access to the plumbing and electrical lines.

The idea for a secret passageway beneath the hotel had occurred to him while he was working on the blueprints in June of 1912. He had heard rumors of secret tunnels George Vanderbilt had constructed beneath the Biltmore House, tunnels designed for him by Richard Sharp Smith that enabled him to move undetected from one end of his mansion to the other.

Tunnels, so the story was told, *that would enable Vanderbilt to slip unnoticed into a guest's bedroom.*

Seely had then begun designing a second set of blueprints, one only a few would ever see. At a glance his set appeared identical to that which Atlanta architect J. W. McKibben had prepared based on Seely's sketches. Seely had first placed a clean sheet of drafting paper over the blueprints McKibben, a talented, but hopelessly alcoholic architect, had dropped off the previous week. He carefully traced the outline of the hotel's foundation, including the location of concrete piers, fireplaces, stairwells and elevators. Then, on his copy, Seely began mapping out passageways that would honeycomb the hotel, making it possible for him to move about without being seen by any guests or employees.

At the core of the hotel was the crawl space beneath the Great Hall. Because of the concrete columns, the foundations for the two fireplaces and the maize of utility pipes, he and Grove had agreed this area could not be utilized for anything other than occasional access to plumbing and electrical lines.

On his plans, McKibben had indicated that the ground beneath the Great Hall need only be excavated to a depth of three feet, just enough to allow any plumbers or electricians to crawl across the floor to make needed repairs. Seely changed it to a minimum of six feet, more in some places, less in others on the rocky hillside, figuring that if either McKibben or the site foreman Oscar Mills noticed, he would simply state that he wanted plenty of room for the workmen should they ever need to run additional lines to new wings.

If the change was ever noticed or discussed, it was never around Seely, who, in truth, wanted the extra height so that he could walk upright from one end of the Great Hall crawl space to the other.

Seely then designated the first room at the bottom of the north stairway leading down from the Great Hall as his primary office, for this room shared a wall with the Great Hall crawl space. On one side he designed an office for Miss Hatch; on the other his darkroom that, once again, no one questioned.

On McKibben's blueprints, which Seely initialed and Oscar Mills carried out to the letter, no doorway appeared between the darkroom and the crawl space.

On Seely's set, a section of the wall became a hidden door.

A few weeks after the hotel had opened, Seely entered the basement crawl space from a locked door in the lower level, the only official entry into the crawl space, one reserved for emergency access only. The two keys to this door always remained in the wall safe in his office, for Seely was not about to let any workmen enter the crawl space outside his presence.

That Saturday afternoon -- he feared making any noise at night would draw attention to him, but any noises made during the day would be attributed to the workmen finishing up some details -- he switched on the single row of light bulbs dangling from the ceiling, making note that he would later want to install a second switch closer to the door to his darkroom.

At the precise spot where he planned to cut his door, Seely

had, during construction of the hotel, casually tossed enough rough pine boards he would need to frame the door. He wanted to be sure to use nothing other than the same lumber the carpenters had used to build the wall of his darkroom.

New lumber, he figured, *might later attract the curiosity of a plumber or electrician.*

Working quickly, yet as quietly as possible, Seely cut each board by hand, then, using a brace-and-bit to pre-drill the holes, he screwed a framework across the top and the bottom of the wall, opting not to use a hammer and nails for fear of being heard by guests a few feet overhead. Holding his handsaw on its side, he then cut through the original wall studs at the top and bottom, freeing a section of framed wall that would become his secret door.

He laughed in delight as he slid the section of wall aside, revealing the interior of his darkroom, the door to which he had earlier locked in anticipation of this triumphant moment. He felt giddy, like a prisoner who had just sawed his way to freedom. Moving faster now, Seely used three brass hinges as templates, scoring an outline around each hinge with a knife.

He then removed the wood to a depth of an eighth-of-an-inch on both the door and the framework, pushing the honed blade of the one-inch chisel he borrowed from the woodshop through the pine with the palm of his right hand rather than risking the noise a mallet would make.

He went through the process six times – twice for each of the three sets of hinges. By the time he was finished he had raised a blister on the palm of his hand, having forgotten to bring along a pair of leather gloves. He attached one side of each of the three hinges to the framework, then wrestled the section of wall back into place, using blocks of wood to suspend it in air while he finished twisting in the last of the inch-and-half wood screws. The blister on the palm of his hand popped, leaking a clear sticky liquid between his fingers.

Pushing the pain out of his mind, he kicked the blocks of wood from beneath the door. When he tested it for the first time, however, he discovered a problem he had not anticipated. The door had to open into his darkroom, he reasoned, to insure that neither the hinges nor any sign of activity in the dirt beneath the door would be visible to any workmen ever in the crawl space. He had already identified a few boards and broken cinder blocks he would carefully place in front of the hidden door to further add to the disguise.

But, as he immediately discovered, the weight of the section of wall he had now transformed into a door caused it to sag to the point where it dragged on the concrete floor of the darkroom. It needed diagonal supports either on the front or the back, diagonal supports Seely could not risk, for they would have revealed from several feet away the presence of a door.

He thought of adding a small wheel or caster beneath the door, but at this point there wasn't enough space for it without him completely removing and dismantling the door, then cutting it down to allow for the height of the caster, which would then be visible to anyone in the darkroom.

It only took him a few minutes to come up with the solution. Seely unlocked the darkroom door leading to his office, whose door was also locked and bolted, then opened the inner door to Miss Hatch's office. Since it was Saturday, she was home tending her garden. Pushed against the far wall was an oak typewriter desk – in truth, more like a small table for her shiny, new black Underwood.

What mattered most to Seely was that this table had what he needed – casters. As he set her typewriter down on the floor, he figured he could call Sluter's later that day – they were open until nine o'clock on Saturday nights – and have them deliver a temporary substitute on Monday morning until a replacement arrived from Berkey & Gay. Miss Hatch would be miffed at the inconvenience for a few days, but he would pay the additional freight and have it rushed down.

And he would send her up to the News Stand to pick out something for her office from the new shipment of items that had just arrived, perhaps a small copper bud vase or a tooled leather handbag. Hopefully, it wouldn't be one of the twenty dollar American Beauty vases….

Seely set the small table against the sagging door in his darkroom, then knelt down and began tapping wooden shims beneath the door until it slowly resumed its original shape. He checked it with his level to make sure it was square with the framework, then squatted on the floor to gauge the gap between the bottom of the door and the floor of the darkroom. He tapped the shims a few more times, checked the door again with his level, then stepped back. He carefully positioned the typewriter table against the door which, because of the shims, was temporarily straight and square again.

Satisfied, he reached for his brace-and-bit, extra screws and screwdriver. Kneeling on the floor, he reached up beneath the top of the table and in a few minutes time had drilled and inserted six screws through the inside of the table and into the oak tongue-and-groove wall paneling – now the face of his hidden door. Holding his breath, he used the handle of his screwdriver to carefully tap the shims out from beneath the door. With a short sigh of relief he could see that the table was now supporting the weight of the door, preventing it from dragging on the floor.

As a final test he grabbed the front of the typewriter table and pulled it toward him. The four steel castors turned in unison, now pointing toward him, and silently rolled across the smooth concrete floor, bringing the door along with them.

Seely never had specific plans for the crawl space, but the secret door in the darkroom provided him with what he really needed: private - and quick - access to the rest of the hotel.

What appeared to be randomly discarded planks were in truth carefully positioned by Seely to provide him with a safe passage around the suspended pipes and over the open trenches. Some planks he purposely placed to discourage any curious intruders by leading them to the brink of one of the four foot deep trenches that had never been backfilled.

> *Just in case,* he murmured to himself as he dragged one of the planks across the dirt floor, *one of the waiters would come looking for a place to take a nip or two.*

The crawl space measured 120 feet long. To his left as he entered from his darkroom was the massive stone and block foundation for the north fireplace. As he had designed it, the granite fireplace, which was nearly forty feet wide, contained three vertical shafts. The center shaft was the chimney flue rising from the over-sized firebox in the Great Hall. On either side of the firebox and chimney flue was one of two elevator shafts.

The public elevator opened at each floor, beginning with the Lower Level, where the operator, typically Frank Mull or Paul Johnson, sat on a chair when not busy. The service elevator, however, by-passed the Great Hall. The doors leading to the service elevator on the guest room floors looked identical to the doors on the guest rooms, causing most people to assume each was a storage closet.

At the opposite end of the crawl space -- 120 feet away -- stood the foundation for the south fireplace. Seely had also divided it into three vertical shafts. The central shaft was for the firebox and chimney flue and a second shaft housed the guest elevator that loaded near the front desk in the Great Hall. Since Fred Seely felt they only needed one service elevator, he directed the carpenters to construct storage closets for the housekeeping staff on each floor inside the third shaft.

Beyond the south fireplace the dark crawl space narrowed, marking the beginning of the south wing. Whereas the central section of the hotel, that portion rising above the Great Hall, stood six stories tall, both the north and the south wings were only five stories high. Like the ground beneath the Great Hall, this area was also scarred by trenches and littered with sections of pipe, broken concrete blocks, rocks, bottles and tools. It reminded him of photographs the newspapers printed of the trenches the doughboys in France were living in. All it lacked were shells whistling overhead and rats racing for cover with coveted pieces of white flesh hanging from their steely jaws.

At the far end of the south wing stood the third of the Grove Park Inn's three fireplaces. This one was slightly smaller than the two facing each other in the Great Hall and its firebox opened onto a covered, outdoor terrace. It had proved to be a popular spot for guests to gather on chilly evenings, regardless of the season, for the tiled roof provided protection from either rain or snow showers. The Old Hickory rockers, with their woven splint seats, could be pulled close to the fire or turned to view the sun setting behind Mt. Pisgah.

While the plans which McKibben had drawn for Seely and Grove showed nothing except a chimney flue behind the granite façade of the outdoor fireplace, Seely pulled Oscar Mills aside one day and explained to him that, although Grove opposed the idea, Seely anticipated a day in the future when a new wing would be added to the south end of the hotel. During their conversation, Seely implied that by then he would be the owner of the hotel – and Oscar Mills would be his full-time contractor.

"This would be the time," Seely pointed out as the two men stood next to the footings being dug for the outdoor fireplace, "to lay up the block for another elevator shaft, one we would just leave empty in case it would ever be needed in the future. One only you and I would know about."

The young contractor from Atlanta could find nothing to argue with the suggestion and was relieved that unlike many of his clients, Seely had come forward with the changes before rather than after his men had started work. Sectioning off an elevator shaft next to the flue presented no difficulties for Mills or his stonemasons as they worked their way from the footings in the crawl space up to the top of the fifth floor roof. Grove, who had returned to his St. Louis offices at the Paris Medicine Company shortly after the July groundbreaking, never noticed the change.

Eleven months later, as the hotel was nearing completion, all of the stonemasons had been dismissed and only the tile layers and finish carpenters remained on the job. Seely was on the site daily, watching carefully, checking details, making sure miter joints were tight and grout lines straight. He took a special interest in two of the oldest carpenters Oscar Mills had hired, two older Dutchmen who between them only knew a few words of English. The men never missed a day of work and, unlike many of the slackers Seely noted, never stopped working before quitting time to gather their tools, wash their hands, locate their lunch pails or chat with their buddies. The hardworking Dutchmen kept to themselves, silently walking down Macon Avenue each evening to catch the streetcar out to West Asheville, where they shared a small, well-kept bungalow with what

Seely, from his car, judged to be a wife or sister of one of them. The oldest had a nasty cough.

Black lung, Seely suspected.

Probably used to work in the mines.

On what would have been their final day working on the Grove Park Inn, Seely had pulled the two aside and indicated he wanted them to return on Monday with their tools. The official opening had come and gone and along with it nearly all of their important guests. Several days earlier Seely had informed Higgins at the front desk that beginning on Monday all of the guests were to be assigned rooms at the north end of the hotel while some work was being wrapped up in the south wing.

He met the two Dutchmen precisely at seven that morning and walked them through the cavernous crawl space beneath the Great Hall and under the south wing until they stood next to the concrete block foundation of the outdoor fireplace. There, beneath the glow of a solitary light bulb, Seely unrolled his plans and showed them what he wanted built: a wooden staircase inside the future elevator shaft.

Knowing he might have trouble communicating with the two Dutchmen, Seely had carefully drawn his design for the staircase, showing the precise locations of the doorways. He had already ordered and had delivered to the far end of the hotel enough lumber and supplies for the two men to get started that morning, including short-handled sledge hammers, masonry chisels and extension ladders. Little was said, but judging by their smiles of recognition and appreciation for the detailed plans Seely had provided, plans that eliminated the need for any awkward attempts to communicate in English, the two men understood what was expected of them.

It took the Dutchmen just five days to build the staircase, but Seely paid them in new silver dollars for two weeks' work. As they smiled in appreciation, Seely reached into his vest pocket and pulled out ten more silver dollars. Tapping the dog-eared blueprints with his index finger, then placing it over his lips to indicate silence, Seely dropped five silver dollars into each of their right hands. The men nodded and Seely knew they would never speak to anyone about their final project at the Grove Park Inn.

A few years later, as he was driving out through West Asheville, Seely turned up Malvern Avenue and drove past their house. The paint was peeling, the screen door leaned against a porch post and toys littered the over-grown yard. The Dutchmen obviously had moved, causing Fred to wonder if the older carpenter had died. The thought saddened him and he wished he could have attended the funeral.

As he stood in the basement of the Great Hall that evening, he thought back to those twelve months of construction, twelve months of noise, confusion, raspy wheelbarrows tottering under the weight of sloshing, wet concrete, men shouting down from the roofs, bridled mules braying, truckloads of rocks barreling down the mountain, the steam shovel chipping through veins of feldspar and mica that had lain undisturbed for millions of years, crowds of bystanders watching from the road, boys playing on pyramids of iron pipe waiting to take their place in the great hotel Fred Seely was building on Sunset Mountain.

For although it was known far and wide as the Grove Park Inn, everyone in Asheville was talking about the young publisher from Atlanta who had rolled into town fresh from having negotiated the sale of his newspaper to the infamous William Randolph Hearst, a young man who reportedly knew President Woodrow Wilson and

Secretary of State William Jennings Bryan – and who, with no training or experience had conceived of the idea for the Grove Park Inn, had drawn the plans for it and now was organizing 400 men who were going to build, furnish and decorate the six story, 150-room hotel in just three hundred and sixty-five days.

It would be a feat the likes of which no one in the region had ever witnessed.

And they would never forget the name of Fred Loring Seely.

Just six years ago, he thought as he scanned the dimly lit crawl space.

It felt like a lifetime.

Satisfied the crawl space was deserted, Seely returned to his office where he deftly scooped up the girl's body from the couch and, keeping the blanket with her, walked through the darkroom and into the crawl space. Twenty yards past the door he turned to his right, off the plank pathway and onto the rocky dirt floor.

Wipe off your shoes before you leave.

Behind one of the massive concrete pillars he stopped and, lowering his left arm, let the blanket fall onto the floor. He used the toe of his black Johnson & Murphy Oxford to spread the blanket out enough to kneel down and, making sure his knee did not touch the ground, slid her onto it.

He quickly arranged her arms and legs, noting, too, that rigor mortis had just begun to set in, then pulled the edges of the blanket over her body, including her face. Before leaving he pulled two empty wooden crates, each stenciled "Haines, Jones & Cadbury – Philadelphia," manufacturers of the bathtubs and sinks in the guest rooms, and positioned them between her body and the doorway to the darkroom.

Before leaving, he turned and surveyed the crawl space, mak-ing sure no one could see the blanketed mound behind the far pillar. Although he was confident no one would notice anything unusual, he knew this was but a short-term solution, designed only to buy him a little more time.

He stepped back into the darkroom, closed and bolted the hidden door, wiped the dust from his hands and shoes with a towel from the darkroom sink and walked into his office.

Guests enjoying the south fireplace in Great Hall.

Chapter 12

*The Grove Park Inn is not intended as a sanitarium
for persons with indigestion, but we recognize the fact
that those who can afford to patronize a place like this
are usually the overworkers, whose digestion needs
best assistance and not our opposition,
as would seem the policy of many hotels.*

Frederick L. Seely, President
Grove Park Inn, Inc.
1918 Brochure

11:05pm
Tuesday
27 August 1918

Back in his office, Fred Seely quickly rearranged the pillows on his
couch, refolded the remaining wool blanket and dropped it into the
bottom of the canvas laundry cart, first checking to make sure there
were no blood stains in it. He picked up the red-stained hand towel
he had taken from the Chiles's room. He realized the housekeeping
report for room 347 that day would show one hand towel missing,
but that wasn't all that unusual and shouldn't attract the attention of
Miss Hatch, who reviewed the reports each afternoon for Seely.

Darting back into the darkroom, he spread the crimson-colored hand towel in the bottom of his cast iron sink, then, pulling a one gallon glass jug down from the cupboard above it, carefully began dowsing it with fixer, the liquid solution he used to remove undeveloped silver iodide from the emulsion on his photographs. As he had hoped, the fixer proved as effective as bleach in removing the blood from the cotton fibers. A blast of hot water sent the final trace of any blood and fixer down the drain. Seely wrung out the majority of the water, then, satisfied no one would ever suspect where it had been, carefully draped it over the edge of the sink to dry.

After checking to make sure the hall outside his office was empty, Seely quickly wheeled the laundry cart down the hallway and parked it outside the door to the housekeeping room. The first maid to arrive in the morning, well aware that one of her staff would be written up if Mr. Seely discovered a laundry cart left in the basement hallway, would be sure to put both the cart and the blanket away without ever mentioning it to anyone. With a final check of his hands, his clothes and his shoes, Fred Seely started up the tiled stairs leading to the Great Hall.

As he pushed open the heavy oak door, Seely was surprised to discover that the room was buzzing with activity. Many of the people from Asheville who had come up to the Grove Park Inn for the evening's movie and the opportunity to see Henry Ford and Thomas Edison were still milling around the lobby. A few could be seen sprawled unhappily across the wicker chairs and couches, still in disarray after the movie. Theodore, upon spotting Seely at the far end of the lobby, quickly made his way over to his employer.

"Everyone's been looking for you, Mr. Seely," he explained. "Seems a big pine tree fell down across Macon Avenue during the storm. Sheriff Mitchell says it just slid down the bank, roots and all.

Saturated from all the rain we had this week. He's been on the phone, trying to get some men and a team of mules to drag it off the road so people can get home."

"Did he say when the road would be open?"

Theodore shook his head. "Maybe not 'til morning. Said it was so big – roots and all – that they would have to saw it up 'for they could move it."

Seely looked around the room. "Where's Sheriff Mitchell now? And Chief Lyerly?"

"Sheriff Mitchell went back down the road. Said to tell you he'd be back in a few minutes. Wants to talk with you. Chief Lyerly's leading a group of cars up Old Toll Road, then back down Town Mountain Road."

Seely shook his head. Old Toll Road led up to his home on Overlook, the top of Sunset Mountain. It was a drive he had mastered, but wouldn't recommend at night to anyone unfamiliar with the road's hairpin turns and sudden switchbacks.

"Mr. Seely!"

It was Higgins, nearly running over from the front desk. Seely frowned at the near panic in his voice.

Higgins had to go. First thing next week.

"Yes, Mr. Higgins?" Rather than looking at him, Seely calmly surveyed the room.

"You know about the road, sir?" he asked breathlessly.

"Yes, Mr. Higgins. I know the road is blocked."

"People want to know what they should do."

Seely glanced at the grandfather clock standing against the pillar in front of the bellstand. "Its late, Mr. Higgins. Too late for people to be driving up Old Toll Road. Start putting people who want them into rooms for the night. No charge. Send any drivers down to Sunset Hall. Call Mrs. Hughes first. Have her get their names and who they are driving for. Tell her to put them on the third floor."

"Yes, Mr. Seely." Higgins turned and started spreading the word through the crowd. Delighted at the prospect of spending a free night at the Grove Park Inn, people eagerly began lining up to get their room keys. A few waved or nodded in appreciation at Fred Seely, still standing near the north fireplace with Theodore.

"Have your boys start straightening up the room, Theodore. As soon as they can, move the chairs back into the dining room. And take down the screen. Leave a note in the kitchen letting Mr. Barvani know he'll have some extra guests for breakfast, but he's still to hold the private dining room for Mr. Ford's party. And tell Mr. Munroe there will be no charge for the Asheville guests at breakfast. But to keep it quiet. I don't want our paying guests to be asking for a free meal."

The swell of people toward the front desk pulled in a few more from the terrace, including Edwin Grove and Cornelia Vanderbilt, who began making their way single file through the jumble of chairs and rockers to where Seely now stood alone. Cornelia came first, closely followed by Edwin who, Seely noted, couldn't take his eyes off her backside.

"Quite an exciting evening, eh, Fred?" Edwin announced, stumbling slightly as he stepped around her.

Seely stood dumbfounded, staring at Edwin's suit where a familiar silk handkerchief with a hand-stitched letter "S" protruded from his breast pocket.

My handkerchief.

In Edwin's pocket.

"Yes," Seely replied, struggling to keep his composure. "Yes, it certainly has been." Turning his gaze to Cornelia, he said, "I'm sorry about the inconvenience, Miss Vanderbilt. I'm afraid it doesn't look too promising right now. Can I arrange for a room for you?"

"Why that's very kind of you to offer, Mr. Seely, but Dr. Battle has already gotten us a room. Mother's gone up to rest until we get word on whether or not the road will be opened tonight."

"That was very generous of him."

Seely gestured toward Edwin's pocket. "Judging by the monogram on your handkerchief, Edwin, I'd say you decided to change your name."

Edwin looked down, making a show of adjusting the handkerchief. "Oh, that," he said looking up at Seely, his words just beginning to slur. "No. Its just something I picked up this evening. Someone must have dropped it, don't you think? Looks very expensive. I was going to check with your Mr. Smith, the Englishman. Architect, I believe. Very proper gentleman, wouldn't you say? And with the right last name, but…." Edwin looked around the room. "Perhaps he was having a nosebleed. Tell me, Fred -- you've probably had experience along these lines -- what's the best thing for getting out blood stains?"

Seely held Edwin's gaze. "I wouldn't know, Edwin. But you might try some hydrogen peroxide. I hear that works."

"Thanks. I just might do that." Edwin paused to look around the lobby. "Quite a crowd you've got here, Fred. Think you'll have room for them all?"

"I think Higgins has it under control."

"Well, if you run out of rooms tonight, you can always use mine. I could just sleep on the couch in your office, right?" Edwin smiled, "unless it's already taken…."

Seely looked at Edwin without blinking.

"No, Edwin. It's available. But I'm sure you can keep your

room tonight. But thanks, just the same." Seely paused. "Are you headed there now?"

Edwin looked around the room. "No, not just yet. We're kinda looking for someone. Two someones, actually."

Cornelia quickly stepped in. "Perhaps you've seen them. Two young women, nurses from the new military hospital out at Oteen. Their names are Daisy Wheeler and Emma Barringer. Mother and I met them a few days ago. Dr. Battle asked us to help the first group get settled in, showed them around Asheville a little. Dr. Westin was there, too. Daisy and Emma were with me, and I told them about Mr. Ford and Mr. Edison being here tonight. They seemed so excited I offered them a ride." Cornelia looked around, "But now I can't find either of them."

"What do they look like?"

"Emma's got short, brown hair. Medium height. Brown eyes, too. She's wearing a cardigan sweater -- light blue -- over a white blouse. With a blue skirt."

Seely nodded, as he felt a bead of sweat trickling down the back of his neck. "And the other? Daisy, I believe, you said?"

"Daisy Wheeler. From Connecticut, though they both just came from New York City, where they were in training. Though she didn't come out and say it, I think her family's pretty well off. She said they were upset when she told them she was leaving Connecticut – and a fiancé – to become a nurse at a hospital for soldiers."

"So, she doesn't have any family down here?"

"No. They're all back in Connecticut. Meriden, I believe."

So, her parents aren't here tonight....

Fred could feel his heart pounding in his chest. He wanted to know more, but he could sense Edwin was studying him. "What does she – this second girl – look like?"

"She's a beaut, Fred. A real looker," Edwin chimed in. "Long blond hair, slender, curves in all the right places. You know, the kind you could die for…."

Seely tried hard to ignore Edwin. "What was she wearing?" he asked Cornelia.

"A pink dress. Silk. It was one of mine," she explained. "Daisy didn't feel she had brought anything nice enough to wear tonight, so I loaned her a dress. She's about my height."

Seely looked around the Great Hall, which was now beginning to empty.

"When was the last time you saw either of them?"

"We got separated just before the movie started. Mother had been introducing me to some people, so they just wandered off. I know Emma was with Dr. Westin part of the time because I ran into her in the Ladies' Lounge during the movie and she was all excited about having met him. She said something about him offering her a position in the new clinic he's building."

Seely groaned silently.

Dr. Westin and his clinic.

It was a line Seely had heard the doctor use more times than he cared to recall -- and usually on the way to his next conquest. Westin's first trips to the Grove Park Inn had always been in conjunction with tours he was giving some of his prospective investors, but after a while Seely noted that Westin was appearing on a regular basis without them.

On one such occasion Seely watched from the back of the front desk as Ron Westin and one of Mrs. Swann's ladies -- Lossie -- left the Plantation Dining Room and strolled about the Great Hall, as Westin pointed out the various quotations Seely had painted on the rocks. Dr. Westin made a point of saying good-bye to her loud enough for several guests to hear, then left through the front door. Lossie, however, who Seely knew was not registered at the hotel, took the elevator to one of the upper floors. When the elevator returned a few minutes later, Seely stepped in.

"Which floor, Mr. Seely?" Frank Mull asked.

"Nowhere in particular," Seely replied. "I'm just checking to see how the equipment is running. Where did you leave your last rider?"

"The lady? Fifth floor."

"That sounds as good as any. Let me hear how the motor sounds."

As the elevator quietly rose in the rock-encased shaft, the call button on the board next to Frank Mull lit up. Fred Seely glanced over at it.

Lower Level.

"Looks like you have another rider, Frank."

"Do you want to get off first, Mr. Seely?"

"No. I'll just ride along. Lets go down and pick him up."

"You know who it is?" Frank asked in surprise.

"I have a pretty good idea."

On their way back up to the fifth floor, Dr. Westin did not mention his luncheon guest, nor did Seely. They passed the time making small talk, then parted with pale promises to get together for lunch sometime soon. Seely could see Lossie waiting not far from the elevator, but Westin made no effort to acknowledge her. As Frank closed the elevator door, Lossie turned and smiled at Seely.

In the weeks that followed Dr. Westin appeared a number of times with one of Mrs. Swann's ladies on his arm, but increasingly Seely saw him with any of the young nurses from Mission Hospital or one of the middle-aged wives sent by their husbands to the Grove Park Inn for a few weeks.

Seely still did not mind providing Westin with a free room, for he continued, as well, with his regular therapy sessions with Evelyn. At times Fred wondered if her treatments were still necessary, but he could not deny the improvement he had seen in his wife, although he sometimes worried that she might have become too dependent on Dr. Westin.

And while Dr. Westin had never asked for any compensation for the business he continued to bring to the Grove Park Inn, Fred Seely still could not bring himself to trust the man.

Someday, he thought, *he'll come wanting something.*

Payback.

A favor.

And if it were something he could not – or would not – provide, what would Westin do?

Take his business elsewhere?

Not likely.

So, what else could he do?

And that was what bothered Fred Seely the most about Ron Westin. While he did not know what it might be, he always suspected that Westin was always watching, hoping, perhaps even working to get something on him. Something he could use.

But what? It was a question he often asked himself.

Something to do with the hotel?

Something with Grove?

Again, not likely, since Grove was opposed to anyone who encouraged tuberculosis patients to come to Asheville, as well as the boarding houses and sanitariums that catered to them. He ranted and raved to anyone who would listen that Asheville could become a leper's colony for dying tuberculosis patients. "Asheville's future," he declared, "is in tourism, not tuberculosis."

On that point he and his father-in-law agreed. Grove went so far as to include a lifetime ban on the construction or operation of any boarding houses or sanitariums in every deed for any property he sold.

Perhaps Dr. Westin would side with Edwin in his attempt to oust Seely from the hotel, but for what purpose?

Perhaps it would have something to do with Evelyn and her treatment. Fred Seely sensed that the day would come when he would find out what Dr. Westin had on him – and what he wanted in exchange.

Which is why he felt he had to come up with a plan.

Fred Seely's secret staircase inside the south fireplace ended in the fifth floor storage room, behind a door hidden by a large, rolling armoire. Inside the storage room a wooden ladder attached to the wall led to a low attic above the ceilings of the ten rooms in the south wing. Seely made it clear to his housekeeping staff that they were never to climb into the fifth floor attic for fear they would frighten or disturb the guests in the rooms beneath them.

Seely did permit – but only under his supervision – the storage of some empty crates in the fifth floor attic, but only because of the same reason that he did not want his staff up there: out of fear they would discover his secret.

At the far end of the attic, where the fifth floor wing joined the central, six story section of the hotel, Seely had recently recalled that the attic wall was also the back of one of the walls in room 641. An alcove formed between the wall and the sloping roof had been hastily sealed by the workmen with just a few boards, which Seely was able to work loose and pry off with his hands. Using an empty crate as a step, Seely could then climb into the alcove and stand upright, just outside room 641.

As soon as the most recent guest had departed, Seely let himself into 641 and surveyed the room. With just a little rearranging of the furniture he was able to free a space on the wall directly in front of the secret alcove. His first thought was to install a peephole, but he immediately realized it could be spotted by anyone in the room.

Then he remembered reading about a recent patent for a transparent mirror. He contacted his friend and Washington patent attorney James L. Norris, who supplied him with a copy of patent No. 720,877 assigned on February 17th, 1903, to Emil Bloch, a Russian citizen residing in Cincinnati. Using Bloch's description of his process and materials, Seely, after much experimentation in his darkroom, was able to transform a one-way mirror taken from one of the dressers into a transparent two-way mirror.

Seely then determined precisely where on the wall in room 641 the mirror should hang, both to appear natural to any guest in the room and to provide Seely with an unobstructed view of the two beds. Using a hammer he had brought with him from his darkroom, Seely tapped a three-inch finish nail through the plaster until it protruded into the dark alcove. With the nail as a reference, Seely then outlined a rectangle slightly smaller than the two-way mirror and carefully cut out the plaster and pine lathe with a keyhole saw. To insure that neither a guest nor one of his housekeeping staff ever moved the mirror, Seely mounted it directly to the wall with four wood screws, taking time to countersink the holes and hide each screw head beneath an oak plug.

In the process of hanging the mirror, Seely made an important discovery. If room 641 were dark, any light in the alcove could be seen through the two-way mirror. Similarly, if someone in room 641 held a lamp up to the mirror, while at the same time pressing their eye as close to the glass as possible, they would be able to see into the alcove. To prevent either from happening, Seely unscrewed the single bulb installed by the original workmen in the fifth floor attic.

As a further precaution – in case one of his staff decided to explore the far reaches of the attic – Seely cut one of the wide boards he had pried off the opening to the alcove and hinged it over the back of the mirror. When he wanted to peer into room 641, he quietly raised the board on its lubricated hinges and secured it with a nearly invisible wire. Before leaving, he would simply lower the board, providing a solid back for the mirror and rendering it undetectable.

Finally, he pulled one of the empty crates into the alcove, giving him a place to sit in his observation post. The remainder of the empty crates he stacked at the end of the attic, effectively blocking anyone's view of the entrance to his secret alcove.

The only other alteration he made to the alcove outside room 641 was a small shelf as high on the wall as he could reach. Positioned between two of the pine studs, the shelf was also cut from an old, discarded board and made to look like part of the original construction bracing. Set on the shelf and pushed as far back into the darkness as it could go was his No. 1-A Autographic Kodak Special with a f6.3 Anastigmat lens.

It had taken several hours of experimentation with various levels of lighting in room 641 to determine the precise aperture and speed settings for his Autographic, but, fortunately for Seely, it was at this same time that Dr. Westin began making his regular Wednesday afternoon appearances. Once the room was ready, it was easy for Seely to tell Higgins to assign Dr. Westin to room 641. The next time Westin appeared for one of his trysts, Seely pointed out to the doctor that the rooms on the sixth floor were generally the last to be assigned each day, insuring him of more privacy -- and room 641 was the closest to the elevator.

From that day on, unless Dr. Westin was known to be back in Miami, room 641 was held out of circulation. As Seely soon observed, each Wednesday a Mrs. Dickerson, wife of a prominent doctor in Asheville, arrived by cab precisely at noon and took lunch by herself, often while reading a book, in the Plantation Dining Room. After lunch she took her customary walk around the hotel, including the terraces in fair weather.

Her routine grew so familiar to the staff that they paid little attention to her – and never noticed that Mrs. Dickerson always made it a point to let herself into room 641 at 1:30 each Wednesday afternoon. About that same time Dr. Westin could be seen parking his automobile – a new Nash 681 – below the hotel, near Sunset Hall, from where he would walk up to the employee's entrance in the Lower Level and call the elevator down to pick him up.

While Seely knew that his housekeeping staff, along with others, such as elevator operator Frank Mull, undoubtedly knew what was going on in room 641 each Wednesday afternoon, he also knew how much they valued their positions. He made it perfectly clear to each new employee that discretion was not only appreciated by their guests, it was expected. *Any conduct to the contrary,* he warned, *would meet with immediate dismissal.*

The first time he had watched Dr. Westin and Mrs. Dickerson having sex – *they really weren't making love,* he observed – Fred became so entranced that he forgot about taking any photographs. It was not, he could tell, their first time together, for there certainly was no seduction involved.

After a few pleasantries they simply disrobed, with Mrs. Dickerson taking time to carefully arrange her dress over the back of the rocking chair. Westin was far more impatient and Seely nearly laughed the first time he saw the distinguished Miami physician, clad only in his wrinkled boxer shorts and knee-high black socks, rush to grope her breasts as she leaned over and shook loose her unclasped brassiere.

Mrs. Dickerson was far more attractive than Seely had noticed when he observed her in the dining room. Her breasts were small, but firm and well-proportioned to her slender, athletic frame. She was taller than many women, nearly as tall as some men, with a long back. What Seely could not understand, as he watched Westin lead her toward the bed, was why she had selected Ron Westin as her lover. She wasn't one of the bored summer tourists or naïve nurses Westin typically preyed upon, coaxing them to his room with promises of positions in his new clinic, shared profits or romantic trips to a Caribbean island.

> Had she wanted, she could have taken any number of young men as her lover, men far more attractive, far more athletic, far more – as Seely discovered as he watched Westin drop his boxer shorts to the floor – endowed.

Westin sat on the edge of the bed, his stubby erection protruding beneath his hair-covered stomach, as he spread his legs to make it clear what he wanted. Without any protest, Mrs. Dickerson sank to her knees. Westin leaned back and held the hairy folds of his bulging stomach in both hands as her head, her brown hair streaked with gray, began a slow, steady bobbing beneath it. After little more than a minute, she stood up and stepped out of her pink lace panties.

On cue, Westin slid further back on the bed, enabling her to straddle him. She reached down and deftly slid him into her, then began to rock back and forth with short, slow motions. As her intensity increased, she took his left hand and held it to her breast, groaning slightly as he rolled her erect nipple between his thumb and finger. In less than ten minutes it was over. She pushed his hand away from her breast, but continued rocking until Westin let out a groan that signaled he, too, had come.

Without a word, without so much as a hug, Mrs. Dickerson backed off the bed and walked into the bathroom. It was then Seely realized that the two had never even kissed.

Dr. Westin, looking even more ridiculous to Seely with his limp, dripping member and dressed only in his black socks and elastic garters, stood up and used his boxer shorts to wipe himself clean before he pulled them and his trousers back on. As he finished dressing, Mrs. Dickerson emerged from the bathroom with a towel wrapped around her, gathered up her underwear and dress, then retreated back to the bathroom.

Dr. Westin took the opportunity to place a phone call. He spoke too softly for Seely to make out who was at the other end of the line, but Fred made a mental note to ask Loretta Franklin at the switchboard to show him her afternoon log. Mrs. Dickerson emerged looking exactly as she had in the dining room, gathered up her book and gave Westin a peck on the cheek as he continued to speak on the phone. Then, with a quick check of the hallway, she disappeared out the door.

Neither their schedule nor their routine varied much during the weeks that followed, enabling Seely to experiment with several different settings on his Kodak Autographic. He kept a small notebook in his pocket, documenting his lens opening and shutter speed with each position he captured on film. Back in his darkroom he transformed the negatives into 8" x 10" photographs, noting on the back of each finished print the precise setting he had used, as well as the lighting in the room. Before long he had assembled an impressive array of explicit photographs of Ron Westin having sex with Mrs. Dickerson, as well as a number of other women. When he knew who they were, he also noted their names on the back, as well as the date, before filing them in a locked cabinet beneath the counter in the darkroom.

More than once Fred wondered what he would do should he ever slip into his dark alcove outside room 641 and find Evelyn in Dr. Westin's bed. Given Evelyn's distaste for sex, he was sure that wouldn't ever happen, but he made it a point to check Westin's room a few times during their regular appointments, and each time found it empty.

Even though his observation post in the alcove enabled him to watch a number of different naked women taking part in a variety of sexual acts with Dr. Westin, he found himself longing to assign other couples to room 641. The results, however, had been largely disappointing, as either the pair slept in separate beds, did not have sex or kept the room dark and the covers on. Westin and his afternoon conquests, especially the new ones, provided Seely with his best entertainment.

He marveled at the doctor's ability to occasionally seduce two different women on one of his Wednesday afternoons without ever failing to achieve and hold an erection. Then, one day after Mrs. Dickerson had left, Seely watched through the mirror as Dr. Westin pulled a packet from his coat pocket and stirred an unmarked powder into a glass of water, which he drank before his second date arrived.

On more than one occasion Seely also watched as Dr. Westin secretly slipped the contents of a different packet into a woman's glass. Seely suspected the doctor was experimenting with various drugs, as in some cases the young women simply became drowsy and offered no resistance to his advances, while in others they became the sexual aggressors. Those instances provided Seely with the photographs he was most likely to pull back out of his locked file and revisit during the times Dr. Westin was back in Florida and room 641 was empty.

Ron Westin had been at the Grove Park Inn several times this month, but Seely had been far too busy preparing for Edison and Ford to spend any time checking on what -- *or who* -- he had been doing in room 641.

Including Daisy Wheeler?

Realizing right then, as he stood in the Great Hall, that Emma Barringer might at that moment be upstairs in Ron Westin's room - - in Ron Westin's bed - - proved unsettling to Fred, even though he had never seen, let alone met the young woman.

Right now, he thought, *she might be the only one who knew what had happened to Daisy.*

But if she did, he argued, *why wouldn't she have come forth immediately? Why wouldn't she have yelled for help for her friend?*

So - Emma must not have been there.

But who was smoking the second cigarette, the Camel?

Luther Hargus?

One of the men in the back of the Great Hall?

One of his own bellmen?

Dr. Westin?

Edwin Grove?

Looking around the Great Hall, Seely knew he had to go back to the Palm Court, but he also had his suspicions about Edwin – and Edwin had his handkerchief, the handkerchief with her blood on it.

I must have dropped it somewhere on the third floor,
> *while we were moving the girl, maybe near the blood*
> *stained carpet beneath the rocking chair.*

So, what did Edwin know?
> *That Daisy was missing, and that my*
> *monogrammed handkerchief had blood on it.*

But that might be all. He might not have made the
> *connection. He certainly didn't seem nervous.*

But could that mean he already knew that Daisy
> *was dead and that someone -- probably me --*
> *had moved her body...?*

But Edwin couldn't know where -- not yet.
> *And he didn't know that my only witness, my only*
> *alibi was Robert, who by now was close to the South*
> *Carolina border....*

So -- where had Edwin been when Daisy died?

Seely turned back to Cornelia Vanderbilt. "Well, I'm sure they're both safe, probably together with Dr. Westin. He might have even taken them back to Oteen in his automobile, up over Old Toll Road -- behind Chief Lyerly. Dr. Westin's been up that road to my house dozens of times."

As he spoke he could see Theodore's crew taking down the screen hanging over the south fireplace. Nodding toward them, he added, trying to appear as casual as possible as he carefully chose his words, "I hope you both enjoyed the movie tonight."

"Yes, we did, Mr. Seely. It was quite enjoyable."

"What did you think of Willard Mack's performance as the prince, Edwin? Pretty remarkable, eh?"

Cornelia's head jerked around, as she stared at Seely with a puzzled look on her face.

She knew Willard Mack had not been in the movie....

Edwin shrugged, hating the thought of either agreeing with his brother-in-law or applauding his choice of a movie, "It wasn't the best I've seen him do. Mack's a good actor, but he wasn't well cast for that role. They should have used somebody else."

Seely looked directly at Cornelia and smiled, "You're probably right. Maybe somebody like John Miltern?"

Edwin nodded. "Exactly. Miltern would have been perfect for that part."

"I agree, Edwin. Well, I had better check to see how Higgins is doing at the front desk. I'll keep an eye out for your friends, Miss Vanderbilt, but, like I said, I'll bet Dr. Westin has already taken them back. If not, I'll leave a message for you at the desk. I'd hate to disturb you or your mother tonight."

"Thank you, Mr. Seely."

Seely started to walk away, then turned back to Edwin.

"Say, Edwin. Have you got a cigarette?"

Without thinking, Edwin reached inside his coat pocket.

"Sure, Fred...." Then, he stopped and pulled his hand back out. "Since when did you take up smoking, Fred?"

"No, it's not for me. A guest asked for one," he explained, "I thought you might have one for him."

Edwin flashed an open hand. "Sorry. Fresh out."

"Thanks anyway. I'm sure he's found one by now."

Fred turned and started back toward the front desk.

"Mr. Seely!" Cornelia called out.

Fred stopped and looked back at the heiress.

"You didn't ask me if I had one."

"No, Miss Vanderbilt, I did not presume…."

"That a woman was bright enough to strike a match?"

Seely smiled. "Not at all."

He stepped toward her.

"Miss Vanderbilt, would you by chance happen to have an extra cigarette?"

"Certainly, Mr. Seely," she replied, reaching into her small handbag and pulling out a sterling silver cigarette case engraved with the Vanderbilt coat of arms. She pressed on its side and the spring-loaded lid popped open. "Help yourself."

Seely reached out, gently withdrew one of her cigarettes and slipped it into his suit pocket. "Thank you, Miss Vanderbilt. I am sure our guest will appreciate it."

"He should," she replied, as Edwin took her by the arm and they began to walk away. "Tell him they're imported."

Stonemasons working inside the Great Hall.

The west side of the Grove Park Inn as it appeared for several years after 1913.

Chapter 13

*We must insist upon protecting the rights of guests
who may have retired, and -- as the Grove Park Inn was located
purposely away from railroads, street cars and other outside
annoyances -- conversations, slamming of doors,
throwing shoes on the floor, and similar unnecessary noises
are liable to annoy guests in adjoining rooms.*

Frederick L. Seely, President
Grove Park Inn, Inc.
1918 Brochure

11:15pm
Tuesday
27 August 1918

Fred Seely watched until Cornelia Vanderbilt and Edwin Grove disappeared from sight onto the terrace, then quietly slipped back down
the stairway leading to his office. Sheriff Mitchell was due to return
any minute and Fred had no interest in talking to him. Higgins at
the front desk had been too busy checking in the last of the Asheville
guests to notice that Seely had again left the Great Hall.

Once in his office, Fred quickly unlocked the door to his darkroom, then exited through the hidden door into the crawl space beneath the Great Hall. Switching on the string of bulbs, he started across the crawl space, glancing over to make sure the two crates blocking the view of Daisy Wheeler's body, now carefully wrapped in her blanket, did not look out of place.

Not that Sheriff Mitchell and his men wouldn't find her if they had a reason to come this far....

At the far end of the basement Seely opened the door to his secret stairwell tucked inside the outdoor chimney. He looked back to make sure he hadn't been followed, then snapped off the lights in the basement. He reached over and flipped on the set his two Dutch carpenters had installed for him in the stairwell, then started up the rough wooden stairs.

On his original blueprints, Fred Seely had assigned to himself a suite of four rooms, all with inner connecting doors, at the south end of the second floor corridor. Two of these bedrooms were fitted with single beds for their children and their nurse. The fourth bedroom and its two double beds, with a view of the golf course to the west, was set aside as their master bedroom. Seely had his staff convert the fifth room, one overlooking the front entrance to the Grove Park Inn, into a living room. He gave Evelyn the closet in their bedroom for her clothes and took the closet in what was now their living room for himself. In the back of that closet, hidden by the large bag containing his tuxedo, the Two Dutchmen had installed a hinged panel opening into his private stairwell.

As he rounded the landing next to the hidden door leading into his closet, Fred noticed a thread of light beneath the door. He paused to listen for the sound of either baby Fred crying or Evelyn in their living room. Hearing nothing, he concluded that Evelyn or the baby's nurse must have left the living room light on, either by accident or anticipating Fred's arrival after they went to bed.

Fred practically sprinted up the remaining stairs to the fifth floor storage room, where he stopped, caught his breath and carefully exited the stairway through the door behind the movable armoire. Once inside the storage room he made his way over to the light switch and the ladder leading to the attic, then tip-toed across the plank floor over the fifth floor guest rooms to the stack of crates disguising the alcove behind room 641.

As he took his seat, he carefully raised the board across the back of the mirror -- and nearly jumped off the crate when he saw the face of Dr. Westin just inches away looking in the mirror. Seely froze, his right arm still in the air holding the top of the board, unsure whether or not Dr. Westin had detected any movement behind the mirror. The two men stared at each other, until Ron Westin opened his mouth and inspected his front teeth.

At that moment a young woman Seely guessed to be Emma Barringer stepped out from the bathroom, her sweater in her hand. "My, it certainly has gotten warm in here, Dr. Westin. And that drink must have gone straight to my head." She staggered slightly, then sat down on the edge of the bed, reaching out with her hand to steady herself. "I really do have to go find Daisy."

"I think you're making a big deal out of nothing," Westin answered, handing her a fresh glass as he sat down on the bed next to her. "It's late, and by now she's asleep in one of the rooms. Besides, if we are going to start drawing out those plans in the morning – and those ideas you had will really make a difference – then you need to get some sleep."

"Do you really think my ideas are good?" she asked. Fred detected a slight slur in her voice.

"Good? Why you've come up with ideas a half dozen architects and twice as many doctors never thought of. You're a natural and gifted designer, Emma. You know what patients want – and what nurses need to do their job. I don't know how I could do it without you. I just don't think I could."

"Oh, you wouldn't need me, Dr. Westin. You've got it all figured out."

Westin put his hand on her shoulder. "Listen to me, Emma. First, if we are going to be partners in this clinic, then you have to start calling me Ronald. I'm not your doctor. I'm your partner. Understood?"

Emma nodded obediently.

"Second, I know medicine, but what I don't know is what patients expect – and what your nurses will need to care for them. This clinic needs a woman's touch – a woman who knows medicine, but who most of all knows people." Westin stared into her eyes. "That's your strength, Emma. You know people. And you care for them. I wish I had but one percent of your compassion. That's my weakness. I spend too much time figuring out the numbers, making sure our clinic is going to show a profit, a really big profit -- for us -- right from the beginning, but you can teach me how to show more compassion, more feeling."

As he spoke his left hand landed softly on her thigh as his right reached across her shoulders. "I've never been more serious, Emma. I don't want to do this without you by my side." He leaned over and quickly kissed her on the lips, gently, then, before she could react, stood up as part of what Seely recognized as a well-rehearsed performance.

"But you're right," he continued, as he began walking around the room, pretending to be deep in thought. "First, we need to make sure that Daisy is safe, then we can get to work making our plans. You both came with Cornelia Vanderbilt, right? So, chances are she's with Cornelia right now."

"But what if they're out looking for me? Shouldn't we call someone? And tell them?"

"You're right, as always, it seems." Emma blushed, as Westin turned around.

Did he just glance at the mirror?

Seely instinctively slid back on his crate.

"Do you know who Mr. Seely is?" Westin continued.

Emma perked up like a bright student. "The man who spoke at the beginning of the movie? The man who introduced Mr. Ford and the others, right? Isn't he the manager or something?"

"Something like that," Westin smiled. "He's a close friend of mine. With the storm and all I'm sure he's still up – and I'm sure he knows exactly where Daisy is. What if I call him, let him know where you are and find out just where Daisy is sleeping tonight?"

"Could you, really? That, that would be wonderful. I would feel so much better."

"Then consider it done, -- partner." Fred Seely watched as Ron Westin stepped to the desk, picked up the phone and asked Miss Howell, the overnight operator, to connect him with Mr. Seely's office. Westin let the phone ring twice, then deftly closed the receiver with his finger as he turned away from Emma and began speaking.

"Mr. Seely? Dr. Westin here." He paused for effect. "Yes, we're alright. No, no problems here. I just wanted to let you know that Emma Barringer, one of the nurses stationed at Oteen, is here with me." Another pause. "Yes, I understand that there are no more rooms available. That's quite alright. We can make due right here."

Another pause.

"You're welcome. Say, Fred, have you seen Emma's friend, another nurse who rode up here with Cornelia Vanderbilt? Her name's Daisy…." Westin looked to Emma for assistance.

"Wheeler. Daisy Wheeler," Emma chimed in.

"Did you hear that, Fred? Daisy Wheeler." He paused. "Yes, long blond hair and I believe you're right, a pink dress." Westin looked at Emma, who nodded vigorously. "You did? Fourth floor? Why, thank you, Fred. That's a relief."

Westin paused again. "Nine o'clock in the morning? In the Great Hall with Cornelia. That sounds fine." He stood silent, nodding. "Yes, I'll tell her. I'm sure she will be relieved. And, Fred, would you please leave Cornelia and Daisy a note at the front desk letting them know Emma's safe?"

Westin nodded again. "Yes, I'll tell her. Thank you, Fred – and good luck getting the road cleared."

Westin put the phone down, then turned and stepped toward Emma, his arms outstretched. "Mr. Seely says everything and everybody is fine. You're to meet them downstairs at nine in the morning." Emma jumped up from the bed to hug him, stumbling slightly as she did. "Thank you, Ronald. I really appreciate it."

"Well, I hope you feel better. It sounds like Daisy and Cornelia must have watched the movie together," he said as he led her back to the bed.

"No, I don't think so," Emma said shaking her head. "Cornelia was talking with some friends of her mother. Daisy was with Mr. Grove. She introduced him to me. He said he owned the hotel."

"Mr. Grove? From St. Louis?"

"Yes, that's where he said he was from. Something about being a pharmaceutical manufacturer."

"Why that old rascal…."

"No," Emma replied, laying her head on his shoulder. "He's not that old. Thirty, maybe."

Westin reached up and began unbuttoning her blouse. "Oh, you don't mean Mr. Grove, then, you mean Edwin, his son."

"I don't know," she mumbled, putting her arm over his shoulder. "He said he owned the hotel."

Westin laughed. "Not 'til the old man dies. And at the rate Edwin's going, he may beat him to it."

"All I know is that he and Daisy hit it off. I had to go to the bathroom and when I came back, just when the movie was starting, they were gone." She murmured something else, but Seely couldn't catch it as she buried her face in Westin's neck as he slipped his hand over one of her breasts.

Seely leaned back on his crate thinking about what he had just heard. Edwin had said nothing to him or Cornelia in the Great Hall about being with Daisy earlier in the evening.

But perhaps Cornelia already knew that....

Could they have all three been together on the sixth floor?

Seely shook his head.

Not Cornelia Vanderbilt.

Not to a young girl she had just befriended.

Then he remembered.

The cigarette. Check the cigarette.

Seely reached into his pocket and pulled out the fresh cigarette Cornelia had given him moments earlier in the Great Hall. There was just enough light filtering in through the two-way mirror for him to read the brand name printed around it.

Arabesca.

No match to either brand -- *Oasis* or *Camel* -- he had found on the sixth floor.

> *So,* he thought, *Cornelia may not have been on the sixth floor when Daisy died, but that didn't clear Edwin.*
> *And Emma saw Edwin and Daisy together before the movie – a movie that Edwin obviously didn't see much of.*

Seely considered staying in the sixth floor alcove to watch Ron Westin seduce the young nurse, but the thought of Westin taking advantage of the poor girl was more than he could stomach.

As he slid his foot across the plank floor, he caught the sound of a cellophane wrapper crunching beneath his shoe. Instantly, he froze, then looked back through the mirror at Ron Westin, but judging from the increased activity on the bed, neither he nor Emma appeared to have heard it.

Fred carefully reached down and picked it up.

> *A peppermint candy wrapper.*
> *Must be one I picked up in the hallway,* he mused.
> *Fell out of my pocket...?*

As he stood up to leave, Seely caught site of Dr. Westin's open bag and Emma Barringer's purse lying next to it on the vanity.

> *Her purse. The missing purse.*
> *Where was Daisy's purse?*
> *And who had taken it?*
> *If Edwin Grove had been with Daisy in the Great Hall,* he thought, *if they had left together, maybe to his room on the sixth floor, then he could have been the last person to see Daisy Wheeler alive.*

And if Edwin had been the one next to her on the
sixth floor when she fell – or was pushed – to
her death, what did he do with her purse?

As Seely quietly worked his way out of the alcove, across the dark attic and down the ladder to the fifth floor storage room, he tried to imagine what he would have done had he been in Edwin's shoes.

The girl is dead, or dying, he can see that from the sixth floor.

If she had just fallen, if it had been an accident, Edwin would have called for help. No one would have thought anything of it. They had tired of the movie and gone for a walk or a tour of the hotel. Perhaps they had been drinking, perhaps she was sitting on top of the wall, lost her balance and fell backwards. Those who knew Edwin might have questioned his judgment -- a married man with a pregnant wife back in St. Louis, alone with a beautiful young woman -- but with no one else around, who could have contradicted his story?

But she hadn't screamed....

And Robert said he heard a door close. Perhaps they weren't alone. Perhaps Edwin knew that. Perhaps he couldn't risk it. Perhaps it hadn't been an accident....

An argument....

A blow to the head. The smoking stand.

Then, push her over the wall, let people think
it was an accident....

What next?

He must have picked up her purse -- and left.

Quickly, yet quietly.

But Edwin would have been on the top floor of the hotel. He had only two means of escape. The south stairway would have brought him out into the Great Hall next to the movie screen – and in front of more than four hundred people. The north staircase would have been safer, but, even so, he could not have gone far without the risk of being seen with her purse, a purse several people could identify has having belonged to Daisy Wheeler, who was then lying in the Palm Court with a broken neck.

He could have run into someone leaving the movie early to go back to their room. Or someone coming out of their room, perhaps after hearing her fall.

Fred shook his head.

Edwin should have left the purse where it was or tossed it down by her body. He must have picked it up in a moment of panic.

Fred sensed that Edwin was too smart to leave the purse in his room on the sixth floor. He knew that too many people had seen him with Daisy before she died, giving Sheriff Mitchell good reason to ask to search his room.

Tossing it out his window would have caught the attention of any number of people right below him on the terrace. Hiding it in the shrubbery around the hotel would have meant bringing it down six flights of stairs, through the Great Hall and across the terrace without being detected.

Unlikely, Fred surmised.

But the fact remains, he quickly reminded himself:

Edwin picked up her purse.

But why?

Fred stopped as the reason suddenly became clear.

To frame him for Daisy's murder.

Why else would Edwin have any reason to want to sleep on the couch in his office?

To slip the purse under a pillow, in a desk drawer or
beneath a stack of papers -- and then, later, when the
moment was right, casually ask Sheriff Mitchell
if they had considered searching Fred's office....

No, Edwin didn't throw her purse away, Fred realized as he carefully let himself out of the fifth floor storage room and into the public hallway, where he took the stairs back up to the sixth floor.

He just hid it for a while.

Until he could come back for it.

Safely.

Fred quickly walked to the spot where he had found the two cigarettes, then turned and began retracing the path Edwin would have taken to arrive undetected back in the Great Hall. The narrow hallway between the row of guest rooms and the balcony wall didn't have space for anything more than a few rocking chairs and small end tables. A quick glance under them revealed nothing.

Although the walls in the Great Hall were made of boulders, those on the guest room floors were of standard construction, with smooth plaster walls providing no crevices as a convenient hiding spot for a small purse.

At the end of the hallway, just past the elevator and the door to Ron Westin's room 641, at the landing for the stairway leading down to the fifth floor, stood one of the oak vanities the houskeeping staff had removed from a bedroom to convert it into a living room as part of a two room suite. Fred opened each of the five drawers in quick succession, pushing his hand to the back of each until he was satisfied it was empty.

As he was about to start down the stairs, something about the vanity seemed out of place to him. The rug on which it stood had a long crease in it, as if the vanity had been pushed back against the wall instead of being lifted and set back down, as Fred Seely had instructed each of his housekeeping staff.

Fred stepped over next to the wall and ran his hand up and down between the back of the vanity and the plaster wall. While he couldn't see it, his fingers soon found the beaded cloth of what he immediately knew to be a purse, a purse someone had wedged between the vanity and the wall. He slid the vanity forward and a purse, a pink purse that matched the dress Cornelia Vanderbilt had loaned Daisy Wheeler, fell to the floor.

The sound of voices drifting up from the lower floors, voices belonging to the last of the guests that Edward Higgins had assigned rooms for the night, reminded Fred that he, too, had to do something with the purse.

If I'm caught with it, and if Edwin claims to have seen me moving a body from the blood stained carpet, then I'm ruined. When Sheriff Mitchell sees that rug, sees me with Daisy's purse, hears Luther's story about the cigarette butts, he'll have no choice but to take the hotel apart, room by room.

Then, it will be just a matter of time before they reach the unmarked door in the hallway outside my office, the only door that leads into the basement crawl space....

With nowhere else to hide it, Fred took a calculated risk. He reached back, lifted up the tail to his suit coat and stuck the purse in the rear waistband of his pants. Fearing it might be visible to someone watching him from behind, Fred unbuttoned his coat, letting the fabric relax so that the outline of the purse would not be apparent to anyone. With a final glance back at Westin's room 641, Fred resisted the urge to knock on the door, to rescue Emma.

After a long, difficult moment, he started down the stairs.

As he hit the fifth floor landing, he paused and looked down the hallway for any guests. He then turned -- and ran right into Edwin Grove coming up the stairs.

"Fred! What brings you up here?" Edwin stopped just three steps below Fred, who could smell the alcohol on his breath.

"Nothing in particular, Edwin. Just checking to make sure everyone found their rooms."

"Well, you had better get your butt back downstairs. Sheriff Mitchell's waiting for you and he's really steaming. Seems a Colonel Hoagland out at Oteen called, worried that two of his nurses – that would be Emma and Daisy – had signed out to come here and haven't made it back yet, but you know that. Higgins said the colonel is threatening to come out here himself if you or the sheriff can't get them to the phone to talk to him."

Edwin took a step toward him, but Fred held his spot on the landing, two steps above Edwin.

"He spoke with Higgins?"

"Yeh. I was there when he called. When Higgins couldn't find you he sent one of the bellmen down the road to bring Sheriff Mitchell back. He was plenty pissed."

"Didn't Higgins tell the colonel about the road being blocked?"

"Oh, yeh, sure he did, but the colonel wanted to know exactly where his two nurses were right then. And he wanted to talk to 'em. And to you. And to Sheriff Mitchell. And probably to President Wilson," Edwin laughed.

"So, what's happening right now?"

"Right now? Well, the sheriff is standing over Higgins having him go through all the room assignments for tonight, looking to see where the girls might be."

"And Colonel Hoagland?"

Edwin smiled. "Don't know for sure, but from what I heard Sheriff Mitchell say to one of his deputies, I'd guess that Colonel Hoagland is headed your way – along with half the United States army. They'll probably take this place apart, room by room, until they find 'em both"

Fred could feel the clasp of the purse biting into the small of his back, and realized Edwin had been heading for the vanity -- and the purse. The thought of dealing with both Sheriff Mitchell and an army colonel sent the blood pounding through his head. He shut his eyes and began massaging his temples.

"Hey, Fred. You okay?" Edwin chuckled.

Fred looked at him. "I'm fine, Edwin. On top of everything else, I'm feeling a cold coming on."

Fred sniffed and nodded toward the stairway below Edwin. "Is that someone coming up after you?"

A slightly drunk Edwin turned to look and, as he did, Fred reached down and plucked his monogrammed silk handkerchief out of his brother-in-law's suit pocket.

"Hey! What do you think you're doing?" Edwin exclaimed as he clutched at his empty pocket.

"Like I said, I feel a cold coming on," Fred explained as he shoved his blood stained handkerchief deep into his back pocket, "and I didn't think you'd mind if I borrowed this handkerchief, right? If you think it belongs to Mr. Smith, I'll be sure to have it laundered before I send it back to him in the morning."

Fred braced himself against the wall in case Edwin tried to wrestle the handkerchief back, but Edwin realized that Seely held the advantage of the higher ground.

"Screw you," he fumed.

Fred stepped aside to let Edwin pass, then reached into the pocket of his suit.

"Edwin!"

Edwin turned, steadied himself against the wall and glared down at Fred, who was taking a key off his ring as he spoke.

"Why don't you do everyone a favor and take Emma down to Sheriff Mitchell?"

Puzzled, Edwin reached out and caught with two hands the key Fred tossed toward him.

"I think Dr. Westin gave her his room tonight – 641."

As Edwin looked at the master room key now in his hand, Fred pulled out his pocket watch and checked the time.

"She's probably asleep by now, so don't bother knocking - – just let yourself in."

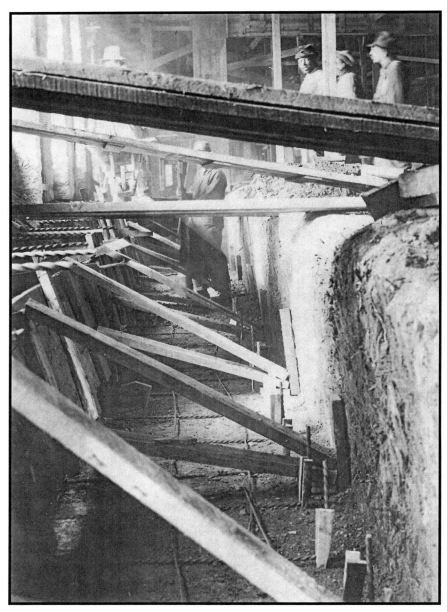

One of the many trenches the workmen dug while building the hotel.

Chapter 14

*Inasmuch as we are frequently asked if it is customary at the
Grove Park Inn to wear evening dress at dinner,
we desire to state that as a rule dinner coats are worn.
This is merely given as information and we wish it distinctly
understood that we do not desire to suggest what our guests
shall eat, drink or wear.*

Frederick L. Seely, President
Grove Park Inn, Inc.
1918 Brochure

11:42pm
Tuesday
27 August 1918

Standing on the fifth floor landing, Fred Seely realized what he now
had to do.

And do it quickly.

In a matter of minutes Sheriff Mitchell and Colonel Hoagland would be waiting for him in the Great Hall, ready to start a
room by room search of the entire hotel, looking for the two missing
nurses.

In less time than that, depending on what was transpiring upstairs, Edwin and Emma would be coming down the stairs from Dr. Westin's room on the sixth floor – as soon as Emma finished getting dressed.

Fred trotted down to the fourth floor landing, where he knew he would find another vanity identical to the one on the sixth floor, the one where Daisy's purse had been hidden. As soon as he did, he lifted one end of it and pushed the rug from beneath two legs with the toe of his shoe. He then went to the opposite end of the vanity and did the same, quickly rolled up the rug, and tucked it under his arm before heading down the stairwell to the third floor.

He could immediately see that the long, narrow Palm Court was now deserted. As he walked from the landing toward the lone rocker slightly out of line from the others, Fred stayed close to the wall, out of sight from anyone – especially Edwin – who might be peering over one of the balcony walls above him.

When he reached room 347, *where,* he hoped, *the Chiles now slept,* to the point where he would have to step out from beneath the protection of the balcony, out into the open Palm Court atrium, out into the view of anyone walking along the fourth, fifth or sixth floors above him, Fred stopped to listen. The only sound he could hear was an occasional snore floating over the open transom window of the Chiles' room. As he stood there, Fred studied the rocker and the French rug a few feet away.

> *The low wicker rocker cast a shadow over the blood stain,*
> > *which,* Seely noticed, *almost blended in with the*
> > *red background of the rug.*
> > *Almost.*

He could see why none of the guests coming back to their rooms after the movie had noticed it, but knew that Sheriff Mitchell would walk straight toward it -- *especially if Edwin Grove was leading the way.*

Like the other French rugs spread about the tile floor of the Palm Court, this one wasn't very large. Seely preferred narrow rugs that he could use in a number of different locations: between two beds, next to a bathtub, under a piece of furniture or in a hallway.

He waited.

Hearing nothing unusual, he drew in his breath and stepped out into the open Palm Court.

If someone sees me, he practiced, *I'll say that a guest spilled some wine on the rug.*

Fred strode confidently over to the wicker rocker, which he easily lifted by its arms and silently set aside. Without so much as a glance upward, he quickly rolled up the blood stained rug, walked it over beneath the fourth floor overhang and brought back the rug he had taken from beneath the vanity.

As he unrolled it, Fred could detect a slightly different weave, but doubted if anyone else could tell the two apart. As the seconds ticked off in his pocket watch, he knelt down and, with his fingernails, revived the crushed fibers in the four, small square indentations left by the feet of the vanity. His back muscles tightened as he readied himself for a shout from above.

From Edwin. Looking down at him. Laughing.

Finally, he stood, rubbed the sole of his shoe over the indentations, then set the wicker rocker back in its normal place. For the first time he looked up, afraid he would see the smiling face of Edwin Grove, alongside that of a puzzled Emma Barringer and Ronald Westin, watching him from the sixth floor. But the balconies were empty.

Forty feet.

That was the distance he judged it to be from where he stood outside the Chiles' room to the far end of the hallway. Picking up the blood-stained rug, he quickly walked past each of the remaining doors facing the Palm Court, then slowed as he approached the third floor landing.

Any minute now he expected Edwin to be coming down.

Edwin wouldn't take the elevator, Fred guessed.

Not this time.

By now Edwin knew he had taken the purse, too, so he would be curious to see what Fred might do next.

The stairwell was silent, giving Fred a brief moment to smile as he thought about the scene that must be unfolding in Ron Westin's room.

With a rush past the open stairwell, Seely continued toward the end of the third floor's south wing, stopping only when he came to a narrow oak door with a small brass plaque that read:

Danger - Electrical Panel – Do Not Enter

Selecting a small key from the ring in his suit pocket, Seely unlocked it, then, with a final look over his shoulder, stepped in and closed the door behind him.

A single 40-watt bulb revealed the stairs his two Dutch carpenters had built for him inside the outdoor fireplace. Fred leaned the rug against the wall and reached back to pull the purse out from beneath his suit jacket: small, flat, with a simple clasp that snapped open as he pressed his thumb and forefinger against it. He could tell it was nearly empty, as he held it beneath the bulb and quickly thumbed through the contents

A military identification card.
Daisy Logan Wheeler.
Meriden, Connecticut.
A ten dollar bill, folded into a small rectangle.
Emergency cab fare. Not a bad idea
for anyone depending on Cornelia.
Smart girl.
A lace hanky. Definitely just a party purse.
Perhaps even Cornelia's, to go with the dress.
No make-up, no matches.
No cigarettes.

Seely snapped the purse shut, stuck it back into the waist of his pants, then leaned over, picked up the rug and hoisted it onto his right shoulder before starting down toward the basement. He frowned when he saw the same sliver of light beneath the secret door leading into the closet of his second floor suite. He paused, this time thinking he heard the sound of the nurse's footsteps coming from their living room, then tip-toed past it as he continued down the rough plank stairs.

Two flights later he reached the bottom of the shaft, switched off the lights inside the stairwell and stepped out into the pitch blackness of the dirt-floor basement crawl space. Fred reached up on the wall and pushed the ivory button that illuminated the string of bulbs stretching across the length of the crawl space. A large rat dived beneath a pile of boards to his right.

Seely had once considered setting out poison, but then decided the rats, so long as they didn't become a bother, might deter a curious employee who stumbled upon the crawl space. Instead, he just left some empty rat poison boxes near this door and the one at the far end -- along with the dried remains of a large black snake

-- as a warning to anyone who might think about exploring the basement crawl space.

At first the room had scared Fred Seely, too, especially as the rats, spiders and green, spindly crickets moved in.

The only way he could overcome his fear, he had reasoned, *was to learn every square foot of it.*

One Saturday, armed with a lantern and the splintered handle of a broken shovel, he slowly and methodically walked the entire length and breadth of the crawl space beneath the Great Hall, as well as the area under the south wing, where he now stood. There was no crawl space beneath the rooms of the north wing, as that area had been finished for the swimming pool, locker rooms, recreation room, barber shop and offices for Seely and Miss Hatch, all built upon a thick concrete slab.

For five years now, Fred Seely had resisted his natural inclination to clean and organize the crawl space, level the trenches and remove all of the trash, shards of glass, dented lunch pails, rocks, concrete blocks, electrical wire, boards and broken tools that littered the area. Instead, he had memorized every square foot and now knew exactly where the round-nosed shovel he needed, the one with the broken handle, had been tossed aside.

Fred started across the basement on his familiar path, but veered off as he approached the base of the pillar near the two Haines, Jones & Cadbury crates. Daisy's body, wrapped in its wool shroud, remained where he had left her. As he stood looking down at her, he tried to think of something appropriate to say, some way to explain what he was about to do, to express his sorrow, his regret, but there were no words.

Nothing he could say.

He could only think of her parents, a father his same age, back in Meriden, who had no idea, no way of knowing that tonight their young daughter, their Daisy was anywhere other than asleep in a military barracks at an army hospital, a barracks far removed from the war, a barracks surrounded by hundreds of soldiers.

How could they fathom, how could they imagine what
had happened to their daughter?
How would they deal with her disappearance?
Would they know where to look?
Would they come to North Carolina?
To the hospital at Oteen? To the Grove Park Inn?
Would they one day -- next week? -- be standing in front
of his desk, describing what she looked like, what she
had been wearing this night, her borrowed pink dress.
There would be the snapshots, he imagined. *Snapshots they*
would show him, would fan across his desk, as if he
could ever forget what she looked like, her soft skin,
those long yellow strands, forever tainted....
Snapshots.
Like those he would have developed and carefully
hidden in his darkroom, locked in his private cabinet.
Snapshots.
Meriden, Connecticut. Silver manufacturing region.
Old family money. Vacations on the coast. Sailing,
picnics, outings in the automobile. Friends from
college. Harvard, Yale, Dartmouth.
That's probably why Cornelia took a shine to her so
quickly. Money smells money.
Ronald Westin, too. Drawn like a spider to a moth,
spinning his web of promises....

And Edwin, naturally.

Cornelia said something about a fiancé, but she wasn't
wearing any jewelry, no engagement ring.

A break-up?

A split from her family?

They couldn't have been pleased with her decision to
leave the safety of Meriden for the Carolina mountains.

An independent spirit? Perhaps a bit too wild for the social
matrons of Meriden? Too bored?

Maybe that's why she ended up with Edwin. Ready for some
excitement - but perhaps not as much as Edwin had in mind.

But she's too smart for him. Is that what got you here?

Were you too smart for him? Did you see him for what he is?

Did your honesty cost you your life?

Edwin. That son-of-a-bitch. How could it be that he was
doing this? How could it be that Edwin had done this
to her, to him, to Emma, to her parents....

Fred shook his head in disgust, anger growing in his gut.

He would find a way.

An eye for an eye.

I give you my word, he whispered down to her.

He will pay for this.

Fred dropped one of the empty wooden crates into a dry trench a few feet away from the pillar. At the bottom, four feet deep, lay a six-inch cast iron waste pipe. Seely remembered that McKibbins' plans had called for a branch line coming down from the pillar to join the main in this trench, which is why this short section had not been backfilled.

As it turned out, the plumbers had determined it made more sense for the branch line to come down the next pillar, but in the rush to complete the hotel by Fred Seely's deadline, no one had time to come back to finish filling in the trench.

Fred stepped down onto the crate, then onto the cast iron pipe. He reached up, pulled the blood stained rug over to him and unrolled it along the bottom of the trench. Smoothing it out like a sleeping bag, he pressed the extra width of the French rug up against the sidewalls of the trench, carefully brushing off the crumbs of dirt that slid down the walls.

Turning back to the crate, Fred stepped back out, being careful not to get his clothes dirty. As he stood looking down at Daisy, he took a slow, deep breath.

This isn't right.
But he could see no other way.
No other way out....

Daisy was dead. Her suffering was over.
But that was no fault of his, so why should he have to suffer -- for the rest of his life....?

He knew this was now his only option and he hated Edwin for having put him, having put her, however it happened, where they both were right now.

You're dead, he thought, *through no fault of your own -- or mine -- and I'm standing here with no choice of what I can do.*

He took a deep breath.

That son-of-a-bitch.

Sliding his arms under the blanket, he lifted Daisy into the air, then turned and carefully stepped back down onto the crate and into the trench. Only by almost standing her up and shifting his hands under her arms could he begin to lay her down onto the rug, stepping forward as he did and straddling her body.

The blanket twisted as he laid her down, so he took a moment to rearrange it, starting at her feet, where he wrapped and tucked it under her shoes, then worked his way up, pulling the blanket taunt around her waist. He parted it over her face, relieved to see that her eyes had remained closed. Kneeling down, he gently lifted her head to arrange her blond hair and straighten the pink drawstring laced across the bodice of her dress.

Then, reaching back, he pulled her small beaded purse out from under his jacket and slipped it beneath her hands crossed over her chest. Finally, he closed the blanket over her face and, as he stepped back, folded the sides of the rug down over the blanket.

Even so, he could not bring himself to begin shoveling any dirt on her. He stood over her, paralyzed.

Then, a sound from above, muffled by twelve inches of concrete, but clearly a chair being dragged across the tile floor of the Great Hall....

My God, there are people up there, people looking for me,
> *for her. People just a few feet away. The sheriff, Grove,*
> *the Miles, T. S. Morrison, Chief Lyerly, the Dunhams,*
> *half of Asheville....*

Sensing he was running out of time, Fred quickly looked about until he spotted what he wanted – some wide, poplar planks leftover from the original scaffolding and two unbroken concrete blocks.

Leaning over, Fred set the concrete blocks in the trench, one just beyond her head and the other beyond her feet, then spanned the distance between them with three wide planks, making an improvised casket.

Satisfied, but not pleased, he then began shoveling the dirt onto the planks. The pile of dry dirt next to the trench proved easy to move and in just a few minutes time Fred had nearly filled the last section of the trench. Before he did, he tossed in the shovel, then used a three-foot long piece of wood to scrape the last of the dirt over it.

What was it Bryan had said at the opening banquet?

Fred had read it a hundred times in the framed newspaper hanging on his office wall, until he practically knew it by heart:

Why should not this hotel stand for all time, for it has none of the elements of decay?

It will be here, as an eloquent monument to its founders, in the centuries to come.

It was built not for the dead, as were the tombs of the kings, but for living human beings that they might find delight here.

Is it not better to build such a monument than a tomb?

I congratulate these men.

They have built for the ages.

Fred closed his eyes.

You would not congratulate me tonight, my friend....

Finally, he casually tossed a few broken bottles, a couple of rocks and the last wooden crate over the spot where he had buried Daisy. Ducking his head and sprinting back to the wall near the hidden stairwell, he grabbed a cobweb-encased jacket one of the men had left hanging on a nail five years earlier and, grasping it by one arm, drug it back and forth on the ground, erasing his footprints as he backed his way out of the area. Shaking off the dirt, he hung the jacket back on its nail and flung the three-foot section of board into one of the dark corners of the basement crawl space.

As he pulled open the door to his darkroom, Fred turned to survey the basement crawl space one last time.

The glow from the row of bulbs did not reveal anything out of place.

Nothing out of the ordinary, nothing to draw your attention. Nothing to lead you to the last pillar.

He reached up, pushed the light switch and dropped the room into complete darkness. Stepping into the darkroom, he turned on the light and closed the door to the crawl space.

Fred sensed that by now Sheriff Mitchell – and perhaps Colonel Hoagland – were impatiently waiting for him upstairs.

By now, he guessed, *Edwin and Emma were there, too, telling them both what they recalled from the evening. That should give me enough time.*

Depending on what happened tonight with Sheriff Mitchell and Colonel Hoagland, Edwin might panic and leave. Once back in St. Louis, protected by his father's money and influence, no one here in Asheville – including Fred Seely – could touch him.

Fred thought for a moment, then shook his head.

No, Edwin wouldn't run.

He wouldn't want to draw any attention to himself by cancelling his afternoon golf game, a foursome Edwin had arranged with T. S. Morrison and two of the managers at Wachovia Bank.

Especially if Daisy's body should suddenly show up -- in Edwin's room.

Edwin couldn't be sure what was going to happen next.

And he would want to know....

No, Edwin would stay the night.

He was sure of that.

Listening to make sure no one was coming down the hallway, Fred picked up his private phone and dialed a familiar number.

She might still be there, he hoped.

"Madame Swann's office."

He recognized Jenny's voice, though it sounded sad and distant. Madame Swann had assigned her to the receptionist desk several months earlier, right after her doctor's diagnosis.

"Its Fred Seely, Jenny. Is Madame Swann there?"

"Just a moment, Mr. Seely."

Less than a minute later he could hear her pick up the extension.

"Hello, Mr. Seely. I hope there's nothing wrong?"

Even in the middle of the night, her French accent was still unmistakable.

"No, not at all, Madame. Everything is fine, just fine."

"Good. Very good. So, am I to assume, then, that this is a business call?"

"Yes, but I know its very late...."

Madame Swann laughed lightly. "My dear friend, for me this is what most would call 'the middle of the day.' There is no need for you to worry about the time. I understand you have some rather important guests at the hotel tonight, oui? Does one of them have a special request?"

"No, not really. But I would like to surprise one of them. You might call it a 'going away' gift."

"This sounds very interesting. Might it be someone I know - or know of?

"I suspect so," he answered, then paused. "Edwin Grove."

"C'est des conneries! Casse-toi! Mr. Seely, there is no way I would ever send one of my girls to him again. Anywhere. He's a mean, sick bastard. Fils de salope! Please, excuse my language, but he's a pig-eyed, son-of-a-bitch. Last time he nearly put my Lossie in the hospital. She was out for three days."

"I know, Madame, but I'm going to ask for an exception," he paused, "and for someone special – Jennie."

The phone went silent. Fred thought she had hung up on him.

"Madame Swann?"

"Yes, Mr. Seely." Her tone had softened. "I'm still here."

The phone went silent again. Fred waited.

Finally, she spoke.

"You know about her 'condition', don't you, Mr. Seely?"

"Yes, I do, Madame. You and I discussed it a few months ago."

"The doctor says she won't make it another year."

"I'm sorry."

"Do you know what it would mean for any man who's with her?"

"Yes, I know."

"Are you sure you do, Mr. Seely? Really?"

"Yes, Madame. I know what syphilis will do."

"Are you prepared to live with that?"

"Yes. I am."

Silence again filled the air. "I don't know, Mr. Seely. I know you must have your reasons, but as much as I hate the bastard, I don't think I could even ask her. And I don't think Jenny would do it."

Fred paused. He had anticipated this moment. "She's still taking care of her son?"

"Benji? Yes, she is."

"Is his father around?"

"No. I don't think she's even sure who Benji's father is."

"How old is Benjamin now?"

"Fifteen."

"What's he do?"

"Odd jobs, mostly. Whatever comes along. I try to find work for him. Clean up after my renters, sweep the shop floors and the sidewalks, that sort of thing. He's a sweet boy and a good worker, Mr. Seely. Its just that...."

"What?"

"Well, Benji, bless his soul, Benji's a half-wit. He's got the heart of an angel, Mr. Seely, but he just isn't the brightest star in the sky. Tell him what to do and he'll do it. Anything. He tries harder than any young man I've ever known. He just can't think things out for himself very well."

Fred paused for a moment.

"Tell Jenny this, Madame. If she will do this for me, just this one time, I will give her – and you – my word that for so long as I am here, Benjamin will have a job at the Grove Park Inn. A real job. Starting tomorrow morning. First thing. At full pay. And I'll pay Jenny triple whatever you normally charge."

It was Madame Swann's turn to pause. "That's a very generous offer, Mr. Seely, and very persuasive, but I still don't know. Give me a minute with her, alright?"

Fred stood motionless, considering his next move, *wondering what was happening in the Great Hall,* until she came back on the line.

"I can have Benji there at seven in the morning, if that works for you, Mr. Seely."

"That will be fine, Madame. We're going to be short a bellman in the morning, so have him report to Theodore." He paused momentarily. "Will Victor be driving Jenny here tonight?"

She paused.

"Yes. But we will need a little extra time to get her ready. Say, forty-five minutes from now, alright?"

"That will be fine. Tell Victor to use the north elevator. Paul Johnson's. He'll have a key for her. Room 655."

"I will."

"And Madame Swann...."

"Yes, Mr. Seely?"

"When Edwin asks, tell Jenny she should say she's a gift from Mr. Coxe. And not to mention my name."

Another pause.

"Whatever you like, Mr. Seely."

As soon as she hung up, Fred called the bellstand. Charles answered on the second ring.

"Charles, its Mr. Seely."

"Yes, Mr. Seely. What can I do for you?"

"Go down to the storeroom, Charles, and fill one of the empty flasks. Then find Edwin Grove - he'll be coming down to the Great Hall shortly - and pull him aside. When you do, slip it into his pocket. Tell him its a gift from a friend, along with something being delivered to his room from Madame Swann's, but don't mention my name, understand?"

"Yes, Mr. Seely"

"Good. Then take what's left in the bottle and leave it for Edwin in room 655, okay?"

"Yes, sir."

"And on your way back, give Paul Johnson a key to Edwin's room. Tell him a young woman will be asking him for it shortly."

"Yes, sir."

Fred was sure Edwin wouldn't turn Jenny away, especially

not at the risk of offending his new ally Tench Coxe, not as he was preparing to go home to a pregnant wife. Seely leaned over his desk and wrote himself a note.

Warn Margerete.

Have E. W. send her to his house in St. Petersburg.

Tomorrow.

Fred spotted his camera still sitting on the end table. He picked it up and, thinking about the undeveloped film still inside it, decided to hide it in the darkroom.

No sense giving anyone any ideas.

He locked the camera in the file cabinet under the counter, then switched off the light. As he turned to close the darkroom door, he stopped.

There, under Miss Hatch's typing table attached to his hidden door, was a tiny beam of light.

Fred stood rigid, unsure what to do.

I know I turned the lights off.

Or did I?

Fred quietly stepped over to the hidden door and listened for any sounds coming from the crawl space.

He heard nothing.

He stepped back into his office and turned off the light, throwing both the darkroom and his office into total darkness -- except for the small pool of light creeping out from beneath the hidden door. He stared at it, still unsure of what to do.

Was someone in there?

Nosing around at the far end?

Looking for Daisy?

Fred reached inside the upper cabinet and released the spring-loaded latch, freeing the door on its hinges. Not knowing what – or who - to expect, he hid behind it, as he slowly pulled the door open, letting the light from the basement crawl space pour into the darkroom.

Again, he listened, then slowly stepped from behind the door into the dimly-lit cavern. No one was in sight, but he felt as if he were being watched.

Was someone hiding behind the fireplace?
Behind one of the pillars? In one of the trenches?
Should I call out?

He shook his head.

No one is there, he reassured himself. *No one knows how to get into the crawl space from that end. You just forgot to turn off the lights.*

But, still, he wasn't sure.

What if someone is there... how much did they see?
Maybe nothing.
But they couldn't. They couldn't get in.
Unless the door on the third floor didn't latch.

He shook his head again.

Did you hear the door latch behind you?
Or were you in too big a hurry to look in her purse?
Did someone follow you down the stairs?
Perhaps Edwin didn't go to Dr. Westin's room....
Perhaps he followed you.
Perhaps he saw you in the Palm Court -- with the rug.
The bloody rug....
Should I call out to him? See what he knows?

Fred stood in the doorway for what seemed an eternity, hearing only the ticking of the clock coming from his office behind him.

Then, a knock on his office door.

Repeated.

Insistent.

They've come for me.

Fred glanced up at the light switch over his head. Slowly, he reached out and turned off the lights in the crawl space, then stepped back into the safety of his darkroom. As once more he began closing the secret door, he looked back a final time across the black depths of the basement - - at the faint, distant glow of a lit cigarette.

Path leading from the streetcar stop to the southwest entrance of the hotel.

Chapter 15

We keep an old-fashioned medicine chest at the Grove Park Inn.
It contains everything from Paregoric to Barbital.
In case you are ill at night, telephone for the night steward
and he will bring you any remedy you may need,
usually two doses in an envelop or bottle,
put up and sealed by our druggist and labeled by him,
so there would not be any risk of a mistake.

Frederick L. Seely, President
Grove Park Inn, Inc.
1918 Brochure

7:30am
Wednesday
28 August 1918

"Wonderful evening last night, Fred."

Fred Seely turned and smiled at Joseph and Victoria Leidy as they stepped off the elevator outside the Plantation Dining Room.

"Why, thank you, Dr. Leidy. I'm glad you enjoyed it."

"Yes, simply delightful," Victoria Leidy added. "We adored Mr. Burroughs. His stories about fly fishing in Alaska were simply mesmerizing. And I had no idea he knew Ralph Waldo Emerson -- and Walt Whitman! You really should have him give one of your presentations some time. He's such a good storyteller."

"That's an excellent idea. Perhaps when I see him this morning I'll be able to persuade him to stay on a few more days."

"Why, that would be wonderful. If you do, please, let us know. We would love to have dinner with him, if he wouldn't mind."

"I'm sure he wouldn't." Seely replied, as he held the door to the dining room open for them. "Enjoy your breakfast. Mr. Barvani is preparing eggs Benedict this morning. I sampled his hollandaise sauce a little while ago and I would declare it the best I have ever tasted."

Though it was still early, the Great Hall was already buzzing with activity, as many of the Asheville guests who had spent the night waiting for the road to be cleared were now making their way to their automobiles. Like Fred Seely, their clothes looked as if they had been slept in.

But Fred had not yet slept.

It was nearly one in the morning when he had arrived back at the Great Hall, where Theodore and his men were still getting everything in order, carrying chairs back to the dining room, straightening the wicker rockers, vacuuming the rugs and picking up the last of the apple cores in their wax wrappers. Their pace quickened once they realized Seely seemed intent on staying in the Great Hall until every piece of furniture was back in its customary place.

As he had hoped, Emma Barringer had been curled up in one of the leather rockers, asleep beneath a light blanket Fred recognized as having come from Dr. Westin's room. Neither Westin nor Edwin Grove were anywhere to be seen. Higgins reported that Sheriff Mitchell had left to check on the progress of the men attempting to pull the tree off the road leading to up to the hotel.

The sheriff returned a little before three with Colonel Henry Hoagland close on his heels. Seely had never met the colonel, though he had read in the *Asheville Citizen* of his arrival this past February to assume command of the Oteen Military Hospital, six miles east of town. Colonel Hoagland, Seely recalled, was also a medical doctor, specializing in the treatment of tuberculosis in soldiers whose lungs had been scarred by German chlorine gas.

After brief introductions, the three men huddled around a groggy Emma Barringer, who attempted to answer their questions as best she could. Fred had decided to let Sheriff Mitchell and Colonel Hoagland handle the questioning, only providing basic information on the time dinner had ended, when the movie started and when it concluded. Everything else he kept to himself.

As Fred expected, Colonel Hoagland was sincerely concerned about Daisy's disappearance, but understood Sheriff Mitchell's reluctance to conduct a room by room search of the entire 150-room hotel in the middle of the night. Neither had the slightest inkling or even raised the possibility of any foul play.

Unimaginable - at the Grove Park Inn.

Not under Fred Seely's command.

Emma had recounted her story of having seen Daisy with Edwin Grove prior to the movie, but once she explained that it had been Edwin who came to Dr. Westin's room to retrieve her, neither Sheriff Mitchell nor Colonel Hoagland showed any inclination to question him.

And knowing what was going on at that very moment between Edwin Grove and Jenny, Fred was relieved no one suggested knocking on the door to room 655.

Although neither of the men expressed their true thoughts in front of Emma, it seemed clear to Fred that they both believed Daisy -- who Colonel Hoagland had met only briefly and who Sheriff Mitchell had never even seen -- to be asleep upstairs, perhaps in a room with someone the sheriff knew, perhaps with someone who would not appreciate being interrupted in the middle of the night.

Given repeated assurances from Fred Seely that he would have his hotel staff watching out for Daisy when she came downstairs in the morning, Colonel Hoagland ushered Emma out to his car and headed back to Oteen. Sheriff Mitchell, more annoyed than upset with the entire incident, thanked Fred for his assistance and promised to call him later. With a final visual sweep of the Great Hall, the sheriff left, announcing his intention to check on the road-clearing crew before heading home to his wife and bed.

Wife and bed, Fred thought.

Knowing Evelyn would be asleep, Fred decided to forego getting any sleep and began making his customary morning rounds. He still had Henry Ford, Thomas Edison, Harvey Firestone and John Burroughs to occupy his mind -- and he wanted to make sure each of the magazine and newspaper reporters found the hotel in perfect order that morning.

After what he was sure would be one of the finest breakfasts any of them had ever eaten, he had arranged for the reporters -- much to their delight -- to have their choice of a guided horseback ride, a round of golf or a hike up to the summit of Sunset Mountain, where from the tower on his Overlook Castle they could see the mountains bordering South Carolina, Georgia and Tennessee.

Today, he declared, *would be the day they turn their attention from Henry Ford and Thomas Edison to Frederick Loring Seely and the Grove Park Inn.*

Today, the tide would turn.

E. W. Grove would retreat to St. Louis, as Fred prepared for the rush of reservations that would follow the front page stories reciting the delectable features of "the finest resort hotel in the world."

Today was the beginning of the end for Edwin Grove.

An eye for an eye.

And, today, the Grove Park Inn was his.

At the conclusion of his inspection, Fred decided to skip his customary Wednesday morning horseback ride and to slip into their room, where he planned to shower and change before returning to the Great Hall to supervise the morning activities. He had promised their older children that they could come down to the hotel after lunch to meet Thomas Edison and Henry Ford, but Evelyn, two-year-old Fred and his nurse, Missy, would still be in their second floor suite.

As he quietly let himself into the outer vestibule, he could hear the soft sound of Marion Harris' hit song "I Ain't Got Nobody" coming from their Sears' Silvertone phonograph. He carefully closed the door and stepped into the living room, where Evelyn stood leaning out the open window overlooking the Inn's front lawn.

"How's little Fred?"

Evelyn jumped back in surprise.

"Fred! I had no idea you were coming." She let out a long sigh. "I was up half the night with him and he just fell back asleep. I told Missy to sleep in the other bedroom. Would you go and check on him, please?"

Fred turned and, as he did, glanced over at the closed door to his closet. He walked into their bedroom where a crib had been set up for their youngest son. Little Fred lay sound asleep in the semi-darkness of the room. Fred patted his son lightly on the back and returned to the living room.

"Sleeping like a baby," he announced.

Evelyn was now sitting with her back to him at the small table where she often took her meals. Fred placed his hands on her shoulders, leaned over and attempted to kiss her, but she turned and his lips landed on her cheek. He caught a whiff of fresh peppermint on her breath.

"Any plans for the morning?" he asked as he glanced at her *Harper's Bazaar* laying open on the table.

"Nothing really. I'm sure the kids will want to go swimming sometime. Papa said he'd have Vincent drive him up to get them, so I'll probably ride along. "

"That sounds fine."

He paused, then decided he would gauge her mood this morning. "Do you want me to have Miss Hatch call Dr. Westin's secretary and re-schedule your appointment?"

Evelyn glanced up at the ceiling for a split second, then softly replied, "No, that won't be necessary."

As she spoke Fred walked to the open window and looked down over the manicured lawn, the lush shrubbery and flower gardens nestled up between the granite walls and the tar-coated driveway leading to the front of the hotel. Some of the early risers were making their way up to the parking area or to the hand-lettered signs marking the beginning of one of the hiking paths. Fred counted seven automobiles parked in front of the hotel, each being attended by one of his uniformed bellmen.

Below him, stepping out from between two six-foot Fraser fir trees planted among the shrubs surrounding the hotel, Fred spotted Benjamin Porter, Jenny's son, who, as promised, had appeared for work promptly at seven o'clock that morning.

I wonder if Victor picked up Jenny at the same time....

Seely frowned as he noted the uniform Theodore had given the slight fifteen-year-old was two sizes too big and his shirt was hanging out the back.

"Benjamin," Fred called down to him.

Startled, Benjamin looked up at the window, then waved as he recognized his new employer. The guests on the driveway looked up as well. Fred waved, then, looking back at Benjamin, pointed toward the rock portico shielding the front doors leading into the Great Hall. "Meet me there. I'll be right down."

Turning away from the window, he hastily explained to his wife, "I've got to take care of something. I'll be right back."

Evelyn nodded without looking up from her magazine.

Benjamin was waiting for him beside the rock pillar.

"Benjamin," Fred asked, looking over at the shrubbery beneath the windows of his second floor suite. "What were you doing over there?"

"Nothing," he stammered nervously. "Nothing, really, Mr. Seely. I was jus' lookin' at somethin'. I wasn't going to keep it, really. I really wasn't, Mr. Seely."

"That's okay, Benjamin," Fred assured him. "There's nothing to get upset about. Now, what was it you weren't going to keep?"

"I, I was going to give it back to her, really, Mr. Seely. I, I really was," he explained.

"Give it to who, Benjamin?"

"To, to that lady, sir."

Benjamin pointed toward the hotel. Fred turned, but could not see anyone.

"I, I just looked up and she, she dropped it, that's all. I, I was going to give it back to her, really, Mr. Seely. I swear. I, I wasn't goin' to keep it."

"I understand, Benjamin," Fred replied, laying his hand on the young man's shoulder to calm him. "You did the right thing, picking it up."

"Really, Mr. Seely. I did?"

"Yes, Benjamin. You did. Now, I'm headed back into the hotel, so why don't I take it? Would you like that?"

"Would you really?" Benjamin exclaimed, fumbling to reach into the pocket of his new, over-sized uniform. "That, that would be great, Mr. Seely, 'cause I, I don't know exactly how to get there, but Mr. Theodore he said he would show me around, first thing, but he's been too busy what with everything goin' on."

"I would be glad to, Benjamin," Fred answered, extending his hand, but with no idea what to expect.

Benjamin pulled a small object out of his coat pocket and carefully placed it in the palm of Fred Seely's hand.

"Are you sure this is it, Benjamin?"

"Yes, sir, Mr. Seely. I seen a lady right there at that window -- the open one -- and waved, but she must not of seen me. Then she looked back in the room and it fell right out of her hand. Right down there," he pointed. "So, I figured I should go get it for her."

Fred glanced at the shrubbery beside the gray granite wall, then looked closely at the lipstick-stained cigarette Benjamin had just given him. He tilted his hand slightly, rolling it until he could read the name.

Oasis.

A slight movement overhead caught his attention.

"There, there she is, Mr. Seely!" Benjamin exclaimed.

Fred looked up from the cigarette in his hand to the open window, where Evelyn now stood, arms crossed, smiling down at him.

William Jennings Bryan (left) and Fred Seely (right) taking
Mary Baird Bryan (rear left), Evelyn Grove Seely (center) and a friend for a ride
in the fall of 1913 near the Grove Park Inn.

Epilogue

For more years than anyone can remember, stories have circulated among the staff and guests at the Grove Park Inn involving a mysterious apparition roaming the hallways around the Palm Court. Although sightings have been sporadic, all have included a fleeting glimpse of a young, beautiful woman in a flowing, pink gown.

These stories prompted paranormal researcher Joshua Warren to undertake a scientific investigation at the Grove Park Inn in 1995, which he documented in his book *Haunted Asheville*. At the close of his study, Warren observed, "Yes, the Pink Lady is real. To try to understand her is like trying to understand the Grove Park Inn itself. It is deep and complex. We look upon the place and we know it is a mystery. A part of us tells us we shall never know all its secrets -- yet we accept that. We accept it because it brings us such a feeling of warmth and comfort to simply walk through its doors. The nature of her existence we may never understand, but she is always out there -- silently watching from a distance."

What eluded Joshua Warren, however, as well as every other researcher before or since then, have been any documents that would confirm the death of a young woman at the Grove Park Inn.

And where history ends, speculation begins.

The majority of the characters in this historical novel were inspired by real individuals, including Fred L. Seely, E. W. Grove, Evelyn Grove Seely, Gertrude Grove, Edwin W. Grove Jr., the guests in the Great Hall and the staff at the Grove Park Inn. Other characters, most notably Daisy Wheeler, Emma Barringer, Dr. Ronald Westin,

Mrs. Dickerson, Luther Hargus, Madame Swann and her ladies, as well as the two women with Edwin Grove in Atlanta, were created for this novel.

Henry Ford, Thomas Edison and their group did, in fact, arrive at the Grove Park Inn on the afternoon of August 27, 1918, during a time when Fred L. Seely and his famous father-in-law, Edwin Wiley Grove (1850-1927), were locked in a personal and public battle over the hotel. That battle was finally fought in a St. Louis courtroom and continued even beyond Grove's death in 1927.

The lawsuit was carried forward by his son, Edwin W. Grove Jr., executor of his father's estate, who won the lawsuit, evicted Fred Seely from the hotel, ignored the terms of his father's will and quickly sold the Grove Park Inn. After a number of affairs, scandals and paternity suits, Edwin Grove Jr. died in 1934 at the age of 44. The cause of death, as reported on the front pages of the St. Louis newspapers, was syphilis.

Fred Seely (1871-1942) managed the Grove Park Inn until 1927, during which time he also operated Biltmore Industries, the woodworking and weaving business he had purchased in 1916 from Edith Vanderbilt. After leaving the Grove Park Inn, Seely operated Biltmore Industries until his death at Overlook Castle at the age of 71. The five workshops he constructed adjacent to the Grove Park Inn have since been restored and now serve as a restaurant, two museums, several artisan workshops and the award-winning Grovewood Gallery (www.Grovewood.com).

Fred and Evelyn Grove Seely (1877-1953) raised their five children at Overlook Castle (today a private residence atop Sunset Mountain), where she remained for several years after her husband's death. Throughout her life Evelyn Grove Seely was torn between two dominant and jealous men: her father and her husband. According to one of their children, when Fred Seely announced he was suing her father, Evelyn refused to speak to her husband for more than a year afterwards.

The Grove Park Inn, which had opened to great fanfare on July 12, 1913, survived the turmoil surrounding the Grove and Seely families to continue to provide its guests -- including United States Presidents Harding, Coolidge, Hoover, Roosevelt and Eisenhower, writers Zelda and F. Scott Fitzgerald, celebrities Will Rogers and Harry Houdini, professional athletes Bill Tilden and Bobby Jones, plus hundreds of prominent business, social, entertainment and political figures -- with the "home-like and wholesome simplicity" that E. W. Grove had promised in his opening night speech.

After the departure of both Grove and Seely in 1927, however, the Grove Park Inn struggled for several years under a series of absentee owners. When World War II erupted, the United States government leased the Grove Park Inn as a detention center for Japanese and German diplomats who had been arrested in Washington, D.C. Later, the government utilized the hotel as a prisoner of war camp and, finally, as the war came to a close in 1945, as a rehabilitation and redistribution center for returning American military personnel.

In 1955, Texas insurance and hotel mogul Charles Sammons (1898-1988) purchased the Grove Park Inn and undertook a series of renovations and additions to the aging hotel. By the close of the century, the Sammons family had expanded the hotel to include 512 guest rooms, two ballrooms, several meeting rooms and restaurants, a restored Donald Ross golf course, a sports complex and, carefully integrated into the historic hotel, one of the world's finest spas.

More recent guests have included President Barack Obama and First Lady Michelle Obama, former President Bill Clinton and

Secretary of State Hillary Clinton, Ambassador Andrew Young, a large number of senators and representatives, and scores of celebrities and entertainers.

In addition, the Sammons family and the Grove Park Inn's management and staff have recognized and embraced the hotel's Arts & Crafts heritage, taking care to preserve its collection of original Arts & Crafts antiques, purchasing additional authentic antiques for the public areas and commissioning accurate Arts & Crafts reproductions for the Great Hall and guest rooms.

Every February since 1988, I and the Grove Park Inn Resort and Spa have hosted the National Arts & Crafts Conference and Antiques Show, celebrating the close connection between this historic hotel and the Arts & Crafts movement (www.Arts-CraftsConference.com).

Additional information can also be found in two of my other books, *Built For the Ages: A History of the Grove Park Inn* and *Grove Park Inn Arts & Crafts Furniture*, winner of the 2009 Thomas Wolfe Literary Award.

> \- Bruce E. Johnson
> August 27, 2010

"Historians want more documents than they can use.
Novelists want more liberties than they can take."
> \- Henry James

A Partial Listing of the 1918 Grove Park Inn Staff
As Recorded in the 1918 Asheville City Directory

Name	Position	Race	Residence
Albert Barvani	Cook	W	Sunset Hall
Kemp Battle	Desk Clerk	W	Sunset Hall
Dallas Benson	Plasterer	B	Asheville
Julie Brookshire	Desk Clerk	W	Asheville
Harriett Bird	Bookkeeper	W	Asheville
Dorothy Blackwell	Maid	W	Sunset Hall
Fred Bluford	Waiter	B	Asheville
Gertrude Brown	Maid	W	Sunset Hall
Dellie Buckner	Maid	W	Sunset Hall
William Burgin	Bellman	W	Asheville
Augustus Caldwell	Laborer	B	Sunset Hall
Lossie Cherry	Stenographer	W	Unlisted
McClelland D. Cochrane	Barber	W	Asheville
Claud Cook	Electrician	W	Asheville
Jessie Couch	Employee	B	Sunset Hall
Robert Creech	Cook	W	Sunset Hall
Edward Crook	House Detective	W	Asheville
Berkley Crump	Waiter	B	Asheville
Walter Davis	Waiter	B	Sunset Hall
Robert H. Dial	Chauffeur	W	Asheville
Joseph Dickerson	Auditor	W	Asheville
Deckard Dover	Porter	W	Asheville
Theodore Elesser	Butcher	W	Sunset Hall
James Evans	Chauffeur	W	Sunset Hall
Theodore Evans	Bellman	W	Sunset Hall
Conway Farley	Desk Clerk	W	Sunset Hall
Arthur Foster	Waiter	B	Asheville
Oscar Francis	Employee	W	Asheville
Loretta Franklin	Operator	W	Asheville
Luther L. Fulton	Waiter	B	Home
G. A. Furgerson	Dishwasher	W	Unlisted
Zana Gallamore	Maid	W	Unlisted
Lawrence Gennari	Cook	W	Sunset Hall
Adam Hall	Bellman	B	Sunset Hall
Frank Harrison	Waiter	B	Unlisted
Ruth Hatch	Secretary	W	Asheville
James H. Henry	Waiter	B	Home
Eldridge Hensley	Employee	W	Unlisted
Joseph Hensley	Fireman	W	Asheville
Edward Higgins	Desk Clerk	W	Asheville
Mae Hood	Maid	W	Sunset Hall
Grace Howell	Operator	W	Asheville
James Howell	Waiter	B	Asheville
Violet Hughes	Matron	W	Sunset Hall

George Iizuka Masa	Photographer	W	Sunset Hall
Paul Johnson	Elevator Operator	W	Asheville
Edward Jones	Chauffeur	W	Asheville
George Jones	Foreman	W	Asheville
Benjamin Jordan	Chauffeur	W	Asheville
Lyda Jordan	Maid	W	Asheville
Nellie Jordan	Maid	W	Sunset Hall
Douglas Justice	Waiter	B	Asheville
Charles Kennedy	Porter	B	Asheville
Jonathan King	Employee	B	Unlisted
Vesta Knight	Storekeeper	W	Sunset Hall
Havon Knuckles	Waiter	B	Sunset Hall
James Lawson	Waiter	B	Asheville
Bertha Littlefield	Housekeeper	W	Sunset Hall
R. P. Logan	Waiter	B	Sunset Hall
Grant McDowell	Doorman	B	Sunset Hall
Jonathan Martin	Bellman	B	Asheville
Jennie Mathews	Stenographer	W	Asheville
Samuel Melton	Dishwasher	W	Unlisted
Gertrude Merrill	Stenographer	W	Asheville
L. Morehead	Waiter	B	Unlisted
Frank Mull	Elevator Operator	W	Sunset Hall
Chester Munroe	Cashier	W	Asheville
Jonathon Murray	Bellman	B	Asheville
Zack Netherton	Checker	W	Sunset Hall
W. B. Owen	Store Room	W	Sunset Hall
G. W. Patterson	Pantryman	W	Unlisted
Daniel Presley	Foreman	W	Asheville
Jason Puckett	Laborer	W	Asheville
Odell Reece	Maid	W	Sunset Hall
Lewis Ricardi	Cook	W	Sunset Hall
Lucy E. Scott	Stenographer	W	Sunset Hall
Fred Shepherd	Dishwasher	B	Asheville
Robert Shepherd	Bellman	B	Asheville
Edward Simms	Waiter	B	Unlisted
Boston Smith	Laborer	W	Asheville
S. S. Smith	Pastry Cook	W	Sunset Hall
Zimmerman Spear	Waiter	B	Asheville
Dan Spearman	Bellman	B	Asheville
Clarence Stewart	Chauffeur	W	Asheville
Eugene Stewart	Porter	W	Asheville
Oscar Stewart	Gardener	W	Asheville
Leslie Streeter	Houseman	W	Sunset Hall
O. Strother	Waiter	B	Unlisted
Robert Taylor	Employee	W	Asheville
Edward Thomas	Employee	B	Unlisted
Earl Trantham	Painter	W	Asheville
Elsworth Trantham	Painter	W	Asheville
William Trantham	Superintendent	W	Asheville

Three Other Books of Interest

Built For the Ages: A History of the Grove Park Inn (hardback, 128 pgs., 2004) chronicles the design, construction and furnishing of the Grove Park Inn in 1913, then traces its history from its opening through the building of its award-winning spa in 2001. Author Bruce Johnson also provides insight into the relationship between owner Edwin W. Grove and his son-in-law and manager, Frederick L. Seely.

The Grove Park Inn Arts & Crafts Furniture (hardback, 175 pgs., 2009) provides an in-depth examination of the Arts & Crafts heritage manifested in one of the most important Arts & Crafts buildings in the country. Author Bruce Johnson explores the relationship between the historic hotel and the Roycrofters, who provided many of the original furnishings and lighting in 1913. Included in the book are detailed drawings for woodworkers interested in building their own Arts & Crafts furniture.

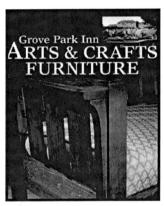

Available at GroveParkInn.com

Is the Grove Park Inn haunted?

Noted author and paranormal researcher Joshua Warren has collected a surreal mixture of history and myth in his well-known book *Haunted Asheville*. In it Warren explores the feasts of legends and searches for the fading morsels of truth surrounding Asheville's famous ghost stories. Explore historical facts, hear the words of eyewitnesses and examine the stunning photographs in this eye-opening book.

www.HauntedAsheville.com

Bruce Johnson has been exploring, researching and writing about the historic Grove Park Inn since 1986. He has also directed the National Arts & Crafts Conference and Antiques Show held at the Grove Park Inn the third weekend in February since 1988. He has written two previous books on the inn, *Built For the Ages: A History of the Grove Park Inn* and *Grove Park Inn Arts & Crafts Furniture*, winner of the 2009 Thomas Wolfe Literary Award. Johnson has also written several books on the Arts & Crafts movement, antique restoration, antiques and home improvement, and frequently appears on HGTV and the DIY television network. He lives on a small farm outside Asheville with his wife, Leigh Ann Hamon, DVM, and occasionally with his two grown sons, Eric and Blake.

For information on Bruce Johnson's next book,
plus how to order additional copies of
An Unexpected Guest
including autographed and inscribed gift books
and discounts for booksellers, please go to:

AnUnexpectedGuest.com

CPSIA information can be obtained at www.ICGtesting.com
Printed in the USA
LVOW080047190911

246827LV00002B/3/P